CHAPTER 1: RACHEL

Then

The tang of wet grass fills my nostrils as I run ghost-like across Stamford Meadows in the thin grey morning light. As I blink away the perspiration that has trickled into my eyes, I can still taste the bubbles of last night's celebratory champagne. My nose wrinkles in annoyance at the reminder of all those empty calories so I force myself to run faster, as penance. My trainers pound the winding concrete path while adrenaline pumps through my veins. Faster, always faster. *Why do you punish yourself so much? Who exactly are you running away from?* These are questions Adie frequently asks me.

I greet the people I typically see on my morning run with a perfunctory 'Good morning'. The portly, retired gentleman and his grey-whiskered Labrador, who is also ancient. Sadly, I imagine that when the dog passes away, he will too. The odd couple, as I refer to them in my head, who jog together, presumably for company, but never speak, even to each other, let alone me. They are still a part of my morning ritual though, and, as such, I look out for them every day. People who know me will attest to the fact that I place a high value on routine. Then there is the soon-to-be-divorced guy in his mid-thirties, a jogger like me, who tries to make eye contact to strike up a conversation. I'm too smart for that, though.

As a mostly unlikeable (so I've been told) woman, I wonder what these individuals think of me. My acquaintances (I don't call them friends) would have you believe that I'm the luckiest woman alive. I have an adoring husband. Two perfectly behaved children. A beautiful home in a sought-after location. And a fantastic job to return to when the children are older.

A strange chill travels over my pale, cold-to-touch skin as I remember Adie's words from last night: 'Why aren't you happy, Rachel, when you have everything you could possibly want?' I recall that his tone had been one of disappointment rather than accusation. My gaze lingered on his dark, unreadable features as I asked, 'What about what I *don't* want?' A strange expression flashed across his face then, followed by a familiar lip-tightening and an unsettling pulse in his chiselled jaw. His features were neutral when he next looked up again. His eyes, as usual, were empty of emotion. He is right, of course. Most women would love to be in my position. On the surface, that is. However, beneath it — lies and secrets are as much a part of my marriage as our two children, Beatrice and Archie.

As someone who has been described as unconventionally attractive, I am too tall, skinny and sharp-featured to be viewed as feminine, but men perversely find me attractive. They claim to see me as something of a mystery, but that's simply not true. When you consider that I am driven by a desire for routine and order, I am rather dull. And I become highly strung when things do not go my way. If every day were the same, I would finally understand what it is to be happy. I only acknowledge to myself in the dead of night that I have turned into a cold wife, a distant mother and an indifferent friend, and that it is *me* I am running away from.

I slow to a walk when I turn the corner, and a familiar row of Georgian townhouses comes into view. With its Regency-Georgian exterior, the Grade II-listed Rutland Terrace is an iconic

Before Us

ALSO BY JANE E. JAMES

BEFORE US

JANE E. JAMES

JOFFE BOOKS

Joffe Books, London

www.joffebooks.com

First published in Great Britain in 2025

Cover art by Nick Castle

ISBN: 978-1-80573-314-0

For my big brother, John
One of the bravest people I know

example of grandeur in the heart of Stamford. My eyes sweep over the timeless elegance of the buildings, which have breathtaking views of the undulating meadows, but as I approach the shiny black door to number thirteen, a nasty feeling of dread swirls in my stomach. It's officially been our home for two days. The selling agent described it as 'character and charm over four floors', and she was not mistaken. Unlocking the door, I'm greeted by a grand staircase, towering ceilings and arched shuttered windows. But silence too. And emptiness.

Where is the sound of children's feet running across the beautiful old geometric tiles to throw themselves into my arms? Likewise, there is no shaggy, wet, fashionably crossbred dog to offer me a welcoming bark. There aren't any toys scattered carelessly across the floor to trip over and no kettle boils endlessly in the background as it did in my own childhood home. Unlike most new homeowners, there isn't any visible chaos, stress or disagreement over where things should go, and more significantly, there is nothing for me to do. The removal firm, who charged a fortune for the convenience, moved everything in effortlessly, following Adie's meticulous plans as to where everything should go. When Adie asks me why I'm not happy, he's referring to this type of privilege.

I keep the fact that I feel unimportant and invisible to my family a secret. Our children attend a private school, have many friends and spend a lot of their spare time partaking in extracurricular activities. Except for driving them to and from school each day, they no longer need me. Adie claims that we are extremely fortunate as they are 'well-balanced and stable' children. This is a dig at me for being 'highly sensitive and volatile', as he calls it. However, I haven't felt like a mother in an exceedingly long time, and I mourn the loss of my children every day. Even though Archie is only six, and Beatrice is eight, they already seem like little adults. They talk only of their favourite activities — netball, hockey, chess, flute and violin practice. Archie follows in his father's footsteps and prefers science and maths, while Beatrice is athletic and musical. Neither takes after me.

Our latest move to Rutland Terrace, which Adie promises is to be our forever home, is only four streets away from our old house, which was already too large for our family of four. Now we have even more space to lose ourselves in. I am not a Stamfordian like Adie, even though I have lived in the town since we were married. I'm originally from London, so I consider it odd that I am stuck here in his hometown while he commutes most days to the city where I grew up. Like many middle-class couples we know, we made the decision that I would be the one to take a break from my career to raise our young children. At the time, it made financial sense because Adie earns five times as much as me.

Even though the children are now older, I'm facing resistance from Adie about going back to work because he claims to want us to have another child. *We have more than enough bedrooms!* Despite not having told my husband yet, my answer is a firm 'no'. Another five years of having nothing to do would send me stir-crazy. It's not as if I can even get stuck into the housework because, at Adie's insistence, we have a cleaner. My secretive husband would prefer me to concentrate on planning and organising the children's lives and occasionally host dinner parties for our friends and colleagues. A stay-at-home traditional wife is something he has always craved as he sees it as a measure of his success as a provider.

Meanwhile, I yearn for companionship. A dog maybe? Something to cuddle and love. But Adie has asthma and is allergic so that is out of the question, even though he goes out of his way to pet other people's dogs at the park. Although I lack culinary skills, unlike his mother, I try to prepare something healthy, fresh and organic every day for us to eat. Adie and I usually have our meals after the children have gone to bed and spend long evenings picking at our food and each other. When he thinks I'm not looking, he stares at me quizzically, and vice versa. We observe each other endlessly across the highly polished dining table, as though we were enemies plotting to destroy each other.

Sadness weighs heavily on my chest as I take off my trainers and store them in the boot room. I give a rueful smile when I see the children's brightly coloured Wellington boots next to my more traditional green ones. It doesn't take long though before darker thoughts begin to crowd my mind. I shuffle barefoot down the concrete steps into the kitchen on the cellar floor and turn on the lights. As the stone-walled, castle-sized room comes to life, I slide out the dark green notebook I purchased this morning from Walkers Books which I have been hiding down my jogging top. There are other people with secrets besides Adie. I've got one of my own now. And I plan to carefully document it in my new journal each day, as evidence.

Adie gets paid a lot of money to foresee threats and keep everyone secure in his role as Chief Information Security Officer at a leading cybersecurity company. It's a shame he doesn't apply the same rules to his family, for I've never felt more in danger of my life than I do right now.

CHAPTER 2: LUCY

Now

As we throw open the peeling painted door to 13 Rutland Terrace, the air inside is thick with dust and smells of ancient wood and crumbling stonework, but it's the faintest smell of perfume that immediately captures my attention. I like to imagine that it belongs to the ghost of a woman who lived here before us. However, since I've always been interested in anything spiritual or otherworldly, I'm prone to such fanciful outbursts. I've had my fortune told enough times to anticipate passing away quietly in my bed at a very old age, surrounded by dozens of children and grandchildren.

Ha. Chance would be a fine thing. I'm already a mother of two but would love more. My plump, matronly body is designed for it. Except Matt maintains that two is enough. What he doesn't say is 'more than enough', but that's what he means. I understand though. Sophie, our second child, was born with Down syndrome, something neither of us could have predicted. Naturally, we wouldn't be without our darling daughter, but even I didn't realise how exhausting caring for a disabled child would be.

'Shouldn't you carry me over the threshold or something?' I tease playfully as Matt pushes past me to go inside by himself, leaving me to juggle our son Jack, who is struggling to get free, with one hand while navigating Sophie's buggy with the other. And let's not forget the Tasmanian devil of a dog that is Casper, whose lead is tightly wrapped around my wrist, cutting into it. Whoever said cockapoos make good family pets obviously doesn't live with one!

'You'd have to lose some weight first,' Matt snorts before vanishing from view.

Knowing that Matt doesn't mean to be cruel, I say, 'Very funny.' It's just his way and besides, he's right. I do need to shed a tonne of weight. I keep promising myself that I'll start a diet soon, but comfort eating has turned into a form of self-medication, and I find it hard to stop.

Matt returns to the door with a shy smile, as though he realises he may have hurt my feelings. For some reason, I'm ridiculously grateful.

'Here, I'll take the buggy,' he offers.

I murmur, 'Thanks,' as I reach out to softly remove a cobweb from his freckly face. I've often questioned what Matt sees in me. He's so good-looking, in a sandy-haired, green-eyed, boy-next-door way. It's certainly not my money. Both of us come from working-class backgrounds, but we're diligent workers and ambitious. As an only child, Matt was and still is the spoiled golden boy, which means his parents are very generous. Without their financial help, we'd never have been able to afford this house. As for me, I'm the youngest of six so I grew up knowing my place in the pecking order, which makes me grounded if nothing else.

When I see my son's downturned face I immediately forget about my husband. 'Jack, what is it?' I ask, instantly alarmed.

'If there are spiders, I'm not coming in,' he protests, warily eyeing the cobwebs in his father's hair and stubbornly folding his arms across his seven-year-old chest.

'Don't worry, Jack,' Matt laughs. 'I have special Spidey senses, so I'll be able to flush them out and make them look for somewhere else to live.'

'Do you promise?' Jack asks hesitantly, wanting to believe his father.

At this, I momentarily turn my back on them because I still remember the mistrust I felt two years ago when I discovered Matt was having an affair with a woman at work and had been lying to me. Since then, I haven't been myself. I became a different, more cynical person because of the betrayal. Before that, I'd been as content as anyone had a right to be. Because I loved my husband, and we were determined to make our marriage work — not just for the kids' sake — I decided to forgive him. And now, forty-two marriage counselling sessions later, we are as devoted to one another as ever and are moving into the house of our dreams that we never thought we could afford. I tell myself how fortunate I am every day.

Pushing any lingering negative thoughts from my mind, I follow my family into the formerly magnificent entrance hall, complete with a grand staircase and large, if a little dusty, shuttered windows that allow in slivers of uneven white light. The room seems older and grimier than it did when we first viewed it. Everywhere is thick with cobwebs and moving shadows. Grim.

'I'll go and put the kettle on, shall I?' I grunt, my nose wrinkling at the stench of mildew and dust.

'Good idea,' Matt suggests vaguely, but I can tell he's not really listening. He has wanted this house for so long, it's become like an obsession with him. I'm reminded of the man he became for a while when he was seeing that would-be homewrecker. I still don't know her name but he was obsessed with her too. I have never been brave enough to ask.

Matt gives me a tight smile, a familiar line growing between his eyebrows as if he knows what I'm thinking. 'Are you okay, love?'

Always 'love'. Never gorgeous, or beautiful. Most likely because I am neither of these things. I can't help wondering if he reserved such affirmations for his bit on the side. A wife who has been wronged never stops wondering, in the same way that a concerned mother never stops worrying. As strands of fair hair fall across Matt's face, I take a moment to examine his expectant features in the late afternoon light. Standing motionless, his feet shoulder-width apart, he is undoubtedly planning how he is going to breathe life back into this house. It has sunk into a sleepy state of neglect after being abandoned. I get the sense that it is full of old ghosts who are waiting to wake up so they can play spooky tricks on us.

As I watch the determined smile slip from Matt's face, something like regret flickers across it — but it's gone before I can identify or call him out on it. I give myself away by stiffening and clearing my throat. Is his lover still on his mind even now? Does he wonder about her as much as I do?

'How about that cuppa? I'm gasping,' Matt prompts, letting out a low whistle, and when I look at him this time, he's properly smiling, not just faking it for my benefit.

'Coming right up,' I exclaim happily, feeling a tiny glimmer of hope as I convince myself that our little family is going to be okay.

Yet, as I turn on the cellar floor lights and go down the concrete steps to the kitchen below, I hear a creaking sound that makes me uneasy. The creak comes again, and the shadows deepen around me as the lights go out, one by one, leaving me in complete darkness. Ears straining in the silence, I imagine I hear my husband's voice behind me urgently whispering his lover's name — just before somebody puts a hand in the middle of my back and shoves me down the remaining steps.

CHAPTER 3: RACHEL

Then

Drinks in the drawing room before dinner are to be a regular thing, apparently. It's another of Adie's efforts to blend in. He claims not to have a chip on his shoulder about his upbringing, but as the only black man among our primarily white acquaintances, he's always trying to prove himself. While he's worked incredibly hard to get to the position that he's in today — at the top of his field — his real luck lay in having a fiercely driven mother who would have 'beaten his ass' — her words, not mine — if he failed to succeed after everything she had sacrificed for her family.

I adore Jonty and was all for her moving in with us after her husband Abel died, but Adie was opposed to the idea, which I must admit stunned me a little. I assumed that, like me, he doted on his mother, but it turns out things are not always as they seem where those two are concerned. Recently, I've observed they maintain a courteous distance from one another that neither tries to bridge. Since Adie's father passed away, it's become very apparent. I understand that it can be challenging for outsiders to understand complex family dynamics and I know I shouldn't consider myself an outsider in my own extended family but being a loner by choice, I've never felt at ease in large family gatherings. Adie appears to have adopted the same solitary tendencies recently. This has resulted in his three older sisters labelling him a 'snob' and someone who 'thinks he is better than them' which I suspect secretly pleases my husband, who seems insistent on distancing himself from them *and* his Nigerian roots.

He's the same with our children, constantly pushing them to outperform everyone else in school as if they aren't under enough pressure as it is. He may not express it verbally, but I'm sure he means that they need to put in more effort to prove themselves due to their mixed-race heritage. I warn Adie that he should allow them to be children and not to instil his own worries into their innocent minds. When this happens, he looks at me as though I am insulting his intelligence. I'm not, but as the sole heir of a well-known, affluent London family that amassed millions in the beauty and cosmetic industry, not only do I not have a leg to stand on, but I also have to watch what I say. Because, clearly, coming from a life of so-called privilege, I don't know what I'm talking about and cannot contribute anything of value. *Except* for more children!

Stony-faced, Adie hands me a gin and tonic that rattles from too much ice. As always, he keeps an eye on my alcohol intake. One shot of gin rather than two. *Because we wouldn't want to turn the clock back to when I had a problem, would we?* As I feel my hand tighten around the glass, I soften my voice to ask, 'How was your day?'

'Back-to-back meetings as usual,' he sighs wearily as he settles into one of the pastel-blue Chesterfield sofas and crosses his long legs. Tall, dark and handsome, my husband casts an impressive figure with his toned body, stylish corporate beard and expressive hazel eyes that he conceals behind designer spectacles.

'Poor you,' I sympathise as I take a sip of my drink, which I discover has very little gin in it. I stand up then and approach one of the two sets of French doors that open onto a pair of wrought iron balconies overlooking Stamford Meadows. Located on the first floor, the drawing room is flooded with natural light due to its impressive high ceilings. The house was kept in immaculate condition by its former owners, a Mr and Mrs Ellis. Sadly for them their daughter fell into a coma following a terrible accident. To relocate closer to Addenbrooke's Hospital in Cambridge, where their daughter Gabriella was, the Ellises wanted a speedy sale and were open to offers. When we signed contracts, I recall thinking that it didn't feel right to be profiting from their misfortune, even if Adie, the businessman, never shared my 'emotional' point of view. Perhaps that's why Rutland Terrace doesn't feel like home and I long to go back to our old house in Scotgate.

I stiffen and begin to shiver uncontrollably despite the late evening's warmth when I sense an Adie-sized creak behind me. As I hear him ask, 'What's wrong, Rachel?' I wince inwardly. When did I begin to fear my gentle giant of a husband?

I turn to face him before he can put his hands on me. 'Nothing,' I murmur, feeling a twinge of guilt at how easily the self-preserving lie comes. He fixes me with an unblinking stare as though trying to read my mind, but I'm not willing to give up every part of who I am, so I remain silent, frustration hardening my features.

He gives me a sceptical frown. 'Are you sure?'

He extends a hand to tilt up my chin, and I feel a flash of rage. The movement sends sharp skewers of agony through my head. After what he did, how dare he touch me? I turn sharp eyes on him and smack his hand away before uttering irritably, 'I said so, didn't I?'

'You've said so before,' he adds glumly, shrugging his annoyance.

The creases on my forehead deepen, and I sigh. 'Let's not start this again.' Like fireworks going off in my head, I sense the start of a migraine.

He protests indignantly, puffing out his chest. 'I'm not *starting* anything. I just wanted to know how you're doing.'

'As you do multiple times a day,' I point out sarcastically.

'We must have a serious problem if I can't ask my wife how she is.'

His angry words send an electrifying pulse of dread up my spine. 'We do,' I hiss accusingly. 'That something being an unfaithful spouse.'

I feel a wave of ice-cold fear wash over me as he looks at me in shock, and my first thought is, have I gone too far? Will he raise his hand to me as he did before, when I first found out about his betrayal?

While the evening sky softens into dusk outside, I watch my husband's eyes sag with fatigue. Voice laced with disbelief, he begs. 'Please, Rachel, don't bring this up again. I'm trying. God knows I'm trying.'

'*You're* trying!' I laugh scornfully, before screaming, 'What about me? After everything you've put me through?'

After that, I don't remember anything, except pain and fear, because the floor comes up to meet me and I black out.

CHAPTER 4: LUCY

Now

No one shoved me down the stairs. And Matt wasn't standing behind me whispering his lover's name either. I panicked, that's all — when the lights went out — and imagined all kinds of things were going on in the dark. This is how I've always been . . . overly sensitive to atmospheres and easily influenced by my overactive imagination. I cannot watch a scary movie to save my life. Embarrassingly, I managed to tumble down the steps all by myself without any assistance at all. As Matt says, I've always been clumsy. If anyone's going to burn themselves by starting a fire or getting an electric shock from a malfunctioning plug it's going to be me. Still, having Matt fuss over me almost makes up for the grazed knee and scraped hand.

'Here you go, love,' Matt says, pressing a mug of tea into my uninjured hand. 'I made it extra sweet for the shock.'

'Thanks,' I mumble dazedly, still feeling a little shaken.

'Drink up,' he orders playfully.

I take several long sips of the milky, sweet, lukewarm liquid before surveying the vast, windowless, stone-walled kitchen. Casper whines in frustration and paws frantically at something behind the large American fridge freezer — I hope it's not mice — and seems at home already. In contrast, my kids are oddly quiet and are staring around them with wide eyes. I admit that the enormity of the house makes me feel uneasy, so I'm sure they're feeling intimidated by it too. I, for one, have no idea how to operate the daunting cream aga, and I can't see myself sipping fancy cocktails at the kitchen island made of black concrete either. Have we taken on more than we can handle? Do we even belong here? Matt seems to think so.

As I'm wondering whose mug I'm drinking from because, given its gold rim and delicate bone-china feel, it most definitely doesn't belong to the Dawson family, Matt leans in and murmurs in a low voice so the kids can't hear, 'I'm sorry about what I said earlier, about you needing to lose weight. You're fine as you are.'

Upon hearing this, I want to do a celebratory cartwheel around the kitchen, chanting, 'My husband loves me,' but the more cynical side of me, which I didn't realise existed until after Matt's affair, recoils at the concept of being viewed as 'fine'. Not *beautiful, perfect* or *sexy* as his affair partner was. Not that I know this for sure, but I suspect her of being everything I was not. If not, why else would my husband have strayed?

When Sophie starts whimpering and struggling to escape her restraints, I unwind my aching limbs and get to my feet because I know Matt won't pick her up unless he's forced to. Our youngest is perfectly capable of walking unaided, but she loves to be carried, and I love carrying her. I can't believe she is almost two-and-a-half already. Before I can reach her flamingo-emblazoned buggy, *bright pink is Sophie's favourite colour*, Jack is undoing her straps.

I give our son a grateful smile and gently tousle his sandy hair as I reassure him, 'It's okay, Jack. I've got her.' Jack is very protective of his younger sister.

'Bless her. She's been good as gold, but she must be starving by now,' I observe to no one in particular as I hug her warm little body against mine and breathe in her unique toddler scent of bananas and milk. But as I look through the buggy bag for the cheese, crackers and grapes I packed for her lunch, she tugs at my top to distract me and whimpers into my neck, 'Want Mama milk.'

Without turning around, I can tell that Matt is glaring disapprovingly at us. This is confirmed by a quick glance at Jack's anxious face. Nevertheless, I still flinch when I hear my husband growl, 'We've talked about this, Lucy.'

'I know we've talked about it,' I remark airily, shooting him a pleading 'not now' look, 'but try telling Sophie that.'

'She's almost three and that's too old to still be breastfeeding,' Matt argues, wrinkling his nose in disgust.

Sophie's cries come again, dissolving into sobs this time. She clings to me like a monkey as I trudge across the dusty floor to sit down at the oak farmhouse table, which I'm quick to notice is something else we seem to have inherited. My heart is thudding painfully in my chest as I expose my swollen, veined breast for her to nurse. It's impossible for me to please both my husband and my child, but with me, my kids come first.

'According to the GP, it's perfectly normal and natural. More so than drinking cow's milk at any rate,' I explain without any malice, and without looking him in the eye because I don't want to witness what lurks there. Whereas I take everything in my stride and laugh at my own embarrassing mistakes — of which there are many — Matt cannot bear to be publicly humiliated. And now that we have a disabled child, I have a suspicion that, despite his inherent goodness, he already feels a great deal of shame about that and despises himself for it. Even though Matt is a fantastic father to Jack, I'm still waiting for him to fall in love with his daughter. I know he is more than capable of it, which is why I remain patient with him.

It's obvious that Sophie's loud, eager suckling on my breast aggravates him even more because the next thing I know, he's scraping back his chair and demanding, 'What happens when you go back to work full time, and Sophie has to go to childcare? You won't be able to breastfeed her then.'

To say I'm shocked is an understatement. 'Who said anything about going back to work full time or childcare?' I ask, my mouth hanging open.

'You're forgetting you have a florist shop to run, and Kerry can't manage on her own indefinitely,' Matt snaps as he stands and paces the floor. When Casper jumps up at him, nearly toppling him over, he lets out a string of oaths under his breath. The next minute he's apologising for this.

It's true that I have taken a much longer leave of maternity absence from the business than planned, largely due to Sophie's medical condition, but although I might be easy-going I'm no pushover — I built that business from scratch without any help from Matt or anyone else — so I purse my lips and retaliate with, 'And because it's *my* business and no one else's, I think I can decide for myself when I go back full time.'

'Let's hope you have a business to return to, that's all I can say,' Matt snorts, turning narrowed eyes on me, 'because the last time I checked it was barely breaking even let alone making a profit.'

'Your point being?' I seethe, incensed that he's poked his nose into my business affairs without telling me. I don't have any secrets from Matt, but still, it would have been nice to be asked before he looked at the accounts.

'The point being,' he grinds out between clenched teeth, 'is that we've taken out a huge mortgage on this place and we need every penny we can get, especially if we are going to do it up. Have you thought about that?'

'Have *you*?' I counter, doing up my milk-stained blouse while simultaneously winding Sophie on my lap as if she were still a young baby. 'Because if I remember rightly, you were the one who wanted this place, and for the life of me I still can't figure out why.'

CHAPTER 5: RACHEL

Then

'Where are you going, Rachel?' Adie asks, looking up from the book he is meant to be reading — *Who Moved My Cheese?* by Dr Spencer Johnson. As always, when observing me, he has the intense stare of a cat.

Surprised by the question, I remark stiffly, 'It's ten o'clock. I'm going to bed.' I might as well have implied, 'Don't you know me at all?' since I go to bed at the same time every night without fail, but that would have been pointless since clearly we don't know each other. At least not anymore. I last recognised my husband three years ago. Since then, I've lived with a stranger that vaguely resembles him.

He sighs and blinks slowly as he places the book in his lap. 'I'm sorry about earlier. I guess we both lost our temper.'

My fingers flutter automatically to my bruised cheek, but I remain silent. The light has faded, and the French doors are now closed. The sounds of Stamford at night are muffled by the heavy, floor-length curtains . . . dog owners taking a last dutiful walk around the block, the hum of slow-moving traffic and the dwindling voices of couples making their way home on foot after a night out at the town's multiple restaurants and bars. For many, it's an ordinary night . . . like any other. Home is meant to be where the heart is but behind the door of 13 Rutland Terrace, only heartache awaits.

'I didn't realise it was that time already,' Adie observes mildly, still watching me. 'Are you sure I can't tempt you with one last drink?'

I take back my words from a moment ago. Adie *does* know me. Another alcoholic drink is the only thing that could tempt me to remain in this room with him for a while longer. As my gaze lingers on the gold, mirrored drinks trolley, where I can make out flashes of blue, amber and green bottles of spirits and Waterford crystal glassware, I force a cheery smile to my face and reply, 'No, thanks,' before pretending to yawn in exhaustion.

As he pours himself another drink, he eyes me boldly and murmurs, 'Wise choice.' My gaze flickers between him and the whisky decanter and I notice that the tawny liquid perfectly matches the colour of his eyes. 'Have you heard from the solicitors lately?' he asks way too casually just as I'm about to leave the room.

Pausing, I gulp nervously before muttering, 'No.'

He scowls. 'I would have thought they'd have sorted out your inheritance by now. It's been almost a year since your parents died.' When the book falls from his lap onto the floor, its pages splayed open, he doesn't attempt to rescue it. Like many things in Adie's life — the book, the house, the cars, the children, the wife — they're for show only.

'That's not that long.' I wrinkle my nose in distaste at his choice of words.

It seems like only yesterday to me that my parents passed away in a helicopter crash while flying over Niagara Falls. After selling up their business assets six months prior, they intended to celebrate their retirement travelling but tragically died during the first stop of their world tour. As a result of being born into wealth, I've never craved it as others do, even though I'm now worth more than ten million pounds. The Beiersdorfs were a close-knit family, but I have seen the harm that money can do. Friends are easily won and lost. No one is to be trusted. Since I was sixteen, men have been chasing after my fortune.

'When my dad died four years ago, probate didn't take any-where near this long,' Adie stresses cynically, giving me a pitying look as if I don't know what I'm talking about.

He is mistaken. I may not be the sharp, clued-up journalist I used to be, living an independent life in the city under a fake surname to hide my identity, but as my extraordinarily successful and entrepreneurial parents' only daughter, I know more about wealth management than most people.

'It's hardly the same,' I remind him. 'Abel didn't have anything to leave.'

At that, Adie raises an eyebrow and grimaces as if I were some-how defying him. 'Forgive me. It seems like I must apologise once again for not being the son of a multimillionaire.'

I cry out, astonished, 'That's not what I meant, and you know it.'

'Do I?' he mutters.

I lower my voice to a soft murmur as I plead, 'I'm sorry, Adie.' Inside, I'm squirming with embarrassment. I couldn't have injured his pride more if I'd tried. This was truly not my intention. I'm not that much of a bitch.

'You've changed, Rachel. You used to say you didn't care about money.'

'I don't,' I gasp, wide-eyed. 'I never have.'

'I'm not sure that's true anymore,' he puffs out his chest and agitatedly gets to his feet, treading on the pages of the discarded book without glancing at it. Then he shoves his hands in his trou-ser pockets and demands, 'Do you remember when we first met, and you said I was the only man who ever loved you for yourself and not for your money?'

Close to tears, I nod sadly, mouthing, 'Yes.' But part of me suspects him of gaslighting me. When we first met and began dating, he didn't have a clue then who I was or that I would one day inherit the Beiersdorf fortune. But when Adie found out about my inheritance, he proposed almost immediately. As we were already passionately in love (at least I was) I persuaded myself this was merely a coincidence, because Adie was nothing like the other men who had pursued me for my money. By the time I realised I was mistaken it was too late. Since then, things have changed. Ten million times over.

I'm not sure how long I can keep him in the dark about receiving my inheritance since it was settled more than three months ago. When he finds out that I have misled him about something so important and that the money has already been reinvested, with trust funds established for the children, there's no telling what he'll do. Without my fortune, Adie's debts, *which he believes I am unaware of,* won't get settled. And he will be unable to maintain the lavish lifestyle he feels he deserves, even with his impressive London salary, since his job is in jeopardy due to allegations of sexual harassment at work. *Again, I'm not meant to know any of this, but due to my wealth I have connections that keep me informed.*

Add to that my hunch that he's seeing someone else, *again*, and plans to leave me for her and take our children with him, because the saying 'once an alcoholic, always an alcoholic' will undoubtedly help him win his custody battle . . . there is a very real and terrifying risk that my husband will do anything to get his hands on my money. And the way it's tied up, the only way he'll see a penny of it is if I'm dead.

CHAPTER 6: LUCY

Now

The metal toe-capped boots of the burly removal men stomp up and down the three flights of stairs and into the adjoining rooms as we tuck into our fish and chips at the oak table in the ground-floor prison cell of a kitchen. Matt went out to fetch them from the Model Fish Bar and we're eating them off paper much like we did when we first got together and had no money. Only one another. And in those days, that was enough. *I was enough.*

I wonder what he'd do if I jokingly threw a chip at him. Would he burst out laughing, like the old pre-affair Matt would, if I started a food fight? One glance at his irritable expression persuades me otherwise. He won't be content until the workers have left and the house is no longer in chaos. He hates the fact that our furniture is being roughly handled and that there are boxes everywhere. A drooling Casper begs at the table, and I turn a blind eye when Jack gives him half his battered sausage, even though I catch Matt rolling his eyes. For some strange reason, I want to laugh. And laugh. And laugh. I question whether I'm experiencing a panic attack.

As the workers move bulky items of furniture into position, noises resembling thunder reverberate down the stairs. 'For God's sake, how difficult can it be!' Matt erupts when he hears a loud clatter followed by a howl of anguish. He then gets up from the table to investigate.

In his absence, the children and I exchange a covert smile, and my peacekeeper of a son immediately wants to know, 'Is Daddy angry?'

'Of course not,' I automatically defend Matt and then take a few of his remaining chips because mine are all gone, before reassuring Jack, 'not with you anyway.'

Although I'm speaking the truth, at least on this occasion, I am worried about my husband's increasingly volatile temper, especially around the kids. Anything can trigger one of his uncontrollable rages — something as innocuous as an inconsiderate remark made by one of my friends, a toilet that refuses to flush or a perceived putdown at work. During our therapy sessions, I expressed concerns about his mental health, and Matt reluctantly acknowledged that he sometimes struggles to control his temper. We were all proven right when the counsellor advised him to take anger management classes because his response was to scream, 'What qualifies you to decide I have a problem?' When it was pointed out to him that her master's degree in psychotherapy made her an expert and her professional opinion shouldn't therefore be questioned, he'd stormed out. He returned home hours later with an apologetic smile, a bunch of flowers bought from the local garage and a half-eaten Dairy Milk bar.

I hear Matt arguing with the person in charge upstairs. Lee, he said his name was. I remember this because he has a cheeky grin, and I caught him looking me up and down when Matt wasn't around. Rather than be offended, I felt absurdly flattered. Matt hasn't looked at me like that in an exceptionally long time — years actually. 'I've still got it,' I remind myself, despite my husband's lack of interest in my curvy body.

The problem with Matt is that, because he is overly confident, he believes he is an excellent communicator — when this simply isn't true — and he even highlights this as a strength on his CV, which he updates frequently. Career moves typically result in pay increases in his sector, and this is the reason he switches jobs roughly every two years. Admittedly, though, that wasn't the reason behind his most recent move to JCB. To save our marriage he was forced to leave his previous employer after admitting to the affair with his female coworker. He'll need to travel more in his new role as a senior global buyer, but at least he is no longer in contact with her.

I pull a face when I hear Matt complaining loudly, 'You're not listening to me.' In response, there's a compliant murmuring of, 'We know what we're doing, sir,' from Lee followed by the shuffling of feet as the harassed worker retreats into another room to escape my husband. Poor Matt. He aspires to be an inspiration to others, but he never listens. Shirley, his mother, is to blame for this. It's not Matt's fault he thinks the world revolves around him. This is why he doesn't have any real pals. And why he doesn't like mine. He labels them as 'superficial' because they're into social media, soaps and celebrity TV shows like *Love Island* and *Strictly*, but the truth is he's really having a dig at me since I also enjoy those things.

'When can we go home?' Jack grumbles from the cold flagstone floor, where he has slipped onto his bottom so he can get Casper in a playful headlock. The two of them are inseparable and even share the same bed, much to my dismay. With one arm raised above her head, Sophie has fallen asleep in the buggy. Curdled breast milk clings to the corners of her mouth and her plump little shoulders twitch with each breath.

'This *is* home,' I sigh, as distressed by this as he seems to be. Rubbing my eyes from a lack of sleep, I drag myself to my feet and tiptoe silently over to the fridge freezer to peer inside. The brightly lit interior throws leaping shadows around the room causing Casper and Jack's ears to instantly prick up. Casper can hear a fridge door open from a mile away.

'I'm thirsty. Is there any pop?' Jack asks eagerly.

I respond distractedly, 'No, sorry,' as Casper joins me to resume pawing at the bottom of the fridge freezer. 'You'll have to make do with water from the tap for now,' I tell Jack, who pulls a face.

I reprimand, 'It won't hurt you for once,' before turning to face the dog whose brown-and-white nose has disappeared beneath the freezer door.

'What is it, Casper? What can you see?' I ask with a hint of annoyance.

The dog gives a frustrated snort, settles back on his haunches and wags his tail expectantly, waiting for his human mum to dig whatever it is out for him. Obediently, I drop to my knees on the sticky floor and scramble around underneath the freezer, fearing that my fingers might encounter something rotting and dead — like a mouse — God forbid, when my hand suddenly clasps itself around a square metallic object.

'What is it, Mum?' Jack is by my side, keen to know what I've discovered. He'll be hoping for a toy car or a forgotten piece of Lego.

'It's a fridge magnet,' I answer, brushing away a thick coating of dust and cobwebs to expose a picture — the kind that would have been taken in a passport photo booth — of a family just like ours. A thirty-something couple with two small children. A girl and a boy. The first thing that comes to mind is why they aren't smiling in the photograph. And why does the woman's dark, haunted eyes appear afraid, as though she needs help?

When Jack sees what I see, his crinkly green eyes fill with interest. 'Who are they?'

'I'm not sure,' I respond, tracing the woman's tormented face with my fingers. 'But I think it must be the family who lived here before us.'

CHAPTER 7: RACHEL

Then

My mother-in-law shows up the following morning. It's pouring with rain outside when I answer her loud knocking on the door, and she greets me from under her orange umbrella with a bright lipsticked smile. This woman is a monsoon of colours, in contrast to her son, who prefers to dress in pale linen suits in the summer and black roll-neck tops with sharply creased trousers in the winter. The outfit Jonty is wearing is flame red and Masai blue, which demonstrates her taste for colourful attire. Tall and slender, she has short, grey afro hair and has on an oversized set of her signature parrot earrings. I've never seen her without them, even at her husband Abel's funeral.

'*Masoyi yarinya*,' Jonty greets me in Hausa as is her custom before stepping inside.

'It's lovely to see you, Jonty. Welcome to our new home,' I exclaim, genuinely pleased to see her.

As soon as she lowers the dripping umbrella, she pulls me in for a tight hug. When she finally releases me, her unique scent of shea butter, cooking oil and spices clings to my skin. It's a reassuring aroma. One I have stored in my memory for when she's no longer around.

I watch Jonty look around the impressive entrance hall, her coffee-coloured, intelligent eyes taking in everything, including the chandeliers made of crystal glass, the ceiling roses and picture rails, the high ceilings and the grand staircase with its ornate spindle banister. She sighs when she turns back to face me.

'Do I take it you're not impressed?' I attempt a laugh.

She purses her lips and grumbles, 'I liked the old house.'

I worry at my lip, afraid Adie will overhear us and think I'm ungrateful, but I'm forced to agree, 'So did I.'

'This one doesn't seem you somehow, dear. Not like Scotgate was.'

'You haven't seen the rest of the house yet,' I gently protest, not wanting to appear disloyal to my husband. But I'm moved that she loved our old house as much as I did and felt that I'd left my stamp on it.

Shuddering as though cold, Jonty mutters incriminatingly, 'This feels more like a show house than a home. I know now why Adie wanted it.'

My eyes fall to the floor in shame as I stand by the glass console table with its extravagant arrangement of fresh lily-white flowers reflected in the art deco mirror. To me, her words sound like a criticism of her only son. Do mothers know their sons best, I wonder? Better than their wives even. If so, what secrets is Jonty keeping from me?

She looks at me sharply then, as if reading my mind, and blurts, 'Where is that son of mine and why isn't he here to greet me?'

Adie surprises us by making a covert appearance above us on the second-floor landing and announcing in a cool, clipped voice, 'I'm here, Mother.' Like Denzil Washington making a celebrity entrance, he sweeps one hand along the oak banister and makes a dramatic descent down the stairs.

Jonty's eyes are frantic as she fastens her gaze on me, as if she's asking for my help. She's worried that Adie might have heard her criticising the house and him. To disguise this, she narrows her eyes and scoffs, 'Mother! I've told you not to call me that. What's the matter with Maami? It's good enough for your sisters.'

Adie scolds, 'You're not in Nigeria now. Besides, I prefer mother.' He smiles charmingly when he says this and opens his arms to receive her as he reaches the ground floor. They hug, albeit briefly, and I notice that Jonty is the first to pull away. I feel sorry for Adie then, who has an injured look. I sigh deeply, realising this is not the start I had hoped.

'So, what do you think of my house?' Adie asks proudly, pointing to the plethora of classic Georgian architecture with both hands.

'*Your* house?' Jonty pouts, defiantly jutting out her chin. 'You mean yours *and* Rachel's house?'

Adie's face darkens when he realises that he has revealed his actual feelings for 13 Rutland Terrace. Jonty is the only family member I know who can embarrass my husband and make him appear tongue-tied. She always has this effect on him. I imagine that's why he hates her so much.

I dare not turn around to witness Jonty's affronted stare as I save the day by declaring, 'She loves the house, don't you, Jonty?' I then grab her arm and push her in the direction of the adjacent rooms, forcefully marching her into the library where she scowls at me. Since Adie is slow to follow, I take this chance to hiss in her ear, 'Just make out you do anyway.'

'You mean like *you* do,' she sniffs sarcastically, but she nods as though she's eager to do what I say.

For a split second, I think that everything is going to be okay, until my husband joins us to enquire, 'How long are you intending to stay, mother?'

'Adie. She just got here,' I gasp, mortified.

'Don't worry, Rachel. I don't pay any attention to him.' Jonty flaps a hand at Adie, but I can see that his comment has stung her. It couldn't not.

'It's just that Rachel hasn't been feeling well lately and tires easily,' he explains, sheepishly avoiding eye contact with me. Even though I know how dishonest he is, I'm angry that my husband can lie to his mother so readily when there is nothing wrong with me that a divorce wouldn't fix.

When Jonty hears this, she becomes instantly anxious and grasps my hand. 'Is that right, love?'

Her eyes are full of concern, poor thing, so I pretend to smile and joke, 'Your son is exaggerating. I'm fine, really.' When Adie's eyes find mine this time, I can tell by the look that he gives me that he thinks I'm the enemy.

'What's meant to be wrong with her?' Jonty gives her son a stern look as she warns, 'I don't know who I'm meant to believe now.'

'You tend to believe anyone over me, so I'm sure it's Rachel in this case,' Adie observes scathingly and walks over to one of the floor-to-ceiling book-lined walls, picks up a book and begins turning the pages.

'Do you want me to stay for a while so I can look after you?' Jonty offers, while casting a suspicious glance at her son over her shoulder, as though he cannot be trusted to do so.

Unlike most daughters-in-law, I would love nothing more than for Jonty to move in with us. Perhaps then I would feel safe. However, Adie would absolutely hate that — he would rather isolate me from the outside world — and would only make things difficult . . . for her and for me. So, rather than accepting her offer, I thank her and explain that it won't be necessary. When I look up, Adie is smirking, as if he is celebrating some sort of victory. I'm convinced now that he wants everyone to believe that I'm not just a recovering alcoholic, but also that I'm mentally ill and incapable. And the only explanation I can think of for that is money.

My money.

CHAPTER 8: LUCY

Now

When I wake up, I'm not that surprised to find the kids snuggled up next to me, their hands and legs tangled in the sheets. At what time they ended up in bed with us, I couldn't say, but I felt Matt impatiently climb out of it around 4 a.m., huffing and puffing like the big bad wolf in the children's fairy tale. Does that make us the three little pigs who are in danger of having their house blown down, I wonder? Matt's body will have replaced the vacant dent left by Jack in his single bed. Even without my husband, there is so much love in this bed, my heart is in its sheets. The mid-range, reasonably priced cotton sheets smell of our family — a comforting mixture of cereal, milk, soap and late-night snacks. Matt doesn't like the kids in bed with us, claiming it's not good for our sex life. I'm tempted to tell him *neither are affairs*, but I've promised not to throw that at him every five minutes. He has no idea how difficult that is for me.

I squint at the buttery sunlight pouring through the curtainless dual-aspect windows, and it takes a few drowsy moments for me to get used to my surroundings. It feels strange to wake up in a house that doesn't feel like home. The door is open, and Casper, who typically shows up with a four-legged muddy dive and a jaw full of partially chewed dog kibble, is nowhere to be seen. That really would take the biscuit where Matt's concerned. Get it. Biscuit . . . Okay, it might not be so funny after all.

I turn to grin mischievously at Jack, whose expectant, mint-green eyes are waiting for me. He knows what to expect next.

I hope I'm not spouting foul morning breath all over his adorable face while I sing, 'Good morning, starshine,' in a terrible out-of-tune manner.

'The earth says hello,' Jack responds dutifully, sounding — at least to me — like an angelic choirboy.

I laugh and pull him in for a hug, singing, 'You twinkle above us.'

'We twinkle below,' Jack murmurs in my ear.

When Matt isn't around, it's our typical morning greeting. Jack's passion for musicals and theatre makes me believe he will make a fantastic singer or actor one day. In that regard, he's just like me. We have an insatiable appetite for films such as *Grease*, *Mamma Mia*, *Hair*, *Oliver*, *Frozen* and *Wicked*. Sophie doesn't join in because she's gazing at the ceiling and blowing wet bubbles. Because of her disability, she learns more slowly than other children and doesn't talk as much yet. But that's okay. She'll learn at her own pace. I just wish Matt and his mother would understand that. Matt's mother! God, I completely forgot about her. She's coming over this morning. 'Early,' she'd said, as though it were a warning — a last chance to get things right. There's no use in pretending I like Sheila or that she has any time for me, but at least I try, which is more than can be said for her.

Panicking, I sit up in bed and exclaim, 'Come on, Jack. We'd best get up.' But the sudden movement makes me feel unexpectedly queasy and I end up swallowing a mouthful of my own vomit. Gross, I know. If I didn't know better, I'd assume I was . . . but, wait, that can't be right, can it? I mean, we hardly ever . . . these days . . . and besides, I'm taking the pill. I scowl at my protruding belly as if it had just given me a mouthful of abuse and say aloud, 'Matt would never forgive me.'

'What wouldn't I forgive?' Matt asks breezily, shooting me a quizzical look as he sweeps into the room armed with a tray, carrying it as if he were a waiter in a fine-dining establishment. His stubble from last night has vanished, his sandy hair is wet from the shower and he's already dressed — albeit in double denim. My girlfriends will attest to the fact that his fashion sense has always been questionable. If his mother showed up right now and discovered her only son serving his fat, lazy wife breakfast in bed, as though it were a daily occurrence rather than an exceedingly rare one, I wouldn't be able to show my face. I feel a little tug of disappointment as I ask myself, *does Matt do it on purpose to make me look bad?*

'Casper getting his dirty paws on the bed,' the lie slips easily out of my mouth. I'm becoming as skilled at deception as Matt. It must run in the family, judging by the accepting look on his face as he grumbles, 'He'd better not or he's for the doghouse,' with a murderous glance at the open door as if expecting the dog to bound through it.

Jack protests, half-jokingly, 'We haven't got a doghouse,' yet he has a worried expression on his face. He takes everything literally, just like me.

'I could soon build one,' Matt observes with a smile, and Jack's face instantly relaxes when he realises his father is not being serious and that Casper isn't about to be banished outside.

'What have I done to deserve breakfast in bed?' I ask, my eyes lingering hungrily on the stack of buttered toast and the steaming mug of tea. I won't lie, my mouth is already watering, but I hold back, not wishing to be seen as greedy. Rather, I take a scalding sip of the tea first, while nursing my mug in one hand.

'Isn't being my wife a good enough reason?' Matt jests, grinning as he sits down beside me on the bed.

This is not the same Matt I encountered at 4 a.m. when he fled our overpopulated bed for an empty room farther down the landing, so I say a little sharply, 'You're on fine form this morning.'

He continues in an unflinchingly cheerful tone, claiming, 'And why not? It's a beautiful summer morning and I don't have to be at work. My mother is coming to visit, and I can't wait to show this house off to her.'

With a sceptical, 'Hmm,' I hand my son a piece of toast, careful not to get buttery fingers on the bed linen. There wasn't any mention of a beautiful wife and two adorable children in that sentence, I notice grudgingly. Maybe I am being too hard on Matt. He hasn't done anything wrong, and he didn't have to make us breakfast. Ungrateful, that is what I am.

As I rub the sleep from my eyes and tell Matt, 'We're very lucky to have you,' I give him an affectionate pat on the hand, forgetting for the time being that the nausea I experienced a few moments ago had reminded me so much of the morning sickness I endured during both my pregnancies.

CHAPTER 9: RACHEL

Then

Tears well in my eyes as I bid farewell to my mother-in-law. You can call me cold-hearted all you want, but I generally don't cry. Nonetheless, I'm moved by Jonty's dejected demeanour as she takes her leave. When I encourage her to, 'Come again soon, Jonty,' she tilts her head curiously at me, as though to convey, 'We both know there's not much chance of that happening.' When I realise that she's right, I fall silent.

I offer her a hug instead, but when I see the resentful expression on Adie's face — since he is obviously standing right behind us . . . watching us — I give up and accept that her visits will be even less frequent going forward after her son's unwelcoming and hostile treatment of her.

I whisper into her parrot-jangling ear, 'I'm sorry you missed the children. They would have loved to have seen you.'

'Why don't you all come for Sunday lunch? The rest of the family will be there. It will be like old times,' she exclaims with a hopeful smile.

'I'd love to,' I admit, while darting a cautious glance over my shoulder. I'm relieved to discover Adie is now nowhere to be seen, but the look isn't lost on Jonty. She's very perceptive when it comes to her son's moods.

'If he doesn't want to come,' she hisses angrily, gesturing to thin air, 'then come on your own. With the kids, of course.'

'We'll see,' I reply tightly, unwilling to commit to a promise I can't keep.

She arches her eyebrows in what can only be described as a cynical gesture and then purses her lips and mumbles disapprovingly, 'Too big for his boots that one. Thinks he's better than the rest of us.'

I nod mutely, indicating that I would rather not talk about it. Not here. Not now. When Adie might still be listening. With a heavy sigh and a helpless shrug, Jonty frowns at the menacing dark clouds in the sky. Her regal form then disappears under the shelter of her vivid orange brolly. As I watch her walk briskly along the puddled path and leave through the wrought iron gate, I have to force myself not to beg her to come back. Feeling very alone, I close the front door with a shiver of unease.

Assuming Adie has disappeared back upstairs to the dining room, where he prefers to work when he is not in the office in London — I wander into the calming oasis of the onyx-green-and-gold library and sit at one of the antique his-and-her writing desks. They stand back to back as if they cannot bear to be separated, like a doting husband and wife, which just makes me feel claustrophobic. Repressed even. Each has a view out of one of the identical sash windows. Adie's desk, slightly bigger than mine, gazes onto the street in a predatory, watchful fashion while mine peers out on the enclosed courtyard garden. At this time of the year, it is filled with a riot of summer colours. The purple blooms of climbing wisteria and blood-red Tess of the D'Urberville roses. The scent of the garden is sometimes overpowering, like a strong perfume that requires time to evolve.

I unlock the drawer to my desk and remove the embossed emerald journal I purchased yesterday. I have been practising my handwriting, perfecting dramatic loops and smooth flowing text because I can't wait to fill its pages with words. Even though I'm not naturally skilled at penmanship, I'm determined that it should be as close to perfect as possible. This journal will be the most important asset anyone could hope to inherit, even more valuable than my fortune. Yesterday, I made a start . . .

> *My husband Adie wants me out of the way. Gone . . . so he can move his new woman (the one he thinks I don't know about) into 'our' so-called dream home as well as get his hands on my money. I don't just think this. I know this. I feel it in my heart, blood and bones. Every time he looks at me, I see a deep-seated hatred in his eyes. He watches me constantly in the hope that I will fail once more. As a wife. A mother. And as a recovering alcoholic. Adie is not alone in having secrets, though, as I remind myself every day.*

When I hear the stifled cough, I experience a moment of full-blown terror. My eyes must be full of horror as I turn to look at the door to see Adie standing there, leaning nonchalantly against the doorframe. It's as though he's been there for a while but didn't want to disturb me.

'You scared me,' I cry, as my hand flutters to my heart which is thudding painfully in my chest.

He smiles apologetically and raises his hands in surrender, saying, 'Sorry. I didn't mean to.'

Didn't you? That is what I want to retaliate with. I mumble instead, 'How long have you been standing there?'

He shrugs as though it doesn't matter, but his look suggests otherwise. 'Long enough' it seems to say, as his inquisitive eyes settle on the green journal. I hold his gaze and say nothing. Eventually, he caves and asks, 'What have you got there?'

'Nothing,' I snip, shutting the journal and returning it to the drawer without locking it this time because that would just raise his suspicions. I'll need to find another hiding spot now where he won't think to search.

As he enters the room, his icy gaze sweeping over the drawer, the desk *and me*, he observes intuitively, 'It doesn't look like nothing.'

I glance at my watch and stall for time by announcing, 'It's almost time for me to pick the children up from school.'

'While we're on the subject of the children,' he warns, pausing to let me know that I have just walked into a trap. 'I think we ought to hire a nanny.'

Startled, I exclaim, 'A nanny!' *This is far worse than I imagined. What is Adie up to?* Shooting him an *over-my-dead-body* stare, I protest, 'I hardly see my children as it is.'

CHAPTER 10: LUCY

Now

Matt's mother is expected to arrive any minute — she never provides an exact time, preferring to catch us on the 'hop', as she calls it — and I am swamped with having too much to do and barely knowing where to begin. I've spent the last hour getting the children washed and dressed in their best clothes while promising to buy them ice cream if they remain on their best behaviour during granny's visit. Right now, they're in the family room on the first floor laughing loudly at cartoons on the TV and Casper has been locked outside in the courtyard, where he keeps whining, barking and jumping up at the French windows, marking them with his paws. Somewhere in the house, the radio is tuned to BBC Radio 1, blasting out lively pop songs that I would once have bopped to. I'm surprised Matt hasn't already switched it back to BBC Radio 2, his preferred station.

'The old fart,' I snort humorously, thinking of my grumpy old-before-his-time husband, as I pick up a discarded pink princess outfit from the floor. I'm positive it's the one Sophie insisted on putting on this morning and she was still wearing it when I last checked. I shudder at what she must be wearing now. My youngest has an unsettling habit of removing all her clothes when in company. Finding her granddaughter naked wouldn't go down well with Sheila. Any more than our dog jumping up at her would. Although Casper wouldn't hurt a fly, Sheila claims he's a danger to the children and professes to fear him because he is 'uncontrollable'.

She's right in a way because none of us can get Casper to do as he's told, but that doesn't stop me wanting to have a pop at her. 'What about your son? He is just as badly behaved, thanks to you.' To be honest, she would still be on Matt's side even if he were found guilty of murdering a dozen innocent people. I guess that's mothers for you. When it comes to *my* son, though, I want Jack to understand the difference between right and wrong and treat women as equals and with respect. Not that Matt doesn't. He simply doesn't listen to anything I say. If it were up to me, we would never have taken on this amount of debt just to purchase a fancy, rundown townhouse when there was nothing wrong with our old home.

From the cellar kitchen, Matt yells, 'Are you there, Lucy?'

He sounds annoyed, as though everything, including the sounds of our home, are too much for him, and yet, as far as I can tell, he has got nothing to do because I've done it all.

'Coming,' I yell back, rolling my eyes as I dutifully make my way to the kitchen.

Unlike Matt, I can't bear silence. I want to be surrounded by the noise made by the people I love. For me, family is everything. I have never been any different, and I used to believe that Matt and I shared the same values. But since his affair, when he changed in many ways, I worry that he has outgrown his small family, or more accurately, me. And I don't know how to keep up or even if I want to. You see, I rather like being me. Without wanting to sound big-headed, I think I'm a nice person. The Lucy Haywood that was . . . had been a popular girl at school, renowned for having a wicked sense of humour, a dirty laugh, and a kind heart. I miss her in the same way I pine for my long blonde hair, which I had chopped into a boring, middle-aged bob after Sophie was born, because, if I'm being completely honest, I couldn't handle it. Or most other things when I found out Matt was having an affair around that time.

Looking back, I believe that my long hair, along with my bold red lipstick, love of ripped jeans and friendship bracelets, played a significant role in who I was. My girlfriends dubbed it 'boho chic' and emulated me. However, Matt asserted that sophisticated women wouldn't be seen dead in such attire. I began to suspect that his lover had not only been smart and attractive, but also classy. A depressing thought indeed, especially since I haven't put a scrap of make-up on, and my unwashed hair is in a messy bun. Why couldn't he have downgraded like most errant husbands do according to TikTok. Something else Matt disapproves of me being into, which I add to my jar of secrets, otherwise known as 'the things Matt mustn't know about', because it will upset the applecart of our marriage.

'Not that he hasn't done that already,' I seethe inwardly. Torn as always between loving my husband, having to walk on eggshells around him and wanting to beat the shit out of him before showing him the door.

He is facing away from me when I enter the kitchen. His tense jaw, pulsing cheek, and stiff posture, which remind me of a prey animal about to take flight has me instantly on high alert. Before I can ask him what's wrong, he asks in a tight voice, 'What's this doing here?'

'Did I forget to put the milk back in the fridge again?' I sigh impatiently, privately thinking it's the least of our problems if that's the case.

He grimaces as he turns to face me and then summons me with an authoritative finger. I sigh once more, this time in relief, as I approach the fridge freezer to see what he is staring at. 'Oh, is that all? I found the magnet yesterday, under the freezer — or rather Casper did.'

Intolerantly, Matt interrupts, 'But what is it doing *here?*'

'I think it's a picture of the family that lived here before us and I didn't have the heart to throw it away. So, I thought I'd put it on the freezer where it belongs, since that's clearly where it used to be before it fell off.'

Matt looks at me in amazement. His complexion is pale and drawn and he looks ill, so I deduce that he might be coming down with the same attack of nausea I experienced earlier this morning. *Hopefully that's all it was.*

He narrows his eyes darkly and argues, 'But they don't live here anymore, and this is *our* house now.' Sometimes, when he looks at me this way, I get the feeling he'd like to hurt me, but I quickly dismiss this absurd idea. Matt isn't like that. He wouldn't do that to anybody, least of all his own family. And yet that's exactly what he did when he had the affair with that homewrecker and his betrayal almost destroyed us.

'They're a very attractive couple, don't you think?' I suggest helpfully, wanting to engage him in conversation about the mysterious pair.

He is scornful. 'I can't say I've given it any thought.'

Then he rips it from the freezer and carries it to the bin.

'What are you doing?' I gasp.

As if it were rubbish, he tosses the magnet into the bin and laments, 'I don't want to see their faces. Besides,' he stresses indignantly, 'even if they did used to live here, and you don't know that for sure, *it's our home now.*'

I scowl. 'How many more times are you going to have to say that word before you convince yourself?'

'What do you mean?' he demands, stumped.

My voice quivers but I manage to say, 'Why won't you admit that this house just isn't home for us?'

'Speak for yourself,' he hisses nastily.

Since I genuinely want him to understand, I try again, but more gently this time, 'Oh, come on, Matt. It's too elegant for the likes of us.'

He just out his chin in defiance, insisting, 'I can be elegant.'

I purse my lips at that. 'Says the man wearing double denim.'

Matt's chin drops forlornly onto his chest as he glances down at his clothes. I almost feel sorry for him when he asks in a hurt, childlike way, 'What's wrong with double denim?'

The sudden and persistent ringing of the doorbell saves me from answering. It has a superior, regal sound, which is not surprising.

'That will be your mother,' I tell Matt bluntly.

As Matt stomps off to answer the door, I retrieve the photo magnet from the bin and wipe away the remaining broken egg-shells and burnt toast from it so I can study it more closely. I'm struck once again by the woman's haunted expression. Who or what was causing her such intense sadness? As I slip the magnet into my pocket for safekeeping, I wonder if the couple in the photo was happy or if they were experiencing some of the same issues as Matt and me. Who were they, I think, *especially her* . . . and how can I find out more about them?

CHAPTER 11: RACHEL

Then

It's Adie's fault I'm late picking the children up from school. There are many gas-guzzling vehicles like mine in the car park — mostly glossy Range Rovers and family-friendly Volvos. This is Stamford after all. Home of the 4x4. I don't congregate at the school gates though to share plant-based recipes, organise sleepovers or boast of my children's accomplishments in swimming, netball and music like the other mothers do, opting instead to stay in my car. *Loner that I am.* The mums all look like they're heading to a summer festival with their floaty dresses and mermaid-wave hairstyles.

After Adie dropped the bombshell about hiring a nanny, we rowed. Of course we did. And, suspecting that this was just the first step of many in isolating me from my children, I did not hold back. I let rip, accusing him of attempting to portray me as an inept wife and mother, who wasn't permitted to clean her own house, much less look after her own children.

Knowing he finally had my full attention; his mouth had lifted into an unpleasant smirk. 'Hear me out,' he'd advised stiffly, as though I were being unreasonable. Careful not to antagonise him, I had inhaled deeply and waited for him to continue.

'You've mentioned several times that you want to go back to work,' Adie had announced unexpectedly, leaving the promise of freedom dangling in the air, and I was like a willing fish at the end of his hook. Filled with hope I dared to ask, 'Are you okay with that now then?'

When he didn't immediately respond, I pressed him further, 'You've always said you'd rather I stay at home with the children a while longer.'

'I might be cool with it if we got a nanny.'

At that moment, I could hardly believe my luck, even though the Rachel Beiersdorf I was in the past would never have sought permission from a man about whether I could pursue a career as a working mother.

My mind screeched at me to stay calm when Adie held up a finger and spelled out for me, 'But on one condition.'

'What?'

Clearing his throat, Adie had declared, 'You know how much I want another child.'

'That's blackmail,' I'd protested, staring at him with barely concealed loathing. 'Besides, I don't need your permission to go back to work,' I'd continued, folding my arms aggressively in what was supposed to be a brave posture. 'You're my husband, not my father. And you don't own me.'

'Maybe not,' he'd conceded, clenching his palms in his pockets as if he were of the opposite opinion and flashing me a brazen grin. 'But after everything that's happened, I feel that I have a right as a husband, and let's not forget . . . the father of my children, to be concerned about how returning to full-time employment and the inevitable long commutes to London could affect your mental health.'

Flabbergasted, I'd insisted firmly, 'I'm not ill. I never was. And you were wrong to tell your mother I was. I just drank a little too much for a while, that's all. And we all know why that was.' I couldn't resist adding another nasty but well-deserved dig, 'Who can blame me after what you did?' as I waited for him to go on digging a hole for himself.

There was a split second of hesitation from him before he replied in a deliberately bored manner, 'If there wasn't anything wrong with you, why would your doctor prescribe antidepressants and recommend that you attend a rehabilitation centre for alcoholics?'

I recall thinking how much I wanted to hurt him at that moment, but Adie is untouchable. Unlike me, he's never publicly put a foot wrong. I have no proof of his latest affair either. Nonetheless, I know my face was unnaturally flushed as I remonstrated, 'I never took the pills, as you're aware, and the doctor only suggested rehab because he knew I could afford it.' My voice had cracked as I finished lamely, 'As much for a rest from you as anything.'

'I believe I've been perfectly reasonable in requesting that our children are adequately cared for by a qualified and responsible person, in the absence of their mother should she choose to return to work or otherwise be absent from their lives for any other reason for a prolonged period,' Adie offers calmly by way of explanation, but his face is pinched with anger.

I'd scowled dismissively to disguise my fear. Because I knew that I would lose if there was a custody battle over the children. Given my history, I wouldn't stand a chance. Adie wins again. But wait! My mind is blown to a million pieces when I figure out what he's secretly keeping from me, and what his true intentions are. But is Adie really that evil?

'Do you already have someone in mind?' I'd probed, adding for clarity, 'for the nanny position?' so he couldn't evade answering.

I'd watched his gaze shift as he glanced uneasily around the room, before admitting, 'I've had a few names recommended to me.'

This implied that my husband had already discussed this with someone else . . . *her*, before raising the subject with me.

'The bastard,' I shriek, viciously pounding my palm on the steering wheel as I recollect his words. Then it's my turn to look around anxiously, hoping that one of the other mums hasn't witnessed my violent outburst. Luck is on my side for once because I soon realise that I'm the only mum left in the car park and all the other vehicles have gone. Praying that the school hasn't marked me down as a non-attending parent, because that will also work against me, I scramble out of the car and search for my children. I smile in relief when I see them barrelling towards me in a whirl of red satchels, blue blazers and matching school caps.

Adie is in for a shock if he thinks he's going to install his whore in my home to look after my children as I'm certain that's what he intends to do.

CHAPTER 12: LUCY

Now

The roast chicken isn't cooked all the way through, so only the crispy outer bits are edible (the best bits in my opinion). Far worse, the Yorkshire puddings are burnt and there are lumps in the mashed potatoes. Casper, who is still locked outside, irritates everyone with his constant barking. The kids can't sit still, and they fidget at the table and try not to laugh. Talk about awkward. Much like the adults around the table, they merely pick at their food. Matt has had too much red wine. Sheila hasn't had enough. She's as tightly wound as a roll of barbed wire. And her husband, John, a man of few words and a miserable expression, has barely spoken a word to me since he arrived, saving all his 'manly' DIY conversation for his son.

Matt likes to make out his father is socially awkward around women, but I don't believe that for one minute. For heaven's sake, he's sixty-two and has been married for a longer period than he hasn't. Sheila at least fakes a polite interest in the house and the kids, but as usual, she doesn't attempt to spend any quality time with her grandchildren.

'I think it's fair to say that lunch wasn't exactly a success,' I say to the hushed table, as I scrape back my chair and stand up, desperate to clear the table of food *and* visitors.

'It wasn't *that* bad,' Matt mumbles for my sake, but he seems glad that the charade of eating is done, and he can finally lay down his knife and fork. As he gets to his feet to help me scrape the leftovers from the plates, his mother's thinly plucked eyebrows skyrocket.

'I can do that, son.' Sheila's piercing voice stabs at us from the other side of the table. 'You go and sit down and rest. You've earned it,' she suggests graciously . . . as though Matt were the one who had been on his feet all morning, peeling vegetables, stuffing the chicken and slaving over a hot oven. Did I mention that I did all of this while also keeping an eye on the kids, who became shy and clingy the second their grandparents showed up? Other than showing his parents the house, I can't for the life of me think what else Matt has done all morning.

Seeing my look of indignation, Matt has the grace to look embarrassed, but that doesn't stop him from taking his mother up on her offer. 'Are you sure?' he asks with a grateful smile, putting down a stack of plates.

Sheila gives an indulgent nod and hauls herself to her feet, using the table's edge for support. She's a big woman; almost obese I'd say. She has been diagnosed with Type 2 diabetes and suffers from poor health as a result. She must be pitied for that, but Matt never urges her to lose weight for her 'own good' as he does me. I've gleaned a lot from listening to Matt and his mum talk over the years. They genuinely need each other, so it's simple for me to fall silent around them. When the two of them get together, even John feels unnecessary.

'Take your father with you. Don't leave him here under our feet,' she commands with an affectionate grin.

I shoot Matt a warning look before he has a chance to vanish upstairs. 'And the children,' I insist bluntly, an edge to my voice.

To be fair to Matt, he tries to persuade the kids to follow him, pulling comical faces and reaching out with both hands, but they react with poker faces. Jack takes one look at his granddad's stern expression, and shakes his head in refusal, muttering, 'We want to stay with Mum.' It goes without saying that Sophie will do the same. Wherever Jack goes, his sister follows.

Matt shrugs stoically, as though expecting me to give him a hard time. 'You can't say I didn't try,' he chirps anxiously, before placing a hand in the middle of his father's back and guiding him up the darkly lit concrete steps. I know exactly where they're going. The largest TV in the house is located on the first-floor family room. Both enjoy motor racing, and the Hungarian Grand Prix is about to begin. We won't see the pair of them for the rest of the afternoon.

When I turn to face my mother-in-law, she's standing over by the big butler sink, armed with a bottle of washing-up liquid and a squeezy sponge.

'You don't have to do that,' I tell her firmly.

'I said I would,' she sniffs, not so eager to lend a hand now that her son isn't around to witness her good deed of the day.

'I meant we have a dishwasher now so there's no need to wash up by hand,' I stammer sheepishly by way of an explanation.

As I point to the black glossy dishwasher in the corner, her eyes meet mine. 'Fancy,' she says with a sneer, adding, 'you really have gone up in the world, haven't you?'

I try not to take offence and say instead — warmly, I might add, 'We couldn't have done it without your help, Sheila.'

Mollified, she snorts, 'I suppose not. Although considering all the money we've given you, I still don't see why Matthew had to quit the job he loved. He's not exactly making a lot more money at his new place, is he?'

'Perhaps not,' I agree, unsure where this conversation is going. 'However, that was his choice.' What I *don't* say is that *it was either that or walk away from our marriage.*

'That's not the impression I got,' she snarls in an accusatory tone, and it seems to me that she has been clinging to this belief for a while and has even been consumed by it.

I sigh and grimace, too tired to play games, and then I ask her straight out, 'What exactly has Matt told you?'

Devoted to her child regardless of the offence, she dutifully responds, 'Nothing he shouldn't have.' However, she can't help but confess, 'With the exception of admitting that he was happy at Caterpillar and made good friends there. He was sorry to leave them, he said.'

Her brief speech has shocked me and made me feel physically ill again in an exact same recurrence of the sickness from this morning. My stomach churns as I ask in a loaded voice, 'Did he mention anyone in particular?' I hold my breath, wondering if Sheila is going to unintentionally reveal the name of Matt's former lover. The female colleague he'd had the affair with.

'No,' she says, shaking her head, and for once, I don't think she's covering up for her son. 'But I do believe that you were the cause of his departure. Or rather, it was your ambition. He hasn't been himself since, you know, and, well, if you don't mind me saying so, he's going to wear himself out before too long and make himself ill if you keep pressuring him to earn more money so he can continue to maintain this lifestyle.'

I harumph as her eyes wander deliberately to the opulent surroundings of our new home. *The house I didn't want.* What I'm hearing is almost unbelievable. Wait until I get my hands on that no-good, lying husband of mine. I'll have his balls on a plate by the end of the day.

As I answer quietly, 'Actually, I do mind,' I look pitifully at Sheila. Because of her toxic and unhealthy relationship with Matt, I find myself making a new commitment to avoid making the same mistakes with Jack.

Something pink and glittery lands at our feet before either of us can say anything else that we might regret. This is followed by a flurry of loud laughter. When I recognise Sophie's princess outfit, I groan inwardly, realising she must have removed it again.

Sheila cries, 'The girl is stark naked,' as though she has never witnessed anything so outrageous in her life. Meanwhile, Sophie clumsily mimics a ballet dancer as she dances around the kitchen, completely unfazed.

'For heaven's sake, Lucy, get your daughter to put her clothes back on before the men come down,' Sheila insists, eyes darting towards the stairs.

I yell, 'She's only two and still a baby so it's hardly a crime.' If looks could kill, she'd be dead right now. The silly mare. Only then do I focus on Sophie, not because she's naked, but because she is clasping something in her hands that I have never seen before . . . an expensive-looking, emerald-green journal.

CHAPTER 13: RACHEL

Then

In the otherwise quiet house, I hear Adie's footsteps creaking heavily on the stairs, and my head snaps up in alarm. Although we have lived at Rutland Terrace for less than a week, I can tell exactly where he is in the house at any time based on his movements. Fear does that to you. It keeps you on your toes. I am aware that I have less than two minutes to stash my journal in its new hiding spot — behind a loose wooden-panelled wall in my dressing room, which is styled in a soft, feminine art deco theme to complement the house's Georgian architecture. In it, I've written:

> *Now that I know what his game is, I am in even more danger. He watches me as if I were the villain in our story and silently works to turn the children against me. He is up there with them now, reading them a story and putting them to bed, even though he knows it is my turn. If Adie gets his way, my children will soon not know me. I can't allow that to happen.*

By the time Adie quietly walks into our bedroom — as though his intention was always to sneak up on me — I'm reclining on the king-sized bed with one palm poised against my scowling forehead, indicating that a migraine is about to strike. When he notices the pill bottle on the bedside table, he nods grimly, a deep frown of concentration on his face.

He observes intuitively. 'Another headache?'

'I'm afraid so,' I groan in fake frustration because there's nothing wrong with me. *As I keep telling him.*

He comes to patiently sit beside me on the bed, his weight disturbing the perfect satin ripples of the duck-egg bedspread, and murmurs, 'That's a shame when I've managed to get the kids down early,' with a teasing, seductive grin. *Too close. He's too close.* I want to scream.

He lazily picks up my hand and holds it possessively to his mouth, which feels as cold as death on my flesh, and I experience a sense of dread. I'm not sure if I should brace myself for another searing slap like the one from last night, so I smile disarmingly at him and murmur an apologetic, 'Sorry,' before nervously asking, 'how were they tonight?'

As I look him in the eye, I watch his jaw tighten. He averts his gaze away from me and mumbles, 'The children were perfect as always.'

'Did they ask for me?' I blurt out, scanning his face.

'No. Should they have done?'

I flinch at his clipped tone and my voice is barely a whisper as I protest, 'But it was meant to be my turn to put them to bed.'

In a flash, he drops my hand and cups a hand to his chin, as if deep in thought, before reflecting, 'But you said yourself you're not feeling well.'

The implicit 'again' in his voice is audible. However, it's a point I can't dispute. He's aware he has me beaten. That doesn't stop me from wanting to wipe the smugness from his face though. Feeling a hint of terror building in my voice, I bluster, 'I'll pop in and see them later to kiss them goodnight.'

Taking the medicine bottle off the bedside table, Adie stands up to examine the small print, before replying unconvincingly, 'I wouldn't do that if I were you.'

It *sounds* like a threat because *it is* a threat. Fighting off a sense of trepidation, I insist, 'Why not?'

He puts down the medication and turns to face me, warning, 'You know why,' and I wince at the way his eyes are narrowed into slits.

I wait a long moment, avoiding eye contact with him, and then I finally muster up the courage to say, 'Actually, I don't.'

He shrugs dismissively and seems to withdraw into himself as he removes his glasses to wipe his eyes and then puts them back on his head.

'Seeing you like this is not good for them,' he admits with a heavy sigh.

'Like what?'

'Upset. Distressed. And in need of medication,' Adie answers curtly.

'Adie, I'm not any of those things,' I object, in what I fear is a pathetic whining voice. 'Why would you say that when I simply have a headache and the only medication I've taken is two paracetamols?'

As I explain this, I point to the pill bottle. However, he is now facing away from me and his gaze is focused intently on the dressing room, where I concealed the journal. It's as if he suspects me of something. But even Adie isn't that clever. *Is he?* He cannot have guessed my secret. *Can he?*

As he finally turns to face me, I can't help but notice how exhausted he looks. His eyes are a picture of misery and if I'm not mistaken, he has also lost weight. Knowing that his deception and infidelity are destroying him gives me a sick sense of satisfaction, and I begin to question whether this man — who once loved me, before lust, greed and crippling debt got in the way — has any regrets and wishes he could go back in time.

I immediately retract my thoughts when he tells me in a guarded, menacing manner, 'The sooner your inheritance is sorted out, Rachel, the better it will be for all of us. You most of all.'

His comment causes a new wave of anxiety to wash over me, until my heart is thudding painfully in my chest as if I had taken a dose of antipsychotic medication. However, I'm brave enough, or foolish enough — take your pick — to persevere, by demanding, 'What do you mean by that?'

Voice loaded with something like greed, he informs me, 'I mean that the money will free us up as a family to concentrate on the important things, like hiring a nanny and getting you the help you need. I fear our family won't be safe until that happens.'

'Safe from what? From whom?'

'Why, you, of course,' he responds sharply, as though it were obvious, before striding abruptly out of the room.

CHAPTER 14: LUCY

Now

'I've said I'm sorry a million times. What else do you want me to do?' Matt complains in a whiny hard-done-by voice while fighting with the pillows on the bed that are too plump for his liking.

I storm out of the ensuite bathroom. 'Not lie to your mother for a start.' He has chosen to launch his defence while I am in the middle of brushing my teeth, but I am as open to a debate on this subject as he is. Yet, there is something unsettling about the way he is staring at me. Not only is there humour behind his eyes but there is something else too. He hasn't made a pass at me in a long time, but if I didn't know any better, I would guess it was lust.

With my hands on my rounded hips, I shake my head angrily and demand, 'What are you staring at?' My voice crackles with tension, but Matt doesn't notice and grins impishly. It's the same smile he uses on his mother to soften her up when he's after something. Money, usually.

He laughs and pats the bed, inviting me in. 'You,' he says.

'You don't get off that easily,' I scowl and stomp back into the bathroom, where I swill my mouth and put my pink toothbrush into the holder next to his blue one. There's something about their togetherness that touches me, so when I return to the bedroom, I have a ghost of a smile on my face.

'You're right,' I tell him. 'Let's change the subject.'

'Does that mean I'm forgiven?' He poses the question flirtingly.

I tut. 'I never said that.'

When Matt folds back the white duvet cover on my side of the bed, I crawl inside, but I don't automatically cuddle up to him like I used to. These days, any advances must come from him. My pride won't have it any other way. When he doesn't pounce on me right away — chance would be a fine thing — and instead begins to scroll through his phone, I ask, 'What do you know about the people who lived here before us?'

Even before he gets a chance to respond, I sense his reluctance. He never engages in gossip or shows more than a casual interest in our acquaintances and friends (especially my girlfriends, who he can't stand). The only exception to this was, of course, his ex-female coworker. Since I don't know her name, let's call her 'homewrecking trash' for now.

He murmurs, 'Why do you ask?' without looking up from his phone.

'I'm curious about them, that's all,' I observe chattily, as I settle comfortably into the bed. 'We seem to have inherited a lot of their things. The freezer, the kitchen table, a writing desk, cups, vases and so forth.'

He turns to face me and says tightly, 'I'm sure they'll come in handy.' His Adam's apple bobbing up and down is a sure sign of his displeasure.

I pull a face and scoff, 'A writing desk? Neither of us has written a letter since we were five years old.' He says nothing in response but shrugs his shoulders as though the conversation has ended. Unwisely, I don't pick up on his irritation, so I rattle on, 'I think we should complain to the solicitors and get the previous owners to pay for their removal.'

'What on earth for? They're valuable pieces,' he objects, sending me a look of derision as if I were crazy for wanting them gone.

'Yes,' I agree grudgingly, before pointing out, 'but their fancy style isn't ours.' To that, he merely frowns, as if 'not having any taste' were just one more nail in my coffin. I'm not deterred by the fact that he has returned to staring at his phone. Never knowing when to stop, I observe, 'They look as if they're a similar age to us and their son must be around Jack's age too.'

Matt now reserves the right to remain silent and just nods in response to my cues. I'm tempted to tell him about the journal and what's written inside it because he couldn't help but pay attention then. But I know if I do, he'll insist that I get rid of it. In fact, he's likely to throw it out like he tried to do with the photo magnet. If he knew that I was reading about another husband's affair, he'd go apeshit and say that it wasn't good for me (by that he'd really mean him) and he would be right because it has brought back memories of Matt's affair, although in all honesty they never truly went away. How could they? Betrayal never dies. Unlike love.

Much to the disgust of my mother-in-law who had quickly left the room, Sophie had to be bribed with 'Mama's milk' before she would relinquish the journal, but as soon as I held it in my hands, I instantly connected with its author, whom I now know is named Rachel. For once, I didn't feel alone. I wasn't the only wife with a cheating husband. Some of the things she wrote about though were scandalous because her husband was allegedly trying to get rid of her so he could move his mistress in, in addition to his having multiple affairs. I started to question if I should believe everything I was reading at that point, particularly the bit about his wanting her money and her fearing for her life. But who would lie about such things? Nobody sane, surely. This woman was obviously not crazy. If anything, her writing was so eloquent and beautiful that it gave the impression that she was extremely intelligent. She's heavily into literature in a way that I am not, and she frequently mentions book titles I've never heard of — which isn't saying much for me — like *Madame Bovary.*

I know I've tried Matt's patience for too long when I hear him blowing out his cheeks in frustration. 'I don't know anything about the previous owners and nor do I want to,' he complains. 'So can we please quit talking about people who have no connection to us at all?' Then, as if to signal that it's time for bed, he finally puts his phone down on the bedside table.

'Whether you like it or not, we *are* connected,' I insist testily. 'They used to live in our house.'

'Exactly. They *used to*,' he sighs as if I had entirely missed the point. Then, using a different strategy — anything to shut me up — he leans in and whispers sexily, 'It's *our* house now.'

When he gazes longingly into my eyes — a burning desire in them — I suddenly feel lightheaded. At that moment, I am willing to forgive him for anything, no matter how terrible. I never once consider the possibility that I might have to do this for real one day.

CHAPTER 15: RACHEL

Then

After we received a reproachful message from the school regarding my lateness yesterday, Adie insisted on driving the kids to school this morning, clearly not trusting me to get them there on time. He's meant to be working in London this week but informed me that he had called in sick because he felt I shouldn't be left on my own. I chose not to call him out for lying, even though I'm aware he has been suspended on full pay while the sexual misconduct case is being investigated. I will finally have all the evidence I want if he is found guilty and fired. If we get divorced and have to go through a custody battle, his character will be called into question. This will finally put us on equal terms.

I had been relying on this, but I've since learned that Adie's female work colleague has dropped all allegations against him and is no longer employed at Prince Tech. I wonder if this news has reached Adie yet. If so, he'll be insufferable when he returns home. Like an all-powerful God who can do no wrong. How do I know this? When the situation originally surfaced, weeks ago, a former coworker of mine had alerted me to the grievance investigation. Juliet Finch, a fellow reporter who is engaged to a man who also works at Prince Tech thought I should be made aware of what

Adie had been up to, if I wasn't already. Everyone was talking about the case, she said, even though it was supposed to be confidential. In her most recent text message sent minutes after Adie left the house this morning, Juliet was unable to tell me if the woman had departed on her own initiative or had been fired for fabricating claims against a senior member of staff.

I take a sip of my scalding black coffee and look around at the dreary stone walls of the dimly lit kitchen and its oppressive concrete island, craving fresh air and light. The remains of the children's breakfast are on the oak dining table. A selection of leftover yoghurt with blueberries and chia seeds, bright yellow free-range scrambled eggs and flaking croissants with apricot conserve are piled onto scalloped bone-china bowls and plates. Not at all like the cold meats and cheese I grew up breakfasting on in Germany before moving to London with my parents when I was eight.

I don't attempt to clear the table or stack the dishwasher since the cleaner will be arriving at 9 a.m. to do that. When I first met Clara (last name unknown) I could tell she took an instant dislike to me. I'd hoped we might become friends, but she is clearly on Adie's side. He's the one who pays her wages — as well as outrageous compliments — even though it's my money he uses. She doesn't know that, though, and sees me as nothing more than a ghost who does extraordinarily little around the house and avoids her presence by moving silently from room to room. We've hardly exchanged more than a dozen words since I moved to Rutland Terrace.

Before heading upstairs to have a refreshing shower after my usual morning run, I tip the remains of my coffee into the double-bowl ceramic butler sink and put a carton of almond milk back in the fridge. At least I can do that without stepping on Clara's toes, I think in satisfaction, as I close the door on the extravagant display of organic fruit and vegetables.

That's when I see it. A magnetic photo of the four of us stuck to the freezer door. One of the children must have put it there. I remember the day it was taken in the supermarket, at Archie's insistence, because he'd never seen a photobooth before and thought it would be fun. Fun! Adie and I had just had another of our terrible arguments, I recall, although not in front of the children. We never did that. The row was over money, of course. And we were barely speaking. Adie and I were happy once. Before his affairs and the gambling debts took precedence and robbed him of his morality. Locking eyes with the woman in the picture, who is a subdued, timid version of the person I once was, I roll my eyes theatrically before asking aloud, 'Who are you, Rachel?' My words hang in the air, bouncing off the stone walls and echoing around me, but all I hear back is silence.

My heart is heavy in my chest as I ascend the first- and second-floor stairs. I'm unsure what to do about Juliet's news and I keep asking myself the same question . . . Why has the woman who made the allegation changed her mind? I shudder at the thought that Adie might have warned her off. He is more than capable of threatening others, as I am well aware.

The champagne queen-sized leather bed in our master bedroom remains unmade, which is another task for Clara. Adie's side is smooth and unruffled as if nobody had slept in it, whereas the Laura Ashley duvet on my side of the bed is wildly tangled, and the goose feather pillows have fallen onto the floor. If this doesn't speak volumes about our individual mental states, I don't know what does. I make sure the journal is still behind the wooden-panelled wall in my dressing room, where I put it, before I take a shower in the marble rainforest shower cubicle. I don't like to think about what would happen if Adie should get his thieving hands on it.

Some, but not all, of the tension leaves my body once I'm in the shower with soothing hot water trickling down on me till my pale skin turns an angry shade of red. As I close my eyes against the stream of filtered water and let my chin rest on my chest, I picture Clara using the key Adie gave her to enter the back door so she can clean my home and launder my children's clothing. I may not be the wife and mother I hoped to be, but one thing I *was* always good at was working as a journalist.

As I come to an impulsive decision, I snap open one eye and stretch my face into a smile that I'm certain resembles the Rachel Beiersdorf BA (Hons), Master of Research and British Association of Journalists member I used to be. The answer to my problems has been staring me in the face all along. I'll put my investigative skills to good use and speak with the woman who made allegations against Adie myself. If anyone can find out the truth, I can. I'll go today before I change my mind. This afternoon even. No. I'll leave before Adie returns later this morning and take the first available train to London. Just as soon as I've rung Julia and wheedled the woman's address out of her.

CHAPTER 16: LUCY

Now

Last night in bed Matt insisted he didn't know anything about the couple who lived here before us. I'm not sure if I believe him, but I've made up my mind that if he won't help me learn more about them, I'll find someone who will. Like our new neighbours. They're bound to know *something*.

After dropping Jack off at school, I returned to Rutland Terrace via Stamford Meadows, which is a picturesque tangle of green fields. I avoided the morning crush of dogwalkers who all appeared to know one another, staying on the winding path as I pushed Sophie's pink flamingo buggy ahead of me. We'd left Casper at home because I didn't think any of our neighbours would appreciate me knocking on their door with a psychopathic hound in tow. An army of joggers has also been enticed out by the morning's promise of sunshine and clear blue skies which reminds me that before I became pregnant with Sophie, Matt and I would often go running together. These days I'm not fit enough to attempt it, so Matt goes alone, although not as much as he used to. He complains, 'The new job takes up too much of my time,' and I have to bite my tongue and not say anything scathing like, 'Not as much as an affair.'

As we exit the park and enter the impressive Georgian terrace, which dominates the whole street, I survey the windows of the houses on each side of ours. When I notice a shadow filling the glass behind number eleven's front door, I point the buggy in its direction and ring the doorbell. As soon as Sophie discovers we are not going straight home she scowls and flaps her arms in protest. 'I'll only be a minute or two,' I promise her.

An elderly gentleman answers the door. He has on a tweed jacket and a shirt and tie despite the heat. He stinks of pipe tobacco and has yellow-stained eyes. He blocks my view with the door, so I only get the tiniest glimpse of his hallway. It smells of fish — kippers, if I'm not mistaken — and has a dark, damp appearance. His unsmiling face registers surprise when he sees us on his doorstep.

'What do you want?' he hisses in an unfriendly manner.

'I'm Lucy,' I reply in the brightest voice I can manage. 'Your new next-door neighbour,' I add, gesturing to number thirteen.

'And?' he grumbles irritably.

Since this first meeting isn't exactly going as planned, I squirm uncomfortably. 'I thought I'd just say a quick hello and introduce myself.'

'Well, young lady, it seems like you've accomplished your mission,' he says with an ugly laugh before slamming the door shut.

'Rude,' I mutter, wondering if I should ring the doorbell a second time and try again in case he misheard me the first time. But I'm distracted by the twitch of a curtain in one of the downstairs rooms of the house next door. After letting out a deep sigh, I turn around and march up the footpath to number nine. I'm not going to let one bad-tempered neighbour distract me from my mission.

The woman at number nine is tall, slender and impeccably dressed. Everything I am not. Flawlessly made up, she wears black chinos and a champagne silk blouse, with dark oversized sunglasses perched on top of her head. Her long ash-blonde hair is styled in an elegant updo as if she were on her way to a wedding. How anyone can look this good first thing in the morning is beyond me and I'm even more impressed when I see the little boy, who is about Sophie's age, clutching timidly to her legs. It's a welcome surprise that one of my nearest neighbours is also a mum. My first thought is that we might wind up being friends. But given my husband's lack of self-control when it comes to the opposite sex, I wonder if it would be unwise of me to befriend someone as attractive as her.

'Can I help you?' she enquires pleasantly, with a hint of something foreign but unmistakably sexy in her tone. I'm guessing she's Latvian or Russian. I make up my mind to keep her away from Matt at all costs.

I automatically repeat, 'I'm your new next-door neighbour, from number thirteen,' and point to our house two doors down.

'Oh, how lovely of you to come and say hello,' she exclaims with a smile. 'We saw the removal lorry arrive.'

'I hope we didn't disturb you. We can be a noisy lot,' I joke.

'Not at all,' she chuckles, extending a softly fragranced hand with French-manicured fingernails to shake mine. 'I'm Alina.'

'Lucy,' I smile back at her but try to hide my own paint-chipped, flaky nails from her since I'm ashamed of them.

'And who's this?' she gestures kindly to Sophie, who is staring wide-eyed at the little boy, her curiosity aroused.

'Sophie.'

'Alex, come and say hello to Sophie,' Alina encourages, but her son hangs back, looking doubtful.

'He's shy around strangers,' she whispers conspiratorially to justify her son's lack of manners.

'As he should be,' I nod, but I can tell it goes beyond that, and Alina is too polite to mention it. When someone usually first sees

Sophie, they can't help but notice the physical characteristics that indicate she has Down syndrome. To me, she is beautiful just as she is, and I find it hurtful when strangers gaze at her as though she were an object of curiosity. Children typically notice these differences first, and I'm proven right when Alex eventually comes out with the inevitable:

'What's wrong with the little girl?'

Mortified by her son's outburst, Alina averts her horrified gaze from mine as if unsure how to respond. Believing her to be kind, I take pity on her and reassure her, 'It's okay, we get this all the time. You can always rely on kids to say exactly what they're thinking.' And then I address Alex directly, saying, 'Sophie may look a little different to other children, Alex, but inside she's just the same. And just like you, she loves to play.'

It's true. My daughter is a fighter and won't be pushed into the background. Right now, she's attempting to break free of her restraints, clearly intent on making a new friend. The next thing I know, Alina is saying, 'Won't you both come in?' while holding the door wide open.

CHAPTER 17: RACHEL

Then

She lives on a quiet tree-lined street in Islington in a self-contained Victorian converted flat. Just around the corner, a multitude of quirky restaurants and bustling bars can be found. I find myself almost envying her lifestyle. Not bad for an information security analyst making £62k a year, which leads me to suspect that Sasha Walker is supplementing her income in other less reputable ways. From here, it's only an eleven-minute tube journey to Tech City in Hackney where the Prince Tech building is. Its 16,000-square-metre offices are spread across three shiny glass-and-chrome floors, with Adie — her tormentor and my husband — sitting at its throne.

After I've rang the doorbell, I stand back to check out my reflection in the blurred metal elevator door. The messy bun is gone, and I'm not wearing jogging bottoms or jeans for once. My shoulder-length brown hair is straightened to a razor-sharp edge and I'm wearing a forest-green linen dress with black patent court shoes (not too high as I'm no longer used to wearing heels). I could almost pass myself off as my old self. *Almost.*

She takes aeons to respond, but I hear a sluggish murmur behind the door, 'Just a minute.' I hover anxiously in the meantime and flinch when I hear a woman's voice demanding, 'What do you want?' through the Ring doorbell camera. I hadn't anticipated that she might not open the door to talk to me, preferring to communicate using the camera, although as a single woman living alone in the city, it makes perfect sense. Realising she can see me but I can't see her is very off-putting, so I put on a fake smile and bluster, 'My name is Rachel, and I was hoping to talk to you.'

Silence.

And then . . . in a voice filled with loathing, she hisses:

'I know who you are.'

Puzzled, I reply, 'You do? But I don't think we've ever met before.'

Accusingly, she barks, 'Adie keeps a photo of you on his desk.'

I feel my cheeks flushing with heat as I process that unexpected information. What a strange thing for Adie to do in the circumstances. I assumed he only ever placed my framed picture on his desk if I happened to drop by his office for a quick visit to go out for lunch, like we used to do when we both lived and worked in London. I always imagined it would be forgotten in a desk drawer the rest of the time. Perhaps he keeps it there for show, to impress his colleagues, or more correctly his superiors by demonstrating that he is not only a perfect employee but a loyal husband. Somebody who can be trusted. Not someone who gaslighted and manipulated his wife into believing she was the crazy one, or who sexually harassed his coworkers.

'If you know who I am, then you must know why I'm here.'

Once more, silence.

Then I hear the gentle rattling of a safety chain being released followed by a soft click as the door reluctantly opens. Suddenly Sasha is standing in front of me. A real person.

'Why *are* you here?' she snaps, jutting out her chin in a childish gesture.

I notice right away that she isn't Adie's usual type. She has bleached blonde hair, a fake tan and is petite, only five feet two. She isn't unattractive. Far from it. She has a pretty, doll-like face. However, she is not the tall, slender, dark-haired, pale-skinned beauty that Adie prefers. Like a lot of young women her age (twenty-eight, I'd guess), she wears false nails and fake eyelashes, and there's nothing wrong with that, but Adie has always favoured 'natural-looking' women.

I go on to say, 'I heard you dropped the charges against my husband.'

'Doesn't good news travel fast,' she snorts nastily, as if enjoying my discomfort. But when she asks cynically, 'And I suppose you're here to thank me,' her sneer vanishes.

I tell her earnestly, 'I'm here for the truth,' wondering if that sounds too dramatic. If I'm not careful I run the risk of coming across as someone who is too good to be true.

'The truth?' she scoffs and pulls her short satin dressing gown firmly around her waist, as if for protection. But from whom? Surely, she can't be afraid of me. In the next breath, she proves she isn't scared of anyone by snarling, 'You rich wives are all the same. You'll do anything to protect your lifestyles, even if it means covering up for your husbands.'

'That's not true,' I protest, my words coming out louder than I intended due to my desperation to be believed. I continue more gently, 'I want to know what really happened. As his wife, I deserve that.'

As soon as the words are out of my mouth, I realise it was the wrong thing to say. She wipes the floor with me by rolling her eyes theatrically, and just when I think she's about to slam the door in my face, she says, scathingly, 'Oh, well, if it's the truth you deserve, you'd better come in.' She then throws open the door and disappears inside her flat. All I can do is follow her inside and close the door quietly behind me.

She certainly has an eye for striking interior design. I'll grant her that. Her open-plan living space features walls that are a deep purple and navy with a pop of blood-stained crimson. There are flowery dresses and strappy sandals all over the sofa, as though she was still contemplating what to wear when I rang the doorbell. Cosmetics and nail polishes in rainbow colours adorn a small glass dining table. It feels like I've walked into the bedroom of a sulky teenager who refuses to clean up after themselves.

If this was a consensual fling that ended badly, and I'm beginning to assume it must have been given that Sasha is not Adie's type (he could never be serious about someone like her), and because she has since dropped all claims of sexual harassment against him — which equates to her formally admitting to lying — I can't imagine him spending any time in this flat. He wouldn't be able to relax in this chaotic environment.

Her next words cripple me as she whips around to say, 'The truth is Adie has told me all about you. He warned me that you might show up.'

CHAPTER 18: LUCY

Now

Sighing regretfully, Alina pours frothy filtered coffee into a pair of identical mugs as she admits, 'I'm afraid we hardly saw the Bellos.' Her ground-floor kitchen has bi-folding doors that open onto a colourful garden with a variety of children's slides and trampolines outside. The room is light and airy in contrast to my gloomy, dark cellar kitchen with its dusty stone walls. Since entering my neighbour's tasteful yet extremely functional and child-friendly home, I've discovered that her husband, an architect, made moving the kitchen upstairs his priority upon relocating here. I hope Matt follows suit one day, but I know it will be years before we can afford it.

'I didn't know that was their surname. It's unusual, isn't it?' I feign a casualness I don't feel as I take a sip of my coffee. Because I'm already learning things about Adie and Rachel, I struggle to contain my excitement.

'He was Nigerian, I believe, but the woman, Rachel, was German,' Alina confirms with a hesitant nod, as though she isn't entirely sure. She then joins me on the slouchy leather sofa that faces the glass doors and glances pointedly at the children who are playing with a collection of toys. 'It's lovely to see them getting along,' she mutters with an endearing smile.

Determined to make Alex like her, my daughter clings to his hand with an open, trusting face. She has an unending love for others. If only Matt felt the same way about her. As I think this, a knot forms in my throat that seems like it might choke me. While Sophie puffs out her cheeks in sheer resolve, I notice that her hair glows golden in the sunlight, like an angel.

As my heartbroken gaze follows her around the room, I feel tears prickle at my eyes. I nod at Alina and stare distractedly into my coffee, before asking, 'Have you lived here long?' Anything to change the subject.

'Ever since Nicholas was born,' Alina replies gently, fixing her empathetic gaze on me as though she can sense my sadness.

'He's your oldest?'

She nods. 'He's seven.'

'He's the same age as our oldest child, Jack.'

Her chiselled cheekbones erupt into a huge smile at that. 'In that case, I have no doubt that they will also become good friends.'

Running a tongue nervously around my lips, I say, 'Don't you think it's a strange coincidence that both you, me and Rachel are all about the same age, have two children of the opposite sex and are stay at home mums?'

She purses her lips as she gives this some thought, 'But Stamford *is* known for its great schools, so you could argue it's not that surprising.'

I mumble vaguely, 'I suppose so,' wanting to get her back on track. My mind is humming with questions, so I come clean. It's the only way as far as I'm concerned. 'I'm dying to know more about the people who used to live in our house. Did you know the Bellos well?' I venture.

Rather than answering straight away, Alina picks up a biscuit and nibbles on it distractedly before returning it to the plate. Not wanting to be judged for being overweight, I do not pick one up, even though I would secretly like to cram a handful of them into my mouth all at once. When she finally responds, she does so in an evasive tone, 'No. I'm afraid not. They very much kept to themselves. As do most of us on the terrace.'

I wonder if that is a dig at me for being too darn nosey, but I can't tell because Alina is now refusing to meet my eye and if I didn't know any better, I would suspect her of lying, but I guess I'm reading too much into things as usual. For what reason would she lie? The air around us abruptly becomes hostile and I can't shake off the sensation that I am no longer welcome. Throwing back the last of my coffee, I clumsily stand up. 'We'd better leave you in peace. I'm sorry to have taken up so much of your time with all my questions. My husband Matt says I'm like one of those TV detectives who enjoys nothing more than solving mysteries.'

'But there is *no* mystery here,' she asserts in a decidedly icy tone, as she stands up, eager, I think, to get me out of the door. Without speaking to her again, I use promises of future play dates to persuade Sophie to let go of Alex's hand and hastily carry her to the front door. When Alina sees how embarrassed I am, she eventually takes pity on me and says in a more encouraging voice, 'You will come again, won't you, Lucy? And next time bring Jack too. I'd love for the boys to meet.'

I retort, 'Well, if you'd really like us to,' and I throw in a shrug for good measure because I feel a little offended by her change of manner.

She gushes. 'Yes, of course,' and adds hastily, 'we all would.'

As if to prove this, she pats me on the arm in a friendly gesture, but when I don't reciprocate (I never claimed I wasn't a person who harbours a grudge) her guilty eyes find mine and she mumbles apologetically, 'I'm sorry if I came across as rude just now. It's just that I don't like to gossip.'

This indicates that there must be something to gossip about, but Alina isn't prepared to let on. I'm certain of it. Naturally, I don't mention any of this. I merely nod in agreement and smile pleasantly.

'Good for you,' I lie enthusiastically, knowing when to cut my losses. Don't get me wrong, I like her, even if she is far too good to be true (can you even call yourself a woman if you don't love a good gossip?) and dangerously attractive to boot (in a sultry Eastern European Bond girl way), but I'm an open book as a rule. There's nothing my girlfriends don't know about me — which is another reason Matt dislikes them so much — so it's unlikely Alina and I will ever become close.

Alina continues to make small talk about schools and the promise of future playdates as I strap a writhing Sophie back into the buggy. By now, Alex is exhibiting signs of tearful tiredness and is being held in his mum's arms. When Alina abruptly stops talking, I turn to look at her and I'm shocked to see her beautiful face going through a slew of emotions, as though she were tormenting herself mentally. Just as I'm about to ask her what's wrong, she leans forward to whisper something in my ear.

CHAPTER 19: RACHEL

Then

Her tiny flat is suffocatingly hot even though the windows are wide open, allowing in the aroma of steak and lobster bistro fare, diesel fumes and the hum of slow-moving traffic as well as the throb of loud music from the nearby bars. Since this woman poses a threat to my happiness, I stand facing her but maintain a combative distance. By dropping the sexual misconduct grievance against my husband, Sasha has unintentionally decreased my prospects of being awarded custody of my children in the event of a divorce taking place. I'm not here to defend Adie's good name, as she seems to think. I'm here to make her change her mind.

I no longer feel out of my depth and unsure of myself, so I open the conversation by asking in a clipped, businesslike tone, 'How much has he offered to pay you to drop the charges?'

Her eyes widen in panic at that. 'He told you?' she gasps disbelievingly.

'Not exactly,' I admit as I gaze around the messy room, trying to visualise Adie here. *With her.* Making love. *To her.* But the image of them together escapes me. I heave a sigh, feeling suddenly weak and gesture to the sofa, silently requesting if I might sit. Sasha nods curtly in response.

'He's my husband and we've been married for a long time, so there's not much I don't know about him. Or the way he works,' I explain matter-of-factly as I sink onto the edge of the small velvet sofa so as not to come into contact with her crumpled heap of clothes.

'Then you'll know that he has promised me a lot of money to keep quiet,' she exclaims, widening her blue eyes at me, almost in triumph.

'How much?' I repeat. Somehow the amount matters. How much does Adie value my children's happiness or our marriage?

'A hundred grand, but I haven't seen a penny of it yet,' she whines petulantly, pursing her over-plumped lips.

'Nor are you likely to,' I snap.

'I'd bloody better!' she erupts. 'Or I'll tell everyone what he did.'

'And what exactly *did* he do?' I bark, angry now and unable to hide it, which startles her into silence. 'Oh, come on, Sasha,' I continue in a wheedling tone. 'We both know it's not Adie's style to make advances to women who aren't interested in him. His ego couldn't cope with the rejection.'

As if realising that she has underestimated my intelligence and that I'm not the kind of wife she envisioned me to be — one who puts up with her husband's affairs for the sake of prestige and wealth — she smirks, as if she agrees with me. She then perches delicately on one of the dining table chairs and looks at me with new eyes.

'We had a brief fling, that's all. It didn't mean anything to me or him,' she mumbles conspiratorially, as if she and I were suddenly confidants.

When I hear this, something inside me dies and I want to scream, 'It meant something to me!' Instead, I urge her to go on, 'And then?'

With a venomous expression, she snarls, 'He ended it horribly. Said some nasty things. Told me I was rubbish at my job as well as in bed.'

Her face crumples and as she impatiently wipes away a tear, I feel unexpectedly sorry for her. She is very childlike and vulnerable. What kind of monster preys on a young woman like that? *How could you, Adie?*

'So, the allegation of sexual misconduct was an act of revenge on your part? And just to be clear, he never improperly propositioned you at all?' I want clarity, so I ask this in my professional journalistic voice.

'Do I really look as if I can't take care of myself when it comes to men?' Sasha objects, seeing this is an attack on her strong, single woman status.

'No, of course not,' I lie, but the poor girl clearly can't, or else she wouldn't have gotten involved with someone as predatory as Adie. 'However, my husband can be very . . . let's say, persuasive. Did he threaten you to make you withdraw your claim, so he doesn't lose his job?'

She throws me another of her infuriated looks and mutters, 'I've said too much already. He warned me to keep quiet or I wouldn't get paid.'

'Do you have any idea where he was going to get such a large sum of money from?' I ask, sighing, and clenching my teeth in frustration.

She shrugs her shoulders, seeming puzzled, as though she hadn't given that major issue any thought. 'Does it matter?' she murmurs.

'Yes, it matters,' I snap, 'because he planned on using *my* money to pay you off.'

'Your money?!' Sasha gasps.

'Yes,' I growl, 'and I'll make sure you don't see a penny of it unless you help me.'

She is incredulous. 'Help you? How am I meant to do that?'

Wanting to shake the girl, I jerk to my feet and jab a finger at her ample chest, insisting, 'By telling HR that Adie threatened you and that's why you dropped the charges against him. Out of concern for your own safety.'

'Are you saying you *want* me to get him in trouble — your own husband — even if I did make up the whole sexual harassment thing?' she asks, astonished. But there's an edge of terror to her voice too that is deliciously addictive. As a long-suffering, deceived wife, I feel I've earned it.

I turn away from her and head for the door, saying in a tight, strained voice, 'Exactly. And if you do as I say, you will get your money.'

'What if I don't?'

I whip around and confront her fiercely. 'Be careful, Sasha,' I warn.

She scoffs, 'I'm always careful,' but the attitude is only for show. She is scared. She ought to be. She is clueless about the situation she finds herself in. God help her. I don't want to think about what might happen to her if Adie finds out she has spoken to me. He'll likely lose his temper big time.

For that reason alone, I throw in one last word of advice as my parting shot, 'And for your own good, stay away from Adie. He's dangerous.'

'That's funny,' she chuckles sarcastically, before adding poison-ously, 'because he said exactly the same thing about you.'

And then, before I do something I might regret, I storm out of her flat.

CHAPTER 20: LUCY

Now

So, this stunning yet somehow cold and indifferent back-to-the-future eco-mansion situated on the edge of Stamford is where Adie and Rachel moved to after leaving Rutland Terrace. That's my assumption, anyway, given what Alina told me after having an apparent change of heart about gossiping. When she revealed, 'I can tell you this much about the Bellos, because it's common knowledge, but, after they sold up, they moved across town to First Drift in Wothorpe,' she looked visibly upset, which continued to baffle me. All I know is that I held the air in my lungs until I was compelled to release it in a deep breath because I now knew where to find Rachel. Or did I? They might have moved on again since then.

I didn't waste any time driving here, leaving Matt to pack his own suitcase for once, he's taking a business flight to Istanbul this afternoon. I had accepted that he would be travelling more in his new role as the senior global buyer for a manufacturing company, but I wasn't prepared for him to abandon us quite so soon after moving into the new house. A part of me thought he was lying when I learned about the upcoming trip and that he was secretly jetting off to somewhere exotic with another woman, but I consoled myself with the knowledge that he could no longer afford covert trysts away. Not now we'd lumbered ourselves with the house of *his* dreams, complete with structural issues and expensive to remedy dry rot.

The cost of the Bello's new, energy-efficient, architecturally designed home is beyond my comprehension, yet it is likely worth more than the whole of Rutland Terrace combined. In a way, I can't see Rachel living inside its glass and steel bachelor-black and concrete-grey walls. To my surprise there is just one car parked in the vast, block-paved driveway and it's an electric Volvo that is safe, sensible and suitable for families rather than a showy Porsche or Range Rover. First Drift is a peaceful, rural oak avenue, lined with multi-million-pound houses that overlook deer-dotted parkland owned by the Burleigh House estate. These houses appear deserted, but they are obviously not. It's simply that nobody is around.

As I'm thinking this, Rachel's front door suddenly opens and a tall man emerges to stand on his doorstep and look around, while keeping his hands on his hips in a proprietary manner. As soon as I see his good-looking features, I experience a feeling of unshakeable sickness and dive down behind the front wall, out of sight, where I wait, trembling, in case he should grab hold of me by the collar and demand to know why I'm spying on his home. When nothing happens, I creep stealthily on all fours towards my battered little car, which is parked along the lane. In the rear, Sophie is still asleep in her car seat, head lolling backwards on her dainty shoulders. She is completely fine because I left the windows wide open and have been gone for just a few minutes, keeping the car in constant view.

Out of the corner of my eye, I catch the owner of the house observing me and I panic and try to start the car without drawing any more attention to myself, but it produces a loud crunch and a whirring sound, instead of turning over. I mutter, 'Oh, for God's sake,' as I keep trying and nothing happens. I should have followed Matt's advice to trade her in for something newer, but after buying the new house I was afraid we couldn't afford it (we can't). Besides, I'm quite attached to Tinker Bell, which is what the kids affectionately call my runaround, having owned her since I passed my driving test. I didn't start taking driving lessons until after Jack was born.

But enough of that because the man is rapidly approaching. I sit paralysed, unsure of what to do. When Sophie wakes up and starts scowling at me in the rear-view mirror, I can tell she's about to start crying. Reluctantly, I wind down my side window when a face appears in the glass.

'Are you okay? Do you need some help?' The man flashes a charming smile, first at me and then at Sophie, his teeth dazzlingly white.

He's like a white knight in shining armour — or, in his case, a black knight — coming to my rescue. Call me overly romantic all you want, but I'm a glutton for punishment when it comes to chivalrous actions. They make my heart flutter. But this man is far from a saint. This is Adie, we're talking about. Rachel's manipulative, lying, cheating, gaslighting jerk of a husband if you can believe everything she wrote in her diary. And all the rage I have felt towards Matt for betraying me and shattering my heart, which I can't express as much as I'd like to — emerges.

Thumping my hand on the steering wheel, I tell him stiffly, 'We're fine,' but my gaze keeps searching for an escape route. Is this man as dangerous as Rachel claimed? Should I even be talking to him? It might be safer for me to start walking, but then I remember that I didn't put Sophie's buggy in the boot. I can't carry her all the way home. I can't call a taxi either because I came out without my purse. Doh. What an idiot.

'You don't look fine,' Adie chuckles as if finding dam-sels-in-distress parked outside his house entertaining. But when he runs a hand over his hair, I notice he is wearing a wedding ring, making me even more curious as to whether he and Rachel are still together. Or did he get his hands on her money in the end, as Rachel feared he might, and move in with his mistress? Is that what the move to this expensive mansion was all about? Is poor Rachel even now confined against her will in a mental health facility?

With a heavy sigh, I get out of the car and prop open the bonnet. As I stand there acting as if I know what I'm looking for, I feel the beginnings of a nervous headache, which isn't like me at all. I'm hardly ever sick. I like to brag that I'm as 'strong as a horse', but then I realise that I've been feeling nauseous for the past few days. This is something I don't want to dwell on, because if I *am* pregnant, Matt will go ballistic.

My skin prickles and a sense of unease slides over me as Adie comes to stand next to me. He's more handsome in person than in his photo. He has surprisingly kind, expressive dark eyes, even behind the round spectacles, and he smells of musk and vanilla, which I'm not averse to.

'Do you live far away?' he asks curiously.

I do not reply with, 'In your old house,' but I can't help wondering how he would react if I did. I've done nothing wrong, other than reading his wife's diary and spying on his house, but the thought of him finding out who I am has my stomach in knots. 'Just across town,' I tell him.

'Do you think you can get it going?' he asks, rubbing his chin thoughtfully as he contemplates the oily engine.

I pull a doubtful face. 'No.'

'Are you with the AA?'

'I'm not an alcoholic if that's what you mean,' I grimace, deliberately misunderstanding him.

I didn't think my joke was all that funny, but he bursts out laughing. 'In this case, I believe the acronym refers to the Automobile Association.'

I shake my head in frustration at myself for not knowing the meaning of the word 'acronym'.

'Well, I *am* a member, so I can call them for you if you like,' he offers with a smile.

'I thought they only came out to cars that are covered on the policy,' I politely protest, debating whether to accept his kind offer.

'As a gold member, I'm covered for any vehicle I travel in, so I can sit in the car with you and pretend to be a passenger if that helps,' he smirks knowingly, as though he has done this before. I immediately think the worst. Perhaps he persuades lone women to let him into their cars so he can murder them. But he doesn't have serial-killer eyes, so I don't really believe this, even if he is dishonest and deceitful. Like my husband.

I grudgingly murmur, 'That's very kind of you,' not wanting to be beholden to him but wanting desperately to get home.

'Not at all,' he objects, suddenly acting all businesslike as he gets his phone out. I move towards the rear of the car and remove Sophie from her seat as he walks up and down the lane with his back to me, talking to the operator. By the time he turns to face me and announces, 'They'll be here in an hour,' she's in my arms. When he asks hesitantly, 'Would you like to come in and wait until then?' my jaw is on the floor.

I'd like that more than anything. To see if Rachel is in there. What if she isn't though? And what happens if he turns out to be a serial killer after all?

'Won't your wife mind?' I enquire pointedly, hoping that I don't come across as distrustful, even though I clearly am.

Adie's eyes briefly cloud over and a vein on his cheek pulses nervously as he gazes at me. 'It's just me, I'm afraid,' he admits with a strained smile.

The next thing I know, he's reaching out to shake my hand, and exclaiming warmly, 'I'm Adie, by the way.'

CHAPTER 21: RACHEL

Then

We are one stop from Peterborough station, where I will need to hurry if I'm going to change trains on time, when the man sits down beside me, sighing heavily. He must have boarded the train at Stevenage, but I didn't see him get on. In contrast to us non-rush hour travellers, he's dressed in a business suit. It looks tired, like him, as if it hasn't been laundered in a while. Without acknowledging him, I shuffle along my seat and rest my cheek against the glass window, gazing out at the dirty grey tower blocks in the distance. The air smells of sweat, the train is packed and the people are loud and irritable due to the oppressive heat. The sound of a wailing infant in the next carriage causes my heart to race involuntarily.

In my mind, I keep playing back the heated exchange I had with Sasha. Will she do as I asked and get her employer to re-open the sexual misconduct case against my husband? She won't see a penny of my money otherwise. I have a lot riding on her telling the truth. Or in her case, *lies*. She must be a vindicative creature to have perjured herself like that in the first place. Although it's not that I don't believe Adie isn't deserving of it given his despicable treatment of her. On that thought, I begin to fret about what mood he might be in when I get home. So far, I have ignored all his frantic texts, demanding to know where I am. He's clearly pacing the floor and getting angrier and more irritable by the second. I will pay for my last-minute trip to London, but it was necessary. He left me with no option.

'Excuse me, but don't I know you?'

It takes me several wretched seconds to comprehend that the man sitting beside me is speaking to me.

'No, I don't think so,' I curtly respond, turning to glare at him for a moment before looking away again.

There's a doubtful pause. Then . . . 'Yes, I do,' he declares, sounding absurdly pleased with himself. 'You're pink shoes.'

I can't resist responding irritably, 'I beg your pardon?' but try not to sound too rude in case he turns nasty. Then, I look around anxiously, hoping to enlist the help of an NLER train attendant, but, as usual, there are none to be seen. *Is it too much to ask to be left alone*, I groan inwardly.

As he waits for me to catch on, he explains patiently, 'I see you jogging in the park most mornings and you always wear pink trainers.'

I furrow my brow as I enquire sceptically, 'In Stamford?'

'Of course,' he laughs. 'Where else?'

'On the meadows?' I probe, still unconvinced.

'Oh, come on. You must have seen me before. I can't believe you don't recognise me. Am I that invisible to the opposite sex?' he objects playfully, covering his heart with one hand as if he were mortally wounded.

That almost makes me smile, but not quite. For the first time though, I notice that he is attractive — in a wholesome boy-next-door kind of way — with his clean-shaven face, floppy fair hair and twinkling eyes. There is something very honest and innocent about him that I find appealing. He will never find that out from me though because, no matter what he says to the contrary, we *are* strangers, and his pretending to know me is nothing more than a well-crafted chat-up line. I'm certain of it.

'You were late for your run this morning,' he points out accusingly as if he were my personal fitness trainer and I was always late for class. But he *is* right. The quarrel with Adie over who was going to take the children to school — which he obviously won — meant I *was* running behind.

'Only by ten minutes,' I insist.

'I don't suppose you saw the old man and his dog this morning?' he asks, bending his head towards me and pulling a worried look.

'No, sorry,' I shake my head, realising that I was mistaken before and he *is* telling the truth, since I see the old man and his dog most days, but not this morning.

With a shy smile, he confides, 'It's just that I haven't seen them for a couple of days, and I'm worried about the old guy. And his dog.'

I can relate to this because I've been having similar concerns. This shows that he is kind and considerate which makes me look at him more intently. Is it possible our paths have crossed before without me knowing? As my critical gaze slides over his unfamiliar face, a fleeting image of a fellow jogger comes to mind. As I recall the man in his mid-thirties blowing out his cheeks and attempting to make eye contact as he ran past me, I realise that even though I've been seeing this man every day for the past six months, we have never exchanged a word except for an occasional brief nod. As I reach this conclusion, I reflect on how coincidental it is that I met him in this manner on the train. Today of all days!

Meanwhile, he is reminiscing, 'And what about the odd couple who always jog together but don't appear to be on speaking terms?'

My mistrust of him dissolves in that instant. Now that I'm on the same page, it truly feels like we are connected. 'You call them the odd couple too?' I roll my eyes in surprise.

'Great minds and all that,' he exclaims, chuckling. As he extends a hand to shake mine, he murmurs, 'Well, now that we've ascertained I'm not a serial charmer who chats up every woman he meets on a train, I suppose I ought to introduce myself.'

'No, hold on, let me guess,' I interrupt, adding with a twitch of a smile, 'you're Soon-to-be-divorced guy.'

He squirms in embarrassment for a moment, but he quickly brushes his discomfort off and asks incredulously, 'How could you possibly know that?'

'You just have this sad look about you whenever I see you,' I shrug, and to my astonishment, I burst out laughing.

'Sad?' he grumbles in a phoney injured tone. 'So, this is how women perceive me?'

I realise that, for once, I am having fun and that I have put Adie and the dreaded return home to the back of my mind. With a wide smile, I introduce myself, 'I'm Rachel,' and offer him my hand.

CHAPTER 22: LUCY

Now

I take back what I said earlier; the interior of the house is stunning, and I could absolutely see Rachel living here. Except, she doesn't. I want to know why, but I need to pick an appropriate moment. My mind is racing with questions, but I can't just blurt them out. Adie has been so kind and hospitable. He even took us on a whistlestop tour of the house where I saw a tonne of photos of his kids, a girl named Beatrice and a boy named Archie, both of whom were at school. But there aren't any of Rachel.

Sophie and I are in the milk-white living room that overlooks a landscaped garden with a striped lawn the size of a tennis court, waiting for Adie to return from the monochrome high-gloss kitchen with cold drinks. There are lots of books and several musical instruments scattered throughout the house, but there are no trampolines or slides in the garden like there are at Alina's. Adie doesn't seem to notice Sophie for being different, even though his children are obviously scholarly and musical and are privately educated based on the pictures I saw of them in their school uniforms. In fact, he appears delighted with her and has even succeeded in making her giggle multiple times. Not once has he lowered his voice to ask, 'What's wrong with her?' as others do. He obviously has a soft spot for all children, not just his own, which is unusual for a man.

This would move me if I didn't know what he was really like. I must admit, though, that my feelings towards him are a muddle of conflicting emotions given that he doesn't act like the man Rachel portrayed in her diary. Once more, I remind myself that I am more aware than most of how a man can deceive you. After all, I had no idea that Matt had been lying to me about having an affair. It nearly killed me when I found out, as honesty is so important to me. Right up there with faithfulness.

As Adie enters the room with a tray, he exclaims cheerfully, 'Elderflower cordial for the adults and a special squash latte for Sophie.'

When Sophie notices a glass of pink squash with a variety of fruit-themed straws in it, she stumbles over to sit next to him on the curved caramel sofa and claps her hands in joy. 'Pretty,' she cries, gazing up at him in awe. As I gaze at my precious daughter, I hold back the urge to cry. I love her so much. Just as she is. Why can't Matt?

'She's special, isn't she?' Adie beams at me, as though he can read my mind. 'My children would adore her,' he continues, tenderly reaching out a hand to tuck back a strand of her hair that has fallen into her eyes. Miraculously, Sophie doesn't move away from him like she does with most men, including her father. Rather, she leans into him.

I nod in agreement, speechless as unexpected emotions catch me off guard. Our daughter has never received a compliment from her father. It's all he can do to look at her, which is something I rarely admit, even to myself. With my jaw clenched in annoyance, I change the subject by asking, 'So, Adie, how long have you lived here?'

'I suppose about a year and a half,' he shrugs noncommittally after considering this.

As I'm about to pose my next question, he holds up a wagging finger and fixes his amused gaze on me, 'Oh, no, you don't, young lady. I've talked quite enough about me. Now it's my turn to ask you a question.'

I can feel the muscles in my neck tensing as I observe him, but I manage to muster up a weak smile, even though I can't shake off the sense of unease that has creeped up on me. I should have seen this coming and been ready with my responses. Naturally, he wants to know what I was doing outside his house, which is situated on a private lane. But I couldn't have foreseen that I would bump into him let alone find myself in his living room having iced drinks.

Though his voice has a hopeful, almost desperate tone, he surprises me by asking a very ordinary and non-intrusive question. 'Do you ever take your children to the park across the road from here?'

I squint my eyes at him. 'Do you mean the one near the golf club?'

He nods. 'Or is it too far for you to come? You mentioned that you live across town.'

I nod back, unsure if he's trying to catch me out so he can establish exactly where I live, but I'm careful not to give anything away. 'Most of the time I take them to a local park, but we sometimes have picnics in the grounds of Burleigh House. The kids love it there and it's free to get in.'

'Yes, we also go there sometimes, or at least we used to,' he finishes lamely, as though he had uttered something he wished he hadn't. His speech is eloquent, velvety smooth, but I've already observed that there is an echo of regret in it whenever he speaks. He's clearly rich enough to own this house and send his children to a private school, but I get the impression that he is lonely.

He doesn't hesitate to express his curiosity. 'And who are *we* exactly? Do you have a husband you need to call to let him know where you are?'

My hands begin to shake, and I spill some of my drink, but luckily, he doesn't make a fuss. I give Sophie a quick warning look, but she remains silent. She doesn't understand the question. I'm not sure I do. I mean, a man like Adie can't be romantically interested in someone like me. I'm nothing like Rachel. Feeling overwhelmed and realising I can't let him discover my true connection to him, because that would mean the abrupt termination of any more conversations about Rachel, I come out with the first thing that pops into my head, 'Not anymore.'

He frowns. 'I'm sorry to hear that.' Then, horrified, he gasps, 'I take it he's not . . . ?'

'Dead? Oh, God no,' I chuckle. The lie comes more easily than it should. 'He's very much alive and kicking. We've recently separated, that's all.'

'That's a relief,' he lets out a sigh and relaxes back into his seat. Then, seeming to realise what his words might imply, he sits bolt upright and adds hastily, 'I meant about him not being dead. Not you being separated.'

'Don't worry, I know what you meant,' I mumble sympathetically, because he's now given me the perfect excuse to ask what I've been dying to know since I first stepped into his house: 'How about you? You said it was just you living here, so how come you ended up with the kids?'

His face unexpectedly collapses with grief, and I watch his head fall to his chest as he replies brokenly, 'I'm afraid my wife is dead.'

CHAPTER 23: RACHEL

Then

I made a friend today. A man, who has promised to help me. It's remarkable that we have been running past each other every day for months without even saying hello, only to meet on the train and find out we have so much in common. When we reached Peterborough, I accepted his invitation to go for a drink and skipped my connecting train. Over the course of the next two hours, we confided in one another about our personal lives while nursing our diluted non-alcoholic drinks. At the end of our time together, I felt as if I'd known him for ever and he expressed that he felt the same way. For his sake, I'll just refer to him here as 'Soon-to-be-divorced guy'. I missed the last train back to Stamford but fortunately, he was able to drop me off near my house because he'd left his car at the station. I don't mind admitting that my heart was thudding in my ribcage when I opened the front door to 13 Rutland Terrace, but I had texted Adie to let him know that I would be late back as I had met up with an old friend.

Adie, who is upstairs putting the children to bed — *again* — said I seemed too pale and worn out from my day of gallivanting around London to read them bedtime stories and advised me to lie down on the bed instead. This I had done, but I used the time to write in my diary before putting it back in its hiding spot and going back downstairs. Naturally, Adie questioned me about the friend I had been seeing, and I trembled as I replied, 'Juliet Finch. We used to work at the paper together,' without glancing at him. I prayed he wasn't aware that Juliet's fiancé was also employed at Prince Tech. Adie would have been suspicious of that, but he seemed oblivious.

'Can I get you a drink?' Adie offers politely as he comes back into the drawing room and settles into a chair.

I mutter, 'No, thanks,' without taking my eyes off the book I'm meant to be reading, even though, in all honesty, I can't concentrate on anything but my new friend. I swear that when I visualise his playful, laughing eyes, my cheeks go red with embarrassment. I haven't felt this way in years.

Unwillingly, I look up at Adie who is swirling his drink around his glass and staring curiously at me, as though he's trying to read my mind. He always has this effect on me, making me feel immediately guilty. It's as if I've done something wrong when we both know who the real culprit is. It infuriates me that all our acquaintances believe Adie to be the perfect husband and father. They say, 'Look at how he dotes on those children,' and give me strange looks wondering why I'm not more appreciative. I've heard their gossipy murmurings, 'What can she have to be depressed about?' on multiple occasions. They would be shocked to learn that Adie is acting, even about my alleged illnesses, and that his wife and children are just for show, like the expensive home and flash cars. Only Jonty and I are aware of Adie's true identity.

In the end, I'm the one to break the long silence that stretches between us, by saying shakily, 'Did you have a good day?'

'Not as good as you, apparently,' he replies with an unpleasant smile.

He doesn't believe me then, about meeting up with Juliet, and is on high alert, churning over the events of the day in a bid to catch me out.

'Did you speak to anyone at work today?' I try again, desperate to know if there have been any developments in his misconduct case. Not that he'd share anything with me, as I'm not meant to know about it.

Adie puffs out his cheeks and demands, 'Why do you ask?'

I comfort him by saying, 'No reason, I just wondered, that's all.'

His smirk sends chills up my spine as he slurps back the rest of his drink. 'If you must know, I had a very productive day.'

'That's good,' I sigh, sitting up straighter in my chair, disappointed that Sasha has clearly not spoken up yet. Already, I can feel tears sparkling in my eyes. I never know where I am with Adie, and he clearly means to punish me for going out without his consent. I don't regret it, though.

To appease him, I get up and head to the drinks trolley where I fix him another whisky, a double this time, and give it to him, saying, 'There you are. Get that down you. You deserve it after having such a productive day.'

That does the trick, at least for the time being, but his suspicious eyes still glower at me. He's got every reason to worry. Because if Sasha is smart and follows my instructions, he could end up losing his job and finding his reputation in tatters, which is exactly what I want. Let him try convincing any judge my children would be better off with him after that. Don't even get me started on the gambling debts and affairs.

'I think I might go up,' I motion with my chin towards the door, adding, 'and have a bath and an early night.' For good measure, I stretch and pretend to yawn. More than anything, I want to be alone with my thoughts.

He gives me a thoughtful nod, as though he agrees, but his voice stops me before I even reach the door. 'You can expect a visitor tomorrow.'

I should have known better. My husband must always have the last word. 'A visitor?' I gulp, turning back to face him.

He goes on to explain in a bored tone as if I should already know this, 'The nanny who was recommended to me, she's going to call on you tomorrow morning. I hope that's all right with you?'

I understand that he's not asking me, he's telling me, so there is no point in arguing with him. 'What time?' I ask as calmly as I can.

He grins effortlessly, undoubtedly enjoying my discomfort. 'I've asked her to come after eleven, so you can go for your run first.'

'Fine.'

He gives a sarcastic eyeroll. 'Aren't you going to ask me about her?'

'I'll find out all I need to know in the morning,' I answer snippily, not wanting to give him the satisfaction. As I stride towards the door, head held high, my legs are like jelly but the rest of me is rigid with pent-up anger.

CHAPTER 24: LUCY

Now

The AA recovery vehicle arrived three hours late, which meant I missed saying goodbye to Matt, who must be halfway to Istanbul by now. He's obviously in a foul mood because he hasn't texted me. Not even to ask whether I managed to pick Jack up from school in time (I did, just). I dare say, he's knocking back free drinks on the plane instead of thinking about us. Two can play that game, and, after the day I've had, I intend to open a bottle of wine later and drink it all myself, while reading more of Rachel's diary. But first, I must see Alina. It might seem unreasonable of me, but I feel compelled to rant at her for not being honest with me and I'm too angry to wait until tomorrow to do this, even though I'm having to drag two tired kids along with me. The memory of what Adie told me about his wife comes flooding back as I pound on my neighbour's door. I still can't believe Rachel is dead.

When Alina opens the door and sees us standing there, she blinks in surprise. I don't blame her when all three of us are scowling at her. Me, for obvious reasons, and because I'm having to jostle a struggling Sophie, who doesn't want to be restrained, in one arm while fiercely hanging onto Jack with the other so he can't drag me back down the path. Having to miss an episode of *The Epic Tales of Captain Underpants* has devastated him.

'I can't believe you didn't tell me!' I hiss furiously at her.

'Tell you what?' she asks, appearing dumbfounded. But to me, she already looks guilty, as if she knows exactly what I mean.

'You know perfectly well what I mean,' I declare.

She doesn't say anything but gives me a pitying glance. It turns out to be my downfall as I'm feeling raw and emotional. *Rachel is dead.* She pleaded for help from the pages of her diary, but I was unable to save her. As for how it happened . . . how could Alina keep that from me?

On hearing her husband call her name from somewhere inside the house, Alina darts an anxious look over her shoulder, as if afraid of being overheard and exclaims nervously, 'I don't know what you're talking about.'

I shake my head in distaste, before launching my attack, 'For someone who claims to be above gossiping, you don't seem to have a problem lying.'

She purses her glossy lips in annoyance at that and sends daggers my way. But before she can get a word in, I jump in with a triumphant, 'I went there, to First Drift, and I spoke to Adie.'

'You did *what?*' she gasps in disbelief.

I grit my teeth and mutter incriminatingly, 'I met Rachel's husband, and he told me what happened to her.'

Alina clenches her eyes shut and sighs deeply, clearly rumbled. When she opens her eyes, she looks at me with something like regret and her voice is barely audible as she admits, 'I thought it best not to tell you.'

'Why?' I stammer, almost tearfully, feeling betrayed all over again — so much for our blossoming friendship. The promised playdates with Sophie, Alex, Jack and Nicholas are unlikely to happen now. After today, I imagine Alina and I will pass each other on the street without even acknowledging each other.

As she watches me closely, Alina seems to come to a decision and offers in a small, helpless voice, 'Won't you come in? So I can explain,' while opening the door wide in a welcoming gesture.

I bristle and shake my head emphatically, saying loudly, 'No, thanks. I can say everything I need to here on the doorstep.'

'Then please keep your voice down,' Alina murmurs, her warning gaze shifting to the street.

At this point, Jack, who is standing silently and looking up at the adults with curiosity, demands to know, 'Who is Rachel?'

'Never mind,' I say, with a comforting touch of his hand, before turning back to Alina, who I'm irritated to see is grinning at my son, as if butter wouldn't melt. My heart hardens towards her and before I know it, I'm barking, 'I'm glad you find a young woman's death so amusing.'

Horrified, she gasps, 'I don't,' and steps back from me as though I'd just punched her, which makes me ask myself, 'Have I gone too far?' I don't think Alina is a bad person, *not that bad anyway*, and she would have had an exceptionally good reason for not telling me about Rachel. Would I have acted so very differently if our roles had been reversed? *Hmm, the jury's out on that one.*

'Who's died? Is it Rachel?' Jack pipes up insistently since any mention of death is guaranteed to pique his morbid curiosity.

I gently reassure him, 'Nobody has died, Jack. Shush now, and let the adults speak.' He makes a face and frowns, but at least he stops talking. I'll have some explaining to do later. I don't want him to have nightmares about dead bodies again. They're becoming a regular thing in our house.

With much less hostility, I address Alina again, 'I just wish you'd told me, that's all, rather than letting me find out from her husband.'

'You're right,' she nods, choking up. 'I should have done. And I apologise for not doing so. I just didn't want to be accused of—'

'Gossiping,' I finish for her, shrugging my shoulders in understanding.

'Are you sure you won't come in?' she implores, looking at us all kindly.

'I need to get the kids home,' I make my excuses because, like her, I'm suddenly overwhelmed with emotion and I find I have to lean against the wall for support since I'm feeling unsteady on my feet. My head is whirling, and I feel sick to my stomach. Could my fear of Matt's reaction to an unplanned, and in his case, unwanted pregnancy be having this effect on me? Or am I in fact experiencing symptoms of having conceived again?

'You don't look well, Lucy. Can I do anything to help?' Alina asks in a worried tone, reaching out to take hold of my arm.

'No,' I brush off her concerns, along with her well-meaning hand, and I am aware that my insisting, 'I'm fine,' sounds utterly unconvincing, as we both know I'm not. And the cause of it.

With a shudder, I lower my voice to a whisper so Jack can't hear as I manage in between silent sobs, 'Knowing that poor woman died in my house has knocked me for six.'

CHAPTER 25: RACHEL

Then

The luxurious perfume of jasmine oil fills my nostrils as I recline in the fragrant bath water. The enormous family bathroom, which is only ever used by me, is a blend of vintage brass and marble. It features a midnight-blue floral wallpaper, art deco lighting and a freestanding brass bath in the middle of the room. From this vantage point, the floor-to-ceiling sash window provides an enviable view of Stamford's darkening skyline. Because of its unapologetic decadence, I usually think of iconic Hollywood movie stars like Ingrid Bergman, Marilyn Monroe and Bette Davis when I am in here. However, they wouldn't have been seen dead with chipped toenail polish like mine, which is visible from the other end of the bathtub.

The rest of my body is submerged, and as I surrender to the peaceful, ambient sounds of 'Rain falling on a forest path' playing on my phone I finally start to relax. Focusing on my breathing, as I have been taught, I inhale deeply — in through my nose and out through my mouth. My eyes automatically close as I begin counting, '1,2,3,4,' and my neck muscles slowly unwind. The tap on the door ruins everything and I shoot upwards in alarm, causing a mini tidal wave of bathwater to splash over on the floor.

'Are you okay?' Adie asks.

'Of course I'm okay,' I grumble irritably. Am I never to be allowed one moment alone?

Adie doesn't give up easily. 'Don't be too long in there,' he advises in an obnoxious doctorly tone.

'I won't,' I respond overbrightly, to convince him that I mean what I say, even though I obviously don't.

'Do you need anything? A hot towel, perhaps?'

I almost exclaim aloud, 'Only to be left alone,' but I catch myself just in time. 'I have everything I need,' I reply instead in a tight voice.

'Do you want me to come in and soap your back?'

The thought makes me shudder, but I politely tell him, 'No, thanks. I'll be out in a minute.' In case he decides to spy on me through the antiquated keyhole in the door, I get out of the bath and wrap myself in a towel.

'Are you sure?' he sounds doubtful.

I'm too angry to respond this time. Unless he ruins everything, including my happiness and peace of mind, Adie isn't happy.

'Don't forget your medication,' he growls, as all pretence of being the considerate husband dissolves. 'I left your prescription by the washbasin.'

I'm about to demand, 'What prescription?' when I turn to stare at the unopened packet of red-and-white pills, which, just as Adie said, is over by the washbasin. I'm shocked that I hadn't noticed it earlier. Who does it belong to and why does my husband want me to take it? Knowing better than to question him, because he will just make out that I know all about it and am being deliberately forgetful, I answer meekly, 'I won't.'

Holding the towel against my body as if it were a protective cloak, I only move over to the double washbasin when I finally hear Adie shuffle away from the door with an impatient grunt.

After gazing at my gaunt reflection in the ornate wall mirror, my hands shake as I pick up the medicine.

My voice quivers with emotion as I read the labelling, 'Risperidone, 5mg antipsychotic tablets taken once a day. Prescribed to Mrs Rachel Bello.'

I crush the packet in my hand and slump to the floor. What is Adie up to now? In my absence, how did he get a doctor to prescribe medicine for me? Or are these black-market drugs, which would potentially make them even more dangerous? How in the world am I going to get the answers to all my questions? There is just one thing I know for sure: my husband is upping his game. He is also moving quickly. Without anybody on my side, how can I keep up with him? Because Adie is the ideal husband, parent and friend, which means no one trusts a word I say.

As I think of the one friend that I *have* made today who *is* on my side, my heart fills with hope, so I scramble to my feet, head across the room and grab my phone. I've saved his real name under 'Geschiedener mann im zug', which translates to 'Divorced man on train', but Adie won't connect the dots even if he does manage to get his hands on my phone. Although he has a German wife, he's never tried to learn the language.

'Did you mean it when you said you'd help me?' I type anxiously.

He responds instantly, as though he has been waiting for my message. He doesn't need to ask who I am because, like me, he has already saved my phone number. 'Of course, anything.'

I feel a wave of relief. Suddenly, I don't feel as alone anymore. However, I must be certain, so I message again, 'Anything?'

'Even though we've only just met, I would do anything for you, Rachel. You can call me a fool, but I believe in love at first sight.'

'Did you feel like that about your soon-to-be ex-wife?' is what my darker, or should I say 'suspicious' side wants to know out of jealousy.

He doesn't pause to reply, 'No. Never.'

I type back, grinning, 'But you must have loved her once?'

There is a small delay this time, and I hold my breath as I wait for the three dots to reappear, indicating that he is composing his reply. 'We were more like brother and sister than husband and wife.'

Deciding his explanation is satisfactory, I ask, 'Can we meet?'

He adds a happy emoji and writes, 'I was counting on it.' Then, 'Rachel, I won't let anything bad happen to you. I promise.'

'What do you mean by that?'

'I noticed the scratches and bruising on your body.'

I now recall that when we first shook hands on the train, he'd glanced at the cuts and bruising on my wrists, before quickly looking away again.

'Are you in danger?' he texts.

I ask myself, can I trust this man who is a stranger? But what other option do I have? As I quickly type, 'I think my husband is going to kill me,' I can feel my cheeks growing red with shame.

CHAPTER 26: LUCY

Now

It's a hot and sticky night, but for some reason, Sophie insisted on having a warm bath before bed. She wasn't content with bubbles and rubber ducks, so she made Jack fetch her a variety of toys, including a water gun that looked scary. The two of them are currently engaged in a water fight, with water spraying everywhere. As always, Jack treats Sophie very gently and doesn't shoot water in her face or eyes, even though she is ruthless in her pursuit of him. My heart isn't in it, but I chuckle along with their playful squeals because their laughter is contagious. They're both saturated, and I am, too. But it feels refreshing after the long, hot, tiring day we've had. In fact, I'd go as far as to say it's exactly what we needed. If Matt were here, he would not be impressed. But since he's not, who cares? It's not as if we can do any more damage to the state of this room.

I imagine this bathroom was once quite spectacular with its big brass bathtub and marble washstand, but sadly the wallpaper is peeling off the walls due to excessive condensation. The house is poorly ventilated, and Matt had to pull up the rotting wooden floorboards as they were riddled with dry rot. We've set up a dehumidifier, which runs twenty-four hours a day to dry everything out, but I haven't noticed any improvement yet.

I hold up a towel for my daughter to crawl into and smile encouragingly, 'Come on, Soph, time to get out.' Her fresh, clean scent makes me want to weep. I help her into her cotton night-dress after drying her off in my lap but she's so tired she nods off in my arms, her little mouth open like a baby bird's. 'Bed,' I command a sleepy-eyed Jack, and he follows me out of the bathroom, dragging his weary feet down the corridor to Sophie's room. I quickly get them settled in their separate bedrooms, and then I'm back downstairs in the kitchen, gazing at the dreary grey concrete steps while taking a chilled bottle of white wine from the fridge. I pour a huge glass for myself, sit down at the table that used to belong to Rachel and stare into my drink. I'm too exhausted to raise it to my lips.

I ignore my phone even though it keeps going off. I know it's not Matt — he won't call until the morning now, and only then to speak to Jack before he departs for school — so I don't bother to look at the screen to see who is calling. I can tell from the Taylor Swift ringtone, 'It's me, hi, I'm the problem, it's me,' that it's my best friend, Beth. Even the memory of switching my ringtone to Taylor's 'We are never ever getting back together' after learning of Matt's affair doesn't bring a grin to my face. Though a bit too booze-mad for my liking and occasionally self-centred, Beth is a great friend who has supported me through thick and thin over the years. Nevertheless, we are vastly different. She is single and has no kids. Because of this, I'm not feeling up to hearing about her amazing new boyfriend and their fantastic sex life tonight. She is aware that Matt is away and is clearly hoping to come around for a drink and a gossip.

After taking a pregnancy test earlier this evening and finding out that I'm not pregnant, the only person I *would* like to talk to, but can't — for obvious reasons — is Rachel, as I feel like she would have understood what I'm going through. The negative result should have been a major relief, as I'm sure it would have been for Matt had he had any notion of it, but even though we are not trying for a baby, and probably never will again, I feel an over-whelming sense of loss. As though I were grieving for a lost child.

To take my mind off the baby that never existed, I open Rachel's diary and force myself to take a sip of wine. I wince at its dry, bitter taste as a burst of woody citrus explodes on my tongue. Determined to drown my sorrows, I take another and another. When it comes to alcohol, I'm a lightweight and one glass is typically my limit, but without it, I won't sleep tonight. Not after finding out what I did about Rachel today. Because of what I now know, I hate Rutland Terrace even more than I did yesterday.

I'm going to insist we put the house back on the market as soon as Matt gets home. I know I'll never be happy here. It's not like we could afford to buy it in the first place. But what if he refuses? And what if he's aware of what happened here and, knowing how much it would have upset me, decided not to tell me? He knows I believe in the spirit realm and I am extremely sensitive to the presence of the dead, even though he is a sceptic and labels my sense of connection to them as 'delusional'. I'm not the only one, though. Jack feels it too. That explains why he's been experiencing nightmares about dead bodies ever since we moved in.

I give an involuntary shudder and find the page I'm looking for (where I last left off) as I try to focus on Rachel's world rather than my own.

> *I made a friend today. A man, who has promised to help me. At the end of our time together, I felt as if I'd known him for ever and he expressed that he felt the same way. Over the course of the next two hours, we confided in one another about our personal lives and I don't mind admitting my heart was thudding in my ribcage . . .*

As I read excerpts of Rachel's outpourings, I feel a sickening surge of anxiety. This stranger she talks of, this man, whoever he is, must be dangerous. What on earth was Rachel thinking? He can't be trusted. Why is Rachel unable to see that? What kind of creep declares his love for a woman he has just met? In addition, his poor wife, whom he considers his sister and says he has never loved, raises alarm bells. I would send this 'soon-to-be-divorced guy' away with a flea in his ear if it were up to me because I have become extremely protective of the woman who used to spend her nights in this kitchen, as I do, mulling over her miserable life.

Rachel can't see this conman for who he is because she has no one else on her side, except for the loving mother-in-law she occasionally mentions, who mistrusts her son just as much as Rachel does. *Did!* I keep forgetting the poor woman is dead. The dimly lit stone steps are a grim and disturbing reminder of how the young mother of two passed away.

Her neck was broken in a tragic but accidental fall. 'She died instantly,' Adie had sadly revealed. And to think, on the day we moved to the terrace, I also took a tumble down those steps. The hairs on the back of my neck stand up as I wonder if this was merely a strange coincidence or something more sinister. A message from the grave.

In any case, I owe it to Rachel, who was helpless and alone, to learn the truth about what really happened to her. Did she fall, as Adie claimed, or was she pushed?

CHAPTER 27: RACHEL

Then

Adie is sleeping soundly next to me. Unlike many husbands, he doesn't snore. Instead, he lies there like a silent assassin, and I lie awake terrified in case his eyes should snap open to stare accusingly at me, as though he has guessed what I'm planning. Thinking about tomorrow, when I've made plans to meet up with my new friend, makes me incredibly anxious. When I feel Adie's body tense next to me, my nerves can no longer bear it, so I swing my legs out of bed and stealthily make my way across the velvety carpet. As I reach the door, I keep one eye on my sleeping husband in case he wakes up — all the while holding my breath — as I open it an inch at a time. Then, as quietly as a shadow, I slip out of the room, resisting the urge to run as fast as I can to escape the prison we call home. But I would never leave without my children. They are the only reason I am here at all.

I rub my eyes as I walk barefoot down the stairs, my toes disappearing into the soft, thick-pile carpet on the various landings. When I turn on the landing light switch to illuminate the cellar kitchen, I realise the lights are not working, which is surprising, given that they were working earlier. I squint into the darkness to see where I am going in the hope of avoiding tripping down the stone steps. The kitchen's flagstone floor is unforgiving at the best of times. I'm constantly reminding the children to use caution when going up and down these steps. The thought of either of them falling and smashing their skulls on that harsh surface makes me tremble.

Using the back of one of the dining chairs as a guide, I feel my way to the table and take a seat. My eyes glisten with unshed tears as I trace the familiar scrawl of my children's names that are engraved into the table. After wiping my nose with the back of my palm and taking a sorrowful sniff, I remove my phone from the folds of my silk nightdress.

It is 3.09 a.m., much too late to be texting anyone, let alone a stranger. Still, I do not hesitate to type the words, 'I cannot wait to see you again.' As I wait for a reply, feeling confident that I will, I feel myself smiling as I reminisce about our long conversation in the hotel bar. His eyes had burned with undisguised desire as if he wanted to kiss me.

When I don't hear back from him after ten minutes, I'm forced to give up. He must be sleeping contentedly like my husband. Wondering how that is possible for either of them considering the current circumstances, I put my phone on silent and get up, letting out a deep sigh as I agitatedly run a hand through my shoulder-length, chestnut-brown hair.

As silent as a ghost, I then ascend two flights of stairs, pausing along the way to glance into unlit shadowy rooms, until I arrive at the third-floor children's bedrooms. They could not be any further away from us, *me*, located on the top floor of the house, which I think of as a mausoleum. Adie says that at eight and six, Beatrice and Archie are old enough to have a floor to themselves, but they are still babies to me.

Beatrice's door is slightly ajar, so I gently push it open, careful not to make a sound. I long to see my children without Adie looming like a prison guard in the background. Is that asking for too much? I can just about see my daughter's adorable face on the pillow because her nightlight has been left on. I long to sit next to her on the bed, but I don't want to wake her. Late at night, she would wonder why her mother was wandering the unlit hallways. She shares Adie's lack of interest in intrigue or drama, thinks logically and is very self-sufficient for an eight-year-old. However, her independence comes at a price. It eliminates the need for a mother.

As I proceed down the landing to Archie's bedroom, I notice that his bed is empty, which makes my heart skip a beat. Fearing that my boy has been abducted, I'm about to turn on the lights and yell for Adie to wake up when I spot the outline of Archie's sleeping shadow in a tent set up on the floor. Like his sister, he is also academic, but he has an adventurous spirit too and hopes to follow in his hero Bear Grylls' footsteps as an explorer.

Knowing there is no chance of Archie waking up if I should kneel beside him to stroke his forehead and kiss him goodnight because he could sleep through a tsunami, I'm about to venture into his room, when—

'What are you doing, Rachel?'

As I spin around in fright to whisper sharply, 'You frightened the life out of me,' I notice that Adie's face is tight and unreadable, yet it's also weighed down with sadness or disappointment. Which one, I can't tell.

'Go back to bed,' he hisses softly, so as not to wake Archie.

'Why?' I mutter crossly, glaring at him.

Frustrated, he shakes his head and rolls his eyes. 'Do you want to wake them up and frighten them again?'

'Again?'

As if sensing that I will not back down, he changes his approach. With a disingenuous smile, he entices, 'Come on, love, let's go back to bed together.' I see that the old Adie charm has returned. Even though I despise the man he has become, I cannot deny that he is still incredibly attractive. He is also in excellent shape. Muscles ripple across his bare chest.

I blurt out rashly, 'Why don't you want me near my children?"

'I've told you, you'll wake them up,' he warns, through clenched teeth.

'So what if I do?' I rage. 'Maybe I'll wake them up right now, load them in the car, and take them away from here and you.'

'You won't do that,' he sighs resolutely.

His lack of concern makes me ask, 'Why not?'

He simply stares at me, as if it were obvious, but I have no idea what he is up to. Is he right? Has the answer been staring me in the face all along, and I have been too blind to see it?

'Why not?' I demand once again, a sense of dread hanging over me.

With a fake look of regret, he informs me in a clipped, clinical tone, 'Because I have applied for a lasting power of attorney on your behalf, due to mental incapacity, and it has since been granted.'

A fresh ripple of fear goes through me as he adds menacingly, 'Which means you are not going anywhere. *With or without* the children.'

CHAPTER 28: LUCY

Now

When I hear a muffled scream, it takes me a moment to digest that it's real and not imaginary. It's 3.09 a.m. according to a quick check of the bedside clock. Neither night nor morning. I quickly toss aside the covers and swing my legs out of the bed to race out of the room. On the landing, I thrust open the door to Jack's bedroom and fumble for the light switch, flipping it on to reveal my son sitting up in bed, tearfully rubbing his eyes. Casper, who is also on the bed, licks Jack's face in concern, but he pauses to wag a tail at me, as if relieved to have some back up.

I quickly run to the bed and embrace Jack, calling out, 'Whatever is it, sweetheart? Are you okay?' while pushing Casper aside.

Jack buries his wet face in my neck and sobs, 'I had a bad dream.' He smells of coconut shampoo and minty toothpaste. Unlike Casper, who stinks of wet dog and foul meaty breath.

'Was it the same one?' I ask with a frown. Like most mothers, I hate seeing my kids upset. It devastates me that I can't eliminate their childhood fears. The bogeyman always wins.

He nods sorrowfully, afraid to say too much in case his nightmare should become real. I ask as gently as I can, 'Was it about the dead body again?'

He draws back to give me a wide-eyed stare, 'She was lying at the bottom of the steps all bloody.' I say nothing, thinking it's best, but as I study his terrified expression, my mind is humming with questions, such as how he could have found out about Rachel's accident. The only conclusion I can come to is that he must have overheard me and Alina discussing it. That'll teach me to keep my big gob shut in future. Because now look what I've done. Given how sensitive my son is, it dawns on me that I should have seen this coming. I have no one to blame but myself.

Jack vocalises for the hundredth time, 'I don't like it here.'

'I know you don't,' I murmur as I get into bed with him, cuddling him and kissing the top of his silky-smooth head. It's all I can do not to cry, because *I don't like it here either!* And I hold Matt fully accountable for that. I now have even more of a case to insist on selling this house because of my son. If only it were possible to go back to our old home.

Out of the blue, Jack wants to know, 'Has Dad left us?'

I freeze on hearing this, but I don't overreact, since I'm afraid I will give myself away. *What has he heard now?* Instead, I chastise in a mock-serious tone, 'Of course not, why on earth would you think that?'

'I heard him on the phone talking to a woman,' he shrugs, a tear leaking onto his cheek.

Squeezing my eyes shut, I stifle a sob, before asking, 'When was this? And how do you know it was a woman he was talking to?'

Slumping against me, Jack swipes a hand across his tear-streaked face and hangs his head, mumbling, 'It was a long time ago but I remember it because he kept calling her *beautiful* as if that were her name.'

Gently does it, I warn myself, as I enquire in an exaggeratedly casual tone, 'And do you know *who* he was talking to? Did he mention her real name?'

He shakes his head and shrugs again, as if bored, but I know better. My son is trying to protect me, his mother, from his father's betrayal.

Jack laments, 'I didn't think dads were supposed to have girl-friends,' sounding deeply offended.

'You're right, Jack. They're not.' I let out a deep sigh, feeling as though my world has been turned upside down again. Is Matt seeing someone new? Or is it the same former coworker from before? Am I wrong to jump to conclusions? The conversation Jack overheard was from a long time ago, he said so himself. But could a seven-year-old remember what his father said over two years ago? It's unlikely.

'But dads are people just like you and me, and they *are* allowed to have friends,' I point out in what I hope is a positive, cheerful voice, despite how I'm really feeling on the inside. Broken. Raw. Furious. Small.

He gives me a withering look and persists doubtfully, 'Even girls?' I'm affected by how much he resembles his father in this moment, although I would really like to kick Matt in the balls right now. For doing this to us. If he's seeing that woman again, I will leave him this time. See if I don't.

'Even girls,' I agree, nodding. My deception does the trick as Jack lies back against the pillow, content to believe what I tell him. The same can't be said of me. I want to bombard my son with a hundred questions. Like, did your dad sound happy or sad when he spoke to her on the phone? Did he tell her that he was leaving me for her? But it wouldn't be fair to put Jack under that kind of pressure, so I bite my tongue.

I can still clearly recall the day I learned about Matt's affair. What cuckolded wife wouldn't? It was a Tuesday and we'd eaten meatballs and pasta for supper. Other than Matt being quieter than normal, I hadn't noticed anything unusual. That is, until I woke up in the middle of the night to discover his side of the bed empty and him sobbing uncontrollably downstairs. He told me everything at that point, claiming that the stress of lying to me was killing him and that he could no longer continue. He assured me that he had ended the affair with his work colleague that very day because he was determined to keep his marriage and family intact. When he acknowledged that he had never loved her, the blow was lessened. They had spent too much time together, he claimed, even travelling abroad for work. 'One thing led to another,' Matt had said. After that, we argued into the night, and it took me a long time to forgive him if I ever truly have.

'Lucy, you are my one true love and always will be,' he'd declared in a very unlike-Matt gesture. I gave him another chance primarily because I shared his desire to save my family. Jack needed his father. And all along, I thought we'd done an admirable job of covering everything up, saving our intense arguments for when the kids were in bed. I was clearly mistaken.

Jack tries to get my attention by tugging on my arm. 'MUM!'

'Yes, love?' I reply vaguely, lost in a world of my own.

He has such a serious expression on his face when I turn to face him that I worry he's going to reveal something even more significant.

'Can we have pizza tomorrow for tea?'

CHAPTER 29: RACHEL

Then

Through the dappled glass of the front door, I can see the top of her head. It looks like a gorgeous auburn shade. She must also be tall if I can see her through the glass panel. Those are two of my husband's desired prerequisites for a female ticked off the list already. It's 11 a.m. precisely. I'm impressed as good timekeeping is important to me. Before I open the door, I inhale deeply and gnaw anxiously at my cheek. I don't think I've ever been so nervous meeting anyone in my life. Not that I'll show it. I wouldn't give her or Adie the satisfaction.

If Adie and his lover, who clearly intends to pose as our children's nanny, mean to intimidate me, they've got a surprise coming. Regardless of Adie's assertion that he is now acting as my lasting power of attorney, I still have the upper hand because what they don't know is that I've already disposed of my fortune. Most of it has been placed in trust funds for the children, out of Adie's reach, but the remainder — still a sizeable amount — has been secreted away in secret offshore accounts that he doesn't know about. He's going to get a serious shock when he investigates my financial matters. When that happens, I would really like to be present.

'Hello, Mrs Bello. I'm Fiona, or Fi if you prefer. I believe you are expecting me,' the nanny announces, as I open the door.

This one is no Mary Poppins, but that doesn't come as any surprise to me. I knew how things would be. How different she is from Sasha, who has gone infuriatingly silent. Fiona is Adie's type. Just as I predicted. Not only is she tall, slender and stunning with milky white skin, she has an abundance of long, dark hair and sultry brown eyes to match. She has cleverly played down her appearance today, but I can see past her make-up-free complexion and plainly styled hair and clothes. Of course, she's younger than me. Much closer than I am to childbearing age. Not that it matters because I don't intend to have any more children, regardless of what Adie says. I have never been able to understand his motive for wanting me to have another child when he is obviously planning to do away with me. All I can think is that he must be using it as a tactic to trick me, and others into believing that he is working hard at saving our marriage.

'Rachel, please, and yes I am,' I make every effort to sound welcoming as I bare my white teeth in a perfect smile. I can pretend to be the perfect future employer to match her perfect would-be nanny disguise.

'Do come in,' I say, opening the door.

She looks shamelessly around her as she enters the grand entrance hall. Does she already see herself living in my home? Becoming both my children's stepmother and Adie's wife?

'You have a beautiful home,' she observes with a fresh-faced smile.

'Thank you,' I say with a stiff nod. 'Follow me, please.'

As I lead her into the library, her flat, functional shoes shuffle on the marble floor behind me. She is at a disadvantage when I sit down at my desk and leave her standing.

'I'm afraid my husband couldn't be here to see you today, so it's just me. But I expect you knew that already.'

She opens her mouth to say something but then seems to think better of it, choosing to remain silent. Adie wouldn't have missed this interview for anything, but first thing this morning he was summoned into the office for an important meeting. He would have liked to have been present when his mistress and wife first met. As it is, he had no say in the matter, which is why I'm hoping Sasha has since come forward. Will he be dismissed and sent home because of this? All I can do is wait and see.

'Where are my manners?' I chuckle conspiratorially as I point to a curved linen-upholstered chair. 'Please take a seat.' Then, bracing myself for the inevitable lie, I enquire politely, 'How did you meet my husband?'

'Through a mutual acquaintance,' she says with a shrug before hurriedly reassuring me. 'But it was just the once and only for a few minutes.'

She is aware that she is on dangerous ground, so I mutter, 'I see,' and glance down at my clenched, white-knuckled hands.

'What would you like to know, Mrs Bello, I mean, Rachel?' Fiona offers me a pile of papers out of her bag and rattles off uncertainly, 'I have my references here if you'd like to see them.'

I'm incredulous, 'You've worked as a nanny before then?' I purposefully do not glance at the papers, which she claws back to save face.

'Yes of course,' she responds, her eyes wide.

I'll give her credit for being a talented actor, but I intend to stay one step ahead of her. If she plans to live in my house, I will have to. The thought of her putting my children to bed causes my heart to twist.

'We both know that personal references don't mean a thing,' I smile to take the sting out of my words.

'I'm not sure I understand,' she begins, but I cut her off brutally.

'What I intended to say was that you have already been recommended to us — well, to my husband, anyhow, and that's more than good enough for me. We just need to work out the details.'

I may not have a choice as to whether I hire her or not as that has already been decided by Adie, but I won't give them the upper hand. I intend to remain in control of my household, if not my husband.

She gushes enthusiastically, 'Oh, thank you so much, Rachel, you won't regret it, I promise. I'll take care of your children as if they were my own.'

Her words slap me in the face. How dare she? Tense with indignation, I do the unthinkable by suggesting, 'Why don't you come for dinner this evening so you can meet the children? Adie will be back by then and I'm sure he'd love to see you.'

'Oh, I'd love that too,' she marvels, clapping her hands together.

With an intentional glance at my stomach that she cannot fail to notice, I simper, 'And when the baby comes, you'll help me with him or her?'

'A baby?' She gasps in alarm, shocked. And if I'm not mistaken, outraged. 'Adie never mentioned anything about a baby.'

I bet he didn't, I rejoice silently, knowing that he will now have even more explaining to do when he comes home to the two of us tonight.

CHAPTER 30: LUCY

Now

After dropping Jack off at school, Sophie and I are heading to Lucy's Blooms, my florist shop in the middle of town, to see how Kerry is doing. I thought I'd best show my face after Matt made that remark about her inability to cope on her own, and let's not forget his dig about the shop not making any money. Kerry has worked for me ever since I opened the business ten years ago. When I took maternity leave with Sophie, I gave her a pay rise and promoted her to manager. We also have another part-time member of staff who helps at peak times, which are usually the summer months during the wedding season (i.e. now). In my defence, I normally try to stop by multiple times a week and stay the odd morning when I can, if Sophie can be persuaded to take a nap out back, but I have been noticeably absent recently due to the house move.

Thank goodness I still have a car to get me there. Tinker Bell has behaved herself since the day I met Adie when the AA managed to get her started again. My phone rings as I'm parking Tinker Bell in the car park behind the shop. I pick it up when I see it is Matt, only to ask in a mock-serious tone, 'What have I done to deserve two calls in one morning?'

'Can't a husband miss his wife?' he jests, from more than two thousand miles away.

Straight away I notice the change in his voice from when Jack and I spoke to him earlier this morning. A shiver runs down my spine as I realise that he's on edge and putting on an act, and that this is how he sounded when he was with her . . . and when he was lying. I'm about to ask him 'What's up?' when I hear smothered female laughter in the background. I'm on it like a tonne of bricks, demanding, 'Matt, who is that?'

'Just one of my colleagues,' he replies sheepishly, and I can practically feel his cheeks smarting down the phone to singe my own.

'You never mentioned anyone was travelling with you,' I stammer, shocked by what I am hearing.

'Didn't I?' he laughs dismissively, as though it doesn't matter, but it bloody well does, so I raise my voice to prove it, 'No. You did not.'

'Calm down, Lucy. I must have forgotten, that's all,' he responds in a tight voice, meaning, 'Now isn't the time to be having this conversation.'

I happen to disagree, so I ask menacingly, 'Who is she?'

He sighs, 'If you must know, her name is Katya.'

'Katya?' I parrot, taking an instant dislike to the exotic-sounding name.

Matt is quick to reassure me, 'But she's not the only one. There are two other coworkers on this trip, so that makes four of us in total.'

'How nice for you.'

'Don't be like that, love,' he murmurs softly, sounding hurt, and I start to feel bad for him. After all, he has done everything I have asked. He quit his old job for one that requires more travel and that he doesn't like as much. He also vowed never to see his former lover again. If I can't trust him to behave himself with a female coworker, what hope is there for us? Besides, she might be as ugly as sin for all I know. I certainly hope so.

'I called to tell you that our trip has been delayed due to the compressors not being ready in time. We won't be back until Friday now.'

'*Our* trip' and '*We* won't be back until' has me on tenterhooks. My nerves are shot. I can't do this again. Deciding that it's not in my best interest to listen to any more of his bullshit, I declare, 'Sorry, I can't hear you. I'm losing you.' *In more ways than one*, I can't stop thinking. And on that depressing note, I hang up. Right before the phone goes dead, I hear him rattle off a dutiful, 'Love you,' but I could have imagined it.

'Bloody men,' I squeal, rebelliously tossing my water bottle into the passenger footwell, next to a dozen other similarly discarded ones, which makes me feel a little better.

'Bloody men,' Sophie giggles from the back seat, only she says it with much less malice. When our eyes meet in the rear-view mirror, we're both smiling. What would I do without my kids? They are my world. And they make everything worthwhile.

'Come on, trouble,' I tell her, as I climb out of the car.

As soon as we enter the shop, Sophie is taken from me. Kerry loves kids and frequently looks after Sophie while I spend time in the back office doing administrative work. Throughout the morning, Kerry is in a quiet, introspective mood and doesn't say much, which isn't like her.

'Is there anything wrong, Kerry?' I ask, concerned.

She flinches when I place a reassuring hand on her shoulder, so I release my grasp and urge, 'If there is. I hope you know you can tell me.'

'I'm fine,' she replies bluntly, and then mindful that I am her boss at the end of the day, she offers me a faint smile and insists, 'really, I am.'

Really, she isn't, but I can't make her tell me what's bothering her if she doesn't want to. I feel hurt though that she doesn't feel she can confide in me as I have her in the past. I've always thought of us as friends rather than just employer and employee.

'Just one thing before you go,' I prompt, before she disappears with Sophie to the park, so I can check the accounts myself without being disturbed. 'Matt said he went over the accounts. Were you here then?'

Kerry's face instantly flushes red in alarm, then she stammers guiltily, 'No, I don't think so,' and quickly looks away from me. Again, this is strange behaviour on her part. Should I be worried?

'Oh, that's odd,' I observe, pulling a mildly puzzled face. 'Because Matt said he was worried about you not being able to cope on your own for much longer, so I assumed he must have spoken to you. But I could have got it wrong.' Since it's not a big deal, I shrug my shoulders.

And then suddenly it is a big deal because she's exclaiming in an unconvincing tone, 'Oh, yes, I remember now. I *was* here, but only for a minute or two, as he caught me just as I was about to leave.' Something tells me that she is lying. But why? And what is she not telling me?

CHAPTER 31: RACHEL

Then

I take my coffee black. He takes his white. He insisted on paying and even treated us to a fancy cake each, which remain untouched on the table. For obvious reasons, I asked to meet him away from Stamford, so we've come to the charming Birch Tree Café in the village of Easton on the Hill, which is partly staffed by young adults with Down syndrome. I'm impressed that he was aware of it and suggested it, even though neither of us have been here before. It demonstrates his compassion for others.

Gazing into his eyes, which are as playful and lively as I remember, I enquire, 'Where are you from?'

'You mean, where do I live?'

'Sorry, is that too nosey of me?'

'Not at all,' he says shaking his head. 'I'm a man with nothing to hide.'

'That makes a change.' I pose this cynically.

Wincing in response to my jab about men in general, he admonishes in a serious voice, 'What you see is what you get with me. I'm an open book.'

'Hmm,' I mumble as I try to process that. 'Where *do* you live, then?'

'At the moment I'm renting a room from a friend in Recreation Road.'

'Would that be a female friend by any chance?' I say flirtatiously, letting him know he won't be in any trouble if it is a woman friend. *Or will he?*

'Talk about suspicious,' he acts all offended. 'You don't let up, do you?'

'I've had my heart broken too many times,' I admit candidly.

He observes me intently for a while, then reaches across and gives my hand a comforting pat. 'You're not the only one,' he confesses.

'You too, huh?' as I say this, I apologetically remove my hand and quickly scan the room to see if someone I know has entered.

He sighs. 'It's the reason we're getting a divorce.'

'You poor thing,' I reply, radiating sympathy.

Cheeks reddening with embarrassment, he goes on to explain awkwardly, 'Don't feel sorry for me, Rachel. I can honestly say it came as a relief. I've been wanting out of my marriage for years.'

I let out a long exhale as I sentimentally admit, 'Adie and I were happy once. At least I thought so.'

Judging by his crestfallen expression, my words have wounded him, but he is intent on not showing it. I don't blame him for this, because I think we both instinctively know what we intend to become to one another. For us, there will be no space for anyone else. Backtracking, I break the tense silence by adding, 'Of course, that was a long time ago.'

He smiles gratefully then, and shoots forward in his seat to exclaim excitedly, 'My wife is currently in the process of remortgaging the family home so she and her new partner, Ian, can buy me out. I'm hoping I'll be able to purchase a house of my own after the divorce is finalised.'

'Good for you,' I throw him a high five, thinking that he deserves it, as it sounds like he's been through a particularly tough time. I then ask, 'What's her name, your soon-to-be ex-wife?'

'Olivia.'

'And do you have any children?'

'One. A boy. And before you ask, his name is Daniel. And he's five. I don't suppose you were a journalist in a previous life, were you?'

'I might have been,' I chuckle provocatively.

He rolls his eyes. 'Seriously?'

'Seriously.'

He blows out his cheeks, suitably impressed. 'You still have the talent for getting the truth out of people. That's all I can say.'

My voice drips with disappointment as I remark, 'If only that were true.'

His lips open and close, unable to form the right words. He then drops his gaze and states, 'If there's anything I can do to help? Anything at all.'

A sudden surge of anger towards Adie bubbles to the surface and I find myself grinding out through clenched teeth, 'In that case, will you help me get rid of my husband?'

'By get rid of, what do you mean exactly?' he stutters in confusion, his voice low and his shocked gaze riveted on me.

I mutter in a resolute, matter-of-fact manner, 'As long as Adie is alive, I am in danger. The children and I will never be safe.'

Eyes wide with incredulity, he gasps, 'When you said *anything*, I didn't think you meant *that*.'

'I see,' I reply briskly, wringing my hands and bowing my head in humiliation. Frustration fills my chest as I realise that I have unsuccessfully let my guard down. And it was all for nothing. This man is not who I thought he was. He is not in love with me at all. He can't be. What a fool I've been.

He whispers across the table, 'Tell me you didn't mean what you said.'

My pulse quickens as I protest, 'It's him or me. What choice do I have?'

'There are always choices, Rachel,' he argues. 'What's wrong with divorcing him.'

'That isn't an option. You don't know what he's like. You don't understand,' I whimper, wiping a tear from my eye.

Brow furrowing in concern, he instructs, 'Then help me to.'

'I've said too much. I apologise. And now I must go,' I stammer as I stand up abruptly, knocking a cup on the floor. 'I clearly misjudged you and what I thought I meant to you,' I snivel heartbrokenly.

He lurches clumsily to his feet to put a restraining hand on my arm. 'Please, Rachel, don't go. Sit down so we can talk this through. You've shocked me, that's all. I am not thinking straight.'

He picks up the shattered cup and gives the pieces to a staff member while I take my seat again. As I rest my hand on my forehead and let out a deep sigh, his gaze shifts to the fresh bruising on my forearm. When I see his jaw clench in rage, I know he will help me no matter what he says.

CHAPTER 32: LUCY

Now

I made the summer bouquet myself, using sunflowers, chrysanthemums, carnations and solidasters — flowers that are known to elevate mood since they are cheerful and bright and can make you smile even when you don't feel like it. When his muscular form emerges behind the glass, I take a nervous step back as he opens the door. Will he be pleased to see me again, or will he find my presence annoying? When he does a double take and then smiles broadly, I feel a wave of relief. And something else, that feels like pleasure, although that doesn't feel appropriate in the circumstances.

'I was just thinking of you,' he enthuses, which I very much doubt. He then frowns and glances over my shoulder to where my car is parked in the lane, with its doors and windows locked. 'What, no Sophie today?' he asks, looking disappointed.

'No. She's with a friend having the time of her life.'

'I'm glad to hear it. Well, come in,' he commands jovially as he swings the door open, revealing a tantalising glimpse of a cemetery-grey hue.

'I wanted to give you these as a thank you for the other day,' I explain, feeling like a clumsy, starstruck teenager as I shove the flowers in his direction. I can't tell him that I arranged them myself, or that I own a flower shop since he would then be able to find out who I really am.

'Oh, wow, thank you so much. They're beautiful,' he says in earnest, sounding like he means it. 'No one's ever bought me flowers before.'

As I follow him inside, I joke, 'Now that I find hard to believe.'

'I don't think you ever told me your name,' he remarks casually over his shoulder as he guides me into the high-gloss, minimalistic kitchen.

I giggle nervously, 'Didn't I?' but my laughter sounds phoney.

He turns to face me with a knowing look and playfully chastises, 'No, you didn't. I'm starting to think you are quite the mystery woman.'

I blush even more as he pulls an expensive-looking vase out of one of the kitchen cupboards and begins to arrange the flowers in it. I resist the urge to do it for him because he doesn't seem to be doing a bad job of it, leading me to suspect he's done it before, although he doesn't follow the 3-5-8 rule for floristry like us professionals do.

When I catch him staring at me through the flower stems, he winks comically, and I get the impression that he is waiting for me to reveal something about myself. This makes me even more tongue-tied in case he has already guessed my identity and is deliberately taunting me.

'There,' he gives a satisfied nod, and steps back to admire the arrangement, all the while ignoring me as if I weren't there.

Unable to bear the suspense any longer, I blurt out, 'It's Sadie. My name is Sadie.' Sadie was the name of a troubled sixth-form student I went to school with, who turned out to be a pathological liar. If the cap fits!

'Sadie and Sophie,' he says, rolling the names approvingly around on his tongue. 'Both names are very lovely.'

'Thank you,' I nod, relieved to have got away with the lie. At least for the time being. A loud ping from somewhere behind him diverts his attention just as I'm about to ask him about Rachel, and what she was like.

'That'll be the oven,' he observes vaguely as he looks at his smartwatch. 'I can't believe it's lunchtime already.'

Disappointed that I'm about to be thrown out, I look at my own smartwatch and pretend to be equally surprised, exclaiming, 'Goodness me. It's almost one o'clock, I'd better be going.'

He frowns. 'But you'll stay for some lunch surely?'

'Oh, I couldn't,' I stammer because his invitation has caught me off guard. It is not what I was expecting at all. He hardly knows me. Or I him.

He winces and pulls an apologetic face. 'It's nothing special, just salmon, new potatoes and green beans.'

That makes me smile. 'It sounds pretty special to me.'

'Then I insist,' he commands, bowing dramatically.

'Oh, well, if you insist,' I laughingly give in, my mouth watering from the delicious aroma coming from the oven now that he has opened it.

He motions for me to sit at the kitchen island, so I oblige, and he swiftly arranges two place settings before starting to dish up. He quickly recalls, 'I'm forgetting the wine,' and reaches for glasses and a bottle of wine.

'Not for me, thanks,' I tell him, holding my hand over my empty glass. 'I'm driving. Besides, I'm not much of a drinker.'

He raises his eyebrows in admiration, 'That's very commendable,' but I notice that he still pours himself a huge glass and has refilled it again before we've even finished our meal.

After swallowing my last bite of the succulent salmon and mopping up the last of the lemon sauce with some sourdough bread he confessed to making himself, I exclaim, 'That was delicious. You're a great cook.'

'You sound surprised?'

I splutter derisively. 'That's because I am. My husband couldn't even reheat a can of baked beans.'

'Us widowers have to fend for ourselves,' he sighs dejectedly.

Feeling like this is the perfect opportunity to question him about Rachel, as I might not get another chance, I rest my chin in the palm of my hand, in what I hope is a seductive gesture, and, as cunning as a coyote, I ask, 'Was your wife very beautiful?'

'Not in the conventional sense, no,' he thoughtfully acknowledges, his gaze elsewhere — in the past, I suspect, 'but she was to me, of course.'

I nod to demonstrate my understanding, which is his downfall because his eyes suddenly start to sparkle with unshed tears. He stands up, mumbles, 'Excuse me a moment,' and leaves the room just as I'm about to reach across to give him a comforting pat on the hand.

I regret causing him such distress. For all I know he's a lonely widower who adored his wife. All that stuff in Rachel's diary about Adie wanting to get rid of her so he could steal her money and replace her with the hot young nanny could have been made up. But why would she lie? And is it just that I like Adie that is making me have a change of heart? I know that Rachel was wrong about at least one thing though since there is no new woman on the scene.

So you can only imagine how horrified I am when the rear door opens and a tall, young woman with long dark hair and sultry brown eyes enters. She is quite beautiful and has milky white skin.

When she sees me seated at the kitchen island, having made myself at home, she demands haughtily, 'Who are you?'

'I could ask you the same question,' I reply, returning her hostile stare.

Adie returns to the room at this point looking embarrassed, as though he has something to hide. Sensing the tension between us, he awkwardly announces, 'I see you've met the children's nanny, Fiona.'

CHAPTER 33: RACHEL

Then

The children adore her. Of course they do. Like them, she is young, energetic and bright, and I pretend to be ecstatic about this over dinner, but I would really like to slit the sly little trollop's throat from left to right with a razor-sharp knife. It was painful to watch Fiona and Adie's awkward and meticulously staged *to-appear-natural* encounter when she first arrived but they're not fooling anyone. I saw the secretive looks they were giving each other, they couldn't keep their eyes off each other.

Adie is in a surprisingly good mood, which leads me to suspect that the meeting in London was not about Sasha or the sexual misconduct case, more's the pity. I'm even more grateful to Soon-to-be-divorced guy for agreeing to help me figure out a way of divorcing my husband that will guarantee I can keep my children — and my fortune — even though he hasn't yet consented to go as far as I wanted him to. Never mind. I'm going to keep working on him and intend to make it worth his while. In every sense.

You would think my philandering husband had something to celebrate, judging by the quantity of red wine he has been drinking, and he does, now that his young lover is here and intends to move into our house. Under the guise of checking on the children, will he be sneaking up to the third floor and into her room at night? I wouldn't put anything past him.

We've finished our meal and everyone, except Adie and the new nanny, have cleaned their plates, but as I recall extremely well, lust has a habit of suppressing appetite. I watched them pushing their food around their plates as though neither of them was hungry. Except for each other!

Any chance she gets, Fiona is keen to impress Beatrice and Archie with how much she shares their interests. Not only does she allegedly play the violin, like my daughter, but she also shares Archie's passion for chess and has already challenged him to a game, much to his delight. When I politely mentioned, 'It would be lovely to hear you play the violin for us,' her eyes had flickered with alarm, before shifting to Adie, who coughed nervously into his hand and guiltily looked away, obviously unable to help. Face reddening, she'd gone on to explain, 'I'd love that another time when I have my violin with me.' When I suggested she could borrow Beatrice's, Adie chose that moment to interrupt, and the subject was then conveniently dropped.

I don't believe a word that girl says. If she can play a musical instrument, I'll eat my hat, as the saying goes. Her talents lie elsewhere.

'Pudding, anyone? I ask wearily, sick of the sight of them.

'Yes please,' both my children squeal automatically, before turning to bombard Fiona, who appears increasingly startled and cornered, with yet more questions. Resignedly, I get to my feet and start gathering plates. 'Apple pie and ice cream coming up,' I beam at the children but fail miserably to get their attention. It's obvious that my son has a crush on Fiona since he blushes whenever she flutters her eyelids at him. Despite being only seven he likes girls. Like father, like son!

'Let me help you,' Fiona offers, following me downstairs to the cellar kitchen. Although she won't admit it, I have a sneaking suspicion that she wants to avoid the intensity of the children's interrogation. How hard must it be to pretend to care about and like other people's children? I don't envy her as I'm not certain I could perform such a task, or that I would be able to pull it off quite so well. Now that it's clearly my turn to be wooed, I brace myself for a barrage of excessive praise. I'm not disappointed.

'I love this kitchen and what you've done with it,' she gushes.

I raise myself to my full height and mutter, 'Really?' in disbelief. 'You don't find it claustrophobic and more like a windowless prison cell?'

She pulls a face and frowns, no longer as captivated. 'Now that you mention it,' she objects, folding her arms and narrowing her eyes.

I can't help but think how susceptible she is to influence. It makes sense that Adie finds her attractive. As I've said before, she's exactly his type.

She goes on in an envious tone, 'You're still very lucky though.'

'How so?' I scowl.

'All of this,' she sighs wistfully, gesturing around the room with one hand. 'A beautiful home, a loving husband and two amazing kids.'

When she slyly adds, 'Not to mention another baby on the way,' my eyes blaze with indignation, and I know that I'm not mistaken when her shrewd gaze deliberately shifts to my flat stomach. My deception has been exposed but she clearly intends to go along with it even though she knows I am not pregnant. She's fast. I'll grant her that. She obviously wasted no time in dragging Adie to one side and demanding to know if it was true.

'It's early days, so we're keeping it to ourselves for now. You mustn't mention it to the children,' I admit frankly, breaking the tense silence.

'Of course, I wouldn't dream of it,' she murmurs in agreement. 'That's your business. Not mine.'

'And Adie's,' I correct her haughtily, as only a millionaire's daughter can. I won't lie. I take pleasure in watching her cheeks burn.

We both jump in alarm when, from behind us, we hear an explosive popping sound. I turn to see Adie standing there, smiling clownishly at us. He has done what he does best, creeped on us unheard, like the snake he is. The fact that he has just opened a bottle of champagne, which is now fizzing out of the bottle onto the flagstone floor, further astounds me.

'Quick, get some glasses,' Adie bids me, trying to save the champagne.

'Ooh, champers,' Fiona exclaims excitedly, clapping her hands in a childish gesture, momentarily forgetting that she is meant to be teetotal.

I locate the glasses, but I cannot keep the sarcasm from my voice as I demand impatiently, 'What exactly are we meant to be celebrating?'

'My promotion,' he boasts dramatically. 'You'll be pleased to know that I have, as of today, been made a director at Prince Tech.'

'A *promotion*?' All my hopes and dreams vanish. How is this possible after what he has been accused of?

'Don't sound so shocked,' Adie snaps in a defensive manner. 'I've worked hard for this, and no one deserves it more than I do.'

CHAPTER 34: LUCY

Now

> *Tonight, the new nanny came for dinner and met the children for the first time. Naturally, they adored her, which broke my heart. My entire family appears to have been bewitched by the scheming Fiona, no one more so than Adie, who also revealed that he had been promoted to director, indicating that the accusations of sexual misconduct against him have not been reopened. I can think of no other explanation for this. But why has Sasha gone silent? It doesn't make any sense. Thank goodness for the distraction of Soon-to-be-divorced guy who has vowed to help me escape my husband's clutches. I'm not sure what he can do to help but we are to meet again tomorrow to discuss it.*

As I read these passages from Rachel's journal, I am deeply outraged on her behalf. How dare Adie move his lover, posing as the new nanny, into the family home? Just wait until I see him again — *if I ever see him again* — because I intend to give him a piece of my mind. As for that piece of homewrecking trash, Fiona, who is clearly a younger version of Rachel given her dark hair, sultry eyes and stunning appearance, I could gladly poke out her eyes. Earlier today when Adie clumsily introduced her as 'the children's nanny' she had scoffed indignantly, 'Nanny? Yeah, whatever,' before sulkily stomping out of the room, leaving a terrible, impenetrable silence behind. After that, I hastily excused myself and left, ignoring Adie's pathetic justifications and apologies for her inexcusable behaviour.

I'm reading while munching on leftover cold pizza and drinking my second can of full-fat Coke. Since I'm constantly telling the kids that sugary drinks are bad for them, I only ever drink them when they're not around, which, as a mum, I think is fair enough. Casper is keeping me company in the kitchen tonight as Jack has the beginnings of a summer cold, and I had to insist that the dog didn't sleep in his room in case its fur made his symptoms worse. Jack was too worn out to argue.

Casper's ears prick up and he begins growling. When he lets out a series of unusually aggressive barks and rushes up the concrete steps with his hackles raised, I follow him. 'What is it, boy?' I ask in alarm. As we enter the entrance hall together, Casper hurls himself at the front door where a darkened silhouette is visible in the dappled glass.

'Who's there?' I call out sharply, pretending at an authority I don't feel. To be honest, I'm shitting myself. Knowing what happened to Rachel in this house only adds to my fear of being alone in it at night, but I'm a mum of two now, I must put on a brave face. I would die before anyone harmed either of my children. Hell, I'd do the same for the dog.

A muffled and disgruntled voice replies, 'John.'

'What on earth are you doing here?' I ask my father-in-law as I open the door, remembering to quickly add, 'not that you're not welcome, of course.'

As he shuffles inside like a much older man, he mutters, 'I should hope so.' His eyes then drop away from mine as he explains, 'I promised Matt I'd look in on you and the kids, seeing as he's not going to be back for a few days and you're all alone.' There's something about the way he says 'all alone' that causes me to shudder. I don't know why.

'That's nice of you,' I tell him, feeling suddenly exposed in my pyjama shorts and strapless vest top. I don't mean to be unkind about Matt's dad, but his peeping-Tom eyes have always freaked me out. I'm groaning inwardly, but I manage to smile as I say, 'But the kids have been in bed for the last two hours.' It is ten o'clock, after all, which seems like a late hour to be paying a visit when as he correctly pointed out, I *am* all alone.

When he doesn't reply, I grudgingly ask, 'Are you staying for a drink?' I obviously don't want him here because, even at the best of times, I can't think of anything to say to him, as he's so socially awkward. Besides, I want to get back to Rachel's diary. After he gives me a lopsided smile, which I assume means yes I put Casper outside in the courtyard before leading hm down to the kitchen. Since neither of Matt's parents can tolerate the dog, it's simpler that way. In Casper's case, the feeling is mutual.

I turn on the kettle and ask, 'Cup of tea, John?' But he makes a face.

'Got anything stronger?'

I sigh as I head to the wine rack and take out an open bottle of red wine that Matt started a few days ago but never finished. To shorten John's visit, I deliberately pour him a small glass, ignoring the resentful look he gives me for being frugal.

Then, unsure of what to say to one another, we take our seats at opposite ends of the table. Eventually, he raises his drooping head from his glass and observes, 'You must be lonely here all by yourself. A girl like you.'

'Not really,' I lie. 'I have the kids, don't I?'

He grins, exposing wine-stained teeth and insists, 'It's not the same.'

'A girl like me — what did you mean by that?' I ask, a little taken aback and insulted now that I've had time to think about his comment.

'Just that you've always been a good-time girl. Haven't you, Luce?'

When did he or anybody else start calling me Luce? It dawns on me then that he is quite drunk and that his late-night call must have coincided with the pub emptying. If I had realised this sooner, I would never have allowed him inside. Father-in-law or not.

'A good-time girl! You're having a laugh, aren't you?' I angrily jump to my feet. 'Do you have any clue how hard I work with two kids, a house to manage, a business to run and Matt away so often?'

He finishes his drink in one go and slams the glass down on the table. 'I meant no harm by it.'

I no longer want to argue, so I stammer, 'I think you should go now you've finished your drink. It's late and I want to go to bed.'

Detecting my fear, his lip curls into a menacing grin as he slurs, 'Now you're talking, Luce.' Then, suddenly, he's lumbering towards me.

CHAPTER 35: RACHEL

Then

I slouch against the wall feeling like an outsider in my own home as I watch Adie and Fiona put the children to bed. They've partnered up under the guise that I am tired and need to rest, plus it will be 'good practice' for Fiona. I know Adie is already filling her head with lies about my mental health and I notice her eyes widen when she stares at me, seeming undecided about whether to be afraid of me. As I return downstairs to my bedroom, I brush a tear from my eye. In a sense, Adie is right. I *am* exhausted.

Later, when Adie is downstairs alone, enjoying a few glasses of expensive whisky to celebrate his new position as a director, I will confide in my journal. Writing everything down gives me a better understanding of what is really happening in this house. If you listened to Adie, who is the biggest liar of them all, he would insist that everything he does is for the benefit of me and the children, but that could not be further from the truth as I am fully aware of his real intentions. How much does Fiona know? I wonder. Would she willingly volunteer to be an accessory to murder? I suspect not, in which case, I might be able to get through to her. Make her understand that my husband intends to get rid of me one way or another. I anticipate having an accident of some kind every day, a warning from Adie, or at the very least, being presented with more false evidence that I am mentally incapable. My nerves are shot to pieces.

I switch on the television to take my mind off the pair of them. I rarely watch the news, because it is so depressing, but the words flashing up on screen immediately capture my attention, and not in a good way.

YOUNG WOMAN (26) FOUND MURDERED AT HER ISLINGTON FLAT. THE WOMAN'S BODY WAS DISCOVERED EARLIER THIS MORNING BY HER LANDLORD AFTER FAMILY AND FRIENDS REPORTED HER MISSING.

I collapse in a heap on the bed, clutching at my throat. My heart is beating so quickly and I can't breathe, my thoughts numb with disbelief. It's Sasha. She's dead. Murdered. Oh, my God. Tears come easily and I try and fail to blink them away because no matter what that poor girl did; she did not deserve this. No one does.

Now everything makes perfect sense: the promotion and Adie's good mood. Sasha had not gone back to Prince Tech to request the sexual misconduct case be reopened because she is dead. Adie killed her. Left with no other option, because he could not get his hands on the blackmail money she was demanding, he had silenced her for good. The only one who stood to benefit from her passing was him. My jaw clenches with terror. This is more than just a warning. It could be me next. What do I do?

I hastily reach for the remote control and turn off the TV when I hear a gentle tapping on the door. Running a hand through my tousled hair, I take a deep, quivering breath, and call out, 'Come in,' as I sit up in bed.

'I've come to say goodnight,' Fiona offers me a tired smile as she hovers uncertainly in the doorway.

'Are you leaving now?' I enquire in the most normal voice I can, given the severe shock I have just experienced.

'Yes, it's gone ten o'clock.'

I sigh wearily. 'But you'll be back tomorrow?'

She exclaims with a girlish laugh, 'I'll be here bright and early with my Mary Poppins umbrella and suitcase.'

Only then do I realise her moving in could be a good thing. It may even save my life. With her around, Adie is unlikely to harm me. Unless, of course, she intends to assist in my murder as well as steal my home and children from me. But since she is so young and naïve, I refuse to believe that, so for the time being I give her the benefit of the doubt by saying, 'Don't stand there in the dark, come in so I can see you.'

'Should I put on the main light?' she asks, as she reluctantly moves a little closer into the dimly lit room.

I bark, 'No,' louder than I intended, not wanting her to witness the emotional state I am in, but it's too late because she's approaching the bed, her dark eyes crinkling in concern as she says, 'You've been crying.'

'Sasha was a warning. It's going to be me next,' I ramble incoherently, fear making me sound like the crazy creature Adie portrays me to be.

At that, she recoils and pastes an unconvincing smile on her face before asking, 'What do you mean? What are you talking about?'

I wring my hands and respond with, 'He's trying to kill me and make everyone think I'm mad.'

'Who?' she gasps, eyes bulging in their sockets.

I throw back my head and laugh before turning to glare at her, 'Adie, of course.' I then shush her, whispering, 'But it's to be our secret.'

She mulls this over before rejecting the idea. 'He wouldn't do that,' she asserts confidently, averting her gaze.

Her words stab at my heart, but I do not blame her. As I watch her sharp face darken, I can tell she thinks I am lying. What must I do to be taken seriously? But I am not doing myself any favours. On some level, I recognise that I am acting strangely — even for me — and begin to suspect that I may be under the influence of drugs. Has Adie found a way of getting those mind-altering antipsychotic pills into me without my knowledge?

Aiming for a more rational tone, I try to impress on her, 'I know what I'm talking about. I may not be myself, but I am not mentally unstable.'

'No one said you were,' Fiona protests unconvincingly as she looks over her shoulder for a way out. I reach out and grab hold of her arm, since I'm not ready to let her go just yet. She tries to back away from me in alarm, but I tighten my hold until I can feel her flesh beneath my fingers.

'I don't know what he's told you, Fiona, or what he's promised you, but if I were you, I would get out now before it's too late,' I hiss.

She viciously snatches her arm away, then rubs it angrily as though it were already bruised. As she gives me a mean-girl stare I ask myself if I was wrong about her. Is she part of the plot to get rid of me? If so, how could I have been so blind? I think I have my answer when she shrugs off her nanny's disguise, curls her lip and torments me by jeering cruelly:

'Adie warned me that you were a mad woman, Rachel, which is why I am here, as your replacement. Should I get him so you can tell him all the crazy things you said?'

CHAPTER 36: LUCY

Now

My father-in-law cowers under my attack and tries to shield his head with his hands, as he cries, 'You're mad, you are, when I didn't do nothing.'

I smack him around the head again and again, shouting, 'I'm not mad! And we both know what you did. You are a horrible, disgusting little man!'

'For God's sake, stop hitting me, Luce,' he begs, his face collapsing with misery.

I snap, 'It's *Lucy*,' and lash out at him once more, even more forcefully this time. 'Your son's wife, in case you've forgotten.'

While I am young, strong and have justice on my side, he is small, mean-minded, and drunk. Never have I been so angry. How dare that dirty little pervert put his hands on me? What made him imagine I would welcome his sexual advances? This family is the worst. Why did I ever involve myself with the Dawsons? I don't exclude Matt from my thinking in this instance. *Like father, like son*, isn't that how the saying goes?

John backs away and sneers from a safe distance, 'I don't forget whose wife you are, but it's a shame that husband of yours has.'

I know my eyes are on fire as I demand, 'What do you mean by that?'

'He's obviously been getting it from somewhere else, hasn't he? And with a fat cow like you for a wife, who can blame him?'

'Get out of my house you lying piece of shit!' I growl, gritting my teeth.

'You can't throw me out of this house when I own half of it,' he scoffs triumphantly, jutting out his chin in a show of defiance.

'We'll see about that,' I threaten as I advance on him again. He's fast on his feet, though, and makes it to the concrete steps before I can grab hold of him. Cowardly, he bolts off as fast as a greyhound and, before I know it, he's up the steps and out the front door, leaving it ajar. Slamming and locking it after him, I lean against it for a moment and heave a shuddering sigh. I'm shaking from head to toe and tears roll down my cheeks.

I hate that I am crying over a lecherous scumbag like my father-in-law, but I am even more disgusted with myself for letting his hurtful remarks about my weight get to me. Flustered, I am unsure what to do next. Do I tell Matt? *Of course you do*, my inner voice insists. *He's your husband and he has a right to know.* But what if he doesn't believe me? And what if John denies laying a hand on me and they gang up on me? *Then divorce the fucker.* If it's 11 p.m. here, though, it's 2 a.m. in Istanbul and too late for me to call Matt now. It may be cowardly of me, but I'd rather wait and do it in person. That doesn't mean I'm not desperate to confide in somebody.

Not Beth. She already despises Matt and the whole Dawson family, so won't be objective. Kerry is next on my list. Before I can change my mind, I return downstairs to the kitchen, get my phone and punch in her number.

'Kerry, I'm sorry to call so late,' I blub as soon as she answers. She doesn't waste any time in asking, 'Are you crying?'

'Yes,' I sob, 'I just found out . . .'

'What did you find out?' she gasps, sounding alarmed.

'It's so upsetting. I mean, how could he do something like that?' I bawl, overwhelmed with anxiety and emotion, and sounding hysterical.

Kerry remains ominously silent as if waiting for me to go on, so I force myself to continue, but I still find it difficult to speak. 'He made a pass,' I stammer, unable to continue due to the restrictive lump in my throat.

'How did you find out? Did Matt tell you?' she demands irritably, before going on the attack with, 'and I suppose that's why you're ringing me at this hour to give me a bollocking even though I'm not the one to blame. It's not like I led him on or anything. And I told him I wasn't interested. Gave him a piece of my mind too.'

My tears instantly stop, and I sit up straight in my chair, as I realise that whatever Kerry is trying to tell me requires a clear, sharp mind.

'What the hell are you talking about? Are you saying that Matt, *my* Matt, made a pass at you?' I exclaim, stunned.

Realising that we have been talking at cross purposes and that she has unintentionally given herself away, Kerry abruptly hangs up. When I redial her number, it goes to voicemail.

I shake my head and stare at my phone as if it holds all the answers, but I can put all of the jigsaw pieces together on my own as I now realise what has been bothering Kerry. No wonder she's been distant. I would kill that useless husband of mine if he weren't in another country right now. It's obvious that all his promises to never repeat the same mistake as before meant nothing. When it comes to Matt, I have been a complete fool. What was he thinking by trying his luck with Kerry, who has been a loyal friend and employee of mine for more than a decade? I can only conclude that he must have tried it on with her when he was at the shop going over the accounts and that's why she has been so evasive about it.

It's not long before I start to question with a heavy heart why I am not enough for Matt, as he is for me. Does this signify the end of my marriage? Is that what I want, or will I forgive him again, despite promising myself that I wouldn't? Am I really that weak? And why does Matt, who used to be my best friend, want to hurt me, *us*, our precious little family, so much? Is he a sex addict who can't help himself and needs professional help or is he just a selfish, lying cheating piece of scum? Like my father-in-law. Like Adie, who is just as evil, if not worse, according to Rachel, and who, until I met the nanny-from-hell for myself, almost charmed me into believing him over her. These men make me so angry. Why bother getting married at all if they don't intend to remain faithful? And even more infuriating, why do women continue to love them when they don't deserve it?

Deciding that this is the worst night of my life, I rest my head on the kitchen table, and sigh for England. After all, it's not every day you find out you're not pregnant but long to be so, that your father-in-law tried to get you into bed and your husband also made a pass at one of your closest friends. When my phone starts ringing and I see that Sheila, my mother-in-law is calling me, I realise I was wrong before. The night isn't over yet.

CHAPTER 37: RACHEL

Then

'Good morning, Rachel. I hope you slept well,' Fiona appears from nowhere to greet me, just as I'm about to slip out of the boot room door and leave by the courtyard entrance. My body ripples with anger as I stare incredulously at her too-good-to-be-true face. There is no trace of last night's callous creature, but that doesn't mean I have forgotten the savage words she said to me. Nor am I likely to. Since all of this is clearly a ruse to trick me, I go along with it for now. But she had better watch out.

'Marvellously well, thank you,' I lie because I hadn't slept a wink all night. Whatever drug Adie had sneakily slipped into my food or drink yesterday, I felt wired and couldn't stop moving. My pacing around the room continued even after he came to bed. I recall standing over his sleeping body at one point, listening to the soft rise and fall of his breathing, imagining what it would be like to place a pillow over his mouth and keep it there until he stopped breathing. *Stopped living.* The image of his glassy-eyed stare and slack jaw is now permanently etched in my brain.

'Who let you in?' I enquire in a brisk, businesslike tone, to show her that I am in charge, even if it doesn't feel like it.

'Clara,' she says, her smile as sweet as apple pie.

I frown, puzzled, 'Who?'

'The cleaner,' she responds, with a bewildered expression.

'Oh, yes, of course,' I reply, dismissive.

'I hope you don't mind,' she explains apologetically. 'But in my eagerness to get started, I arrived earlier than expected and Clara saw me waiting outside and invited me in for a cup of tea.'

Thinking this sounds plausible, I try not to appear bothered as I observe jealously, 'No doubt you're the best of friends already.' Given that neither of them is a fan of mine, it's easy to imagine that they will get along.

Fiona laughs nervously and claps her hands together in a cute, childlike manner. I notice she does this a lot, but I'm not charmed by it.

'Are you going out?' she says with a forced smile, but I detect a worried tone in her voice.

I give her the briefest of nods and pull my cap down over my eyes, 'For my morning run, yes.'

She grimaces, as though eager to put me off, 'What time will you be back?'

I look at my smartwatch and remark drily, 'I'll be around an hour. That should give you time to settle in and make yourself at home.'

'Oh, yes, thank you very much,' simpers Fiona.

I turn away from her then, assuming that our conversation is over, but when I hear her add in a voice laced with menace, 'Actually I feel very much at home already,' my stomach lurches. Or am I being overly suspicious and paranoid? Always thinking everyone's out to get me. However, in hers and my husband's case, I remind myself that this is true.

As I hurry up the courtyard steps and open the arched metal gate into Rutland Terrace, her spiteful words from last night continue to stab me in the back. They even accompany me on my flat-out run across Stamford Meadows. 'Adie warned me that you were a mad woman, Rachel, which is why I am here, as your replacement.'

Pressing my lips into a firm line, I'm more determined than ever not to let her take my home, my children and my inheritance from me. She is welcome to have Adie without any of those things, of course, but I don't think he would be as appealing to her without the Beiersdorf fortune.

I'm about to head down to the River Welland to complete my typical morning circuit of five miles, meticulously worked out at a pace of twelve minutes per mile, when I hear a familiar voice shout, 'Well, if it isn't pink shoes,' which puts me off my stride and nearly makes me trip and fall.

I turn around, startled, and am both relieved and delighted to see that it's him . . . Soon-to-be-divorced guy. As he jogs purposefully towards me, in a bid to catch up, I assume that he must have followed me.

'It's you,' I exclaim breathlessly, lifting my cap's sun visor to get a better look at him as he skids to a halt in front of me. His fair hair is blonder than I remembered in the sunlight. But his sparkling eyes remain the same.

'Of course it's me,' he chuckles. 'Who else would it be?'

'How did you know where to find me?'

'You're a creature of habit, remember? I could set my watch by you.'

'Shall we talk as we run?' I suggest, encouraging him with a wide and welcoming grin. The kind a bride usually reserves for her wedding day.

'Why not? It's not as if I'm not dressed for it,' he gestures to his jogging attire of shorts, T-shirt and trainers.

'Shame about the white socks, but nice knees,' I compliment him with a playful nudge in the ribs. The desire to touch him is overwhelming.

'If only I could see yours,' he grumbles, pulling a hard-done-by face.

'My fair skin burns easily, so I always wear leggings,' I inform him, as we jog side by side, ignoring everyone else we pass.

As he wonders, 'Tell me, Rachel, do you ever do anything spur of the moment?' he darts me a teasing smile.

'Like what?' I raise my eyebrows, unsure if he is laughing at me or not.

'Like choose a different sports brand, run in a new direction just for the hell of it or ever be late for anything?'

'You think I'm ridiculous?' I pout, not liking the version of me he sees.

'Not at all,' he assures me.

My eyes sting when I look up at him and confide brokenly, 'Without routine I suffer with extreme anxiety. The doctor says it's a control thing because everything else in my life is unpredictable.'

'I like that in this uncertain world you at least *are* predictable. Knowing where you are at any given time, and that you are safe, makes me feel close to you even when I can't be with you,' he admits in a strained voice, nodding to demonstrate his understanding of my situation.

His intensity, at this early stage of our relationship, would be too much for anybody else but I have my own calculated reason for excusing it. My mouth curls into a smile again as I insist on knowing, 'And do you?'

'Do I what?'

'Want to be with me?'

In a dramatic, thespian accent, he drawls, 'For eternity and beyond,' which makes me feel alive — almost reckless. And so, I find myself teasing him in a flirtatious manner, 'Fair skin doesn't burn in hotel rooms.'

'Are you suggesting what I think?' he exclaims, widening his eyes gleefully and pretending to be shocked.

I bat my eyes at him. 'How is that for spur of the moment?'

CHAPTER 38: LUCY

Now

I shake my head in disgust and mutter aloud, 'My mother-in-law can do one,' for what feels like the hundredth time today. This time, though, I'm overheard by a middle-aged female shopper who shoots me a snobbish, disdainful glance. 'Oh, sod it,' I explode, stomping off, because Sainsbury's in Stamford is apparently not the place to let off steam or rant.

Sophie giggles from her perch in the shopping trolley, 'Sod it,' which makes me feel guilty. I dart a quick look over my shoulder to make sure the prudish shopper hasn't heard my daughter. The next minute, I tell myself that, given the mood I'm in, I couldn't give a damn. I've been spoiling for a fight ever since I got into a row with Sheila on the phone last night, which ended abruptly when the battleaxe hung up on me.

How dare she accuse me of lying and trying to divide the family by claiming I wouldn't be content until we were all ruined? This came after she tried, and failed, to convince me that John was just being friendly and that I had misinterpreted his intentions. *Misinterpreted, my eye*, the creep had put both hands on my breasts! Because she was constantly covering up for her husband and son's mistakes and acting as though they were perfect and incapable of doing anything wrong, I in turn blamed her for the way they'd turned out. Furthermore, could she even call herself a grandmother when she consistently ignored her own grandchildren? As you might imagine, that did not go down well, even if it was the truth, and did not end well either. She had it coming, though, particularly after that remark she made about Matt ruining himself financially due to my selfish demands for an extravagant lifestyle that he could not afford. Ugh. Infuriating woman!

As for John's cruel taunt that Matt was getting 'it' elsewhere, I have to acknowledge that there may be some truth to that. Is he having another affair? Could it be with Katya, his new work colleague, or is he seeing the same woman from his old place of work? If so, I haven't decided what I intend to do about it yet. Although now I know Matt tried it on with Kerry, I can't keep giving him the benefit of the doubt. I sternly remind myself that I am not his mother, and I for one will not tolerate his behaviour.

When I realise that Sophie is trying to get my attention, I shake my head to get rid of all the anxiety inside it. No such luck.

'Mummy,' Sophie begs, pointing to something in the distance, probably the sweet section of the supermarket, which I deliberately ignore.

'What is it, sweetheart?' I fuss, watching her frown deepen as I tuck a stray lock of her blonde hair back behind her ear. My beautiful daughter who I love with all my heart. And who means more to me than any man.

From somewhere behind me, a male voice calls out, 'Sadie, Sadie.' As I picture his child slipping out of his grasp and escaping down the chocolate aisle with him in hot pursuit, I smile to myself. We've all been there.

'I thought it was you. I called out your name, but you didn't answer,' the same male voice says in my ear, making me jump.

I spin around and find Adie standing in front of me, looking ridiculously pleased to see me. I realise, stupidly, that I hadn't responded to my fictitious identity of Sadie — in fact, I'd completely forgotten that I had posed as someone else — and hadn't considered the possibility that I might run into him while shopping, even though Stamford is a small town.

'Sorry, I was miles away,' I stammer out an apology. But he has already turned away from me and is grinning down at Sophie.

'Hello, trouble,' he booms, tickling her under the chin to make her giggle. I can't express how relieved I am not to have Jack with me because if he had heard someone calling me Sadie, he would have dobbed me in on the spot, whereas Sophie doesn't seem to care. I'm simply 'Mum' to her.

While Adie is preoccupied, I notice a woman patiently waiting for him. She is older than Adie and they share similar features, so I assume this must be his mother. When Adie looks up and sees me staring at her he signals the woman to approach.

'Sadie, this is my mother, Jonty.'

'Pleased to meet you, Jonty,' I remark, tongue-tied, because I feel like I'm being presented to a queen. Her clothes are extraordinarily colourful and her enormous, dangling parrot earrings sway with every movement of her neck. No matter where she goes, she must attract admiration.

'So, you're Sadie. I've heard so much about you from Adie,' she gushes, energetically pumping my hand. I get the feeling she'd rather smother me in kisses and hugs, but I'm relieved she doesn't.

'I doubt that very much,' I laugh shyly, out of embarrassment. Even Adie seems a little uncomfortable at that point, but Jonty notices and smiles indulgently at her son, suggesting, 'I'll leave you two to chat for a bit while I go and rummage through the reduced section.'

'I had you down as a Waitrose man, so I wasn't expecting to bump into you at Sainsbury's,' I prattle, for something to say.

'I'll have you know I've even been known to shop at Aldi,' he chuckles.

'I don't believe that. Not for one minute. Your mother seems lovely by the way,' I observe, because while she is exactly as Rachel described, what does feel off is that she and Adie seem to get along, which is not how Rachel described their relationship.

As though he can read my mind, Adie replies stoically, 'She's been my rock. After what happened, I don't know what I'd have done without her.'

'You mean with what happened to Rachel?'

He gives a sorrowful nod as if the very mention of his dead wife's name had crushed him, then goes on to say, 'In any case, I'm glad I ran into you because I wanted to explain about Fiona.'

'Oh, please don't. You don't owe me any explanation,' I say quickly.

'No, I insist.' Then, he takes me to one side and whispers, 'The thing is, Fiona is working out her notice, but she doesn't want to leave.'

'You mean you've sacked her?' I reel, shocked.

He pulls a tormented face, 'It's not something I'm proud of, but after Rachel died, Fiona got the wrong impression about us, and, well . . . she was clearly mistaken and that complicated things, so I had no choice but to let her go, even though the children are fond of her and will miss her.'

I remark sympathetically, 'That does sound complicated,' while privately believing that no one deserves to be handed their marching orders more than the nasty, hot nanny who made poor Rachel's life such a misery.

When Adie goes on to confess, 'I want you to know that I didn't do anything to encourage Fiona,' I'm really confused as I don't know who to believe at this point. Because one of them is clearly lying, I ask myself, 'Is Adie telling the truth or is Rachel?'

CHAPTER 39: RACHEL

Then

I didn't find the sex particularly satisfying. Despite his many flaws, Adie has always been a considerate and skilled lover, never leaving me unfulfilled, unlike Soon-to-be-divorced guy, who, after finishing quickly, fell onto his back in a sweaty heap looking absurdly smug. If I were to cut him some slack, though, I would have to acknowledge that it was our first time, and he did seem anxious. With time, I am sure things will get better. What concerns me more is that he seemed blissfully oblivious of my frustration. It shows an aspect of selfishness that I hadn't expected from him. For now, I grudgingly put this down to inexperience. Before marrying Adie, I had many lovers, whereas — I suppose I should call him by his real name of *Tony* now that we have been intimate — has only ever slept with two women. His wife and a girlfriend before that.

With only a sheet wrapped around me, I'm lying here naked, in the William Cecil Hotel's blue room, with one leg hanging out of the covers touching the floor: ready to run at a moment's notice. As I tug a hand through my tangled bed-head hair, he puffs up his chest and lets out a deep sigh beside me. His pale skin, covered in a sparse layer of golden hair, intrigues me. It contrasts so sharply with Adie's silky coffee-coloured flesh.

'That was amazing,' he drawls, squeezing my hand as an afterthought.

I throw him a charming smile and comment innocently, 'Wasn't it just?'

He brushes off his embarrassment with a boyish chuckle, saying, 'Next time I promise to last longer.'

Curling up to him, I purr seductively in his ear, 'We've got all afternoon,' because I feel hopeful now that he has recognised his shortcomings.

'Don't you have to be back for the kids?' he asks, blinking open his eyes to stare at me.

I shake my head. 'Isn't that what nannies are for? To look after the children when you're not there.'

He shakes his head before protesting, 'I can't stay, I'm afraid. I've got work calls to make and I've promised to pick my kid up from school.'

'Oh, no, I was really hoping we might, you know . . .' I protest weakly, leaving the words 'fuck again' implied but unsaid.

He sits up in bed and reaches for his phone on the bedside table. 'I'm sorry,' he mumbles, avoiding my gaze. 'But it's almost two already.'

For his benefit, I fake a smile and mutter nonchalantly, 'That's okay. Another time then,' because it is expected of me, but inside I'm furious. I have risked everything to be with him. Adie's wrath. Fiona's critical assessment of my parenting skills — or lack thereof — since I have abandoned my children to be with a man I barely know, who hasn't done any of the things he has promised to do so far, like help me escape my husband.

I draw the sheet tightly around me as he gets out of bed and goes into the adjoining bathroom. I see that he has stretchmarks on both bum cheeks and that his buttocks dimple when he moves. Since he doesn't close the door behind him, I also hear the repulsive splash of his urine in the toilet. On arrival at the hotel, we'd found it remarkably quiet, and they had rooms available, so we were permitted to check in early. Located in the historic grounds of Burleigh House, this Elizabethan gem is a landmark in Stamford. Every room, including ours, has a classical charming design. I doubt that many couples splash out on rooms here though just to have afternoon sex.

'Can't your wife collect your son?' I grumble as he shuffles back in.

He shakes his head emphatically and begins tugging on his clothes, 'Not today. Olivia's out with her friends having a boozy birthday lunch. Besides, I promised Daniel.'

I scowl and raise my eyes to the ceiling, 'Seems a waste of all this.'

As he sits down on the bed to put on his awful white towelling socks, his lips start to twitch in annoyance. 'Why don't you stay and take a long, relaxing bath to make the most of it?'

I give him a feral look. 'On my own?'

He responds, 'Why not?' as his patience frays even more. 'You're always saying you feel like a prisoner in your own home.'

'That's true,' I groan, burying my nose deeper in the bed that still has his scent on it. 'Adie is always watching me.'

'Will you be in a lot of trouble when you get back?' he asks, concerned.

Tears cloud my vision as I admit forlornly, 'I was mad to come here. I don't know what I was thinking. I just wanted to shock you by proving I could be spontaneous and now you're the one with a timetable.'

Seeing how miserable I am, he exclaims, 'You don't regret it, do you? Because I don't. I loved every minute and can't wait to do it again.'

Ego soothed, I'm about to reply when the hotel phone rings. Both mine and his eyebrows soar at that point, and we hold our breaths for a second, although I couldn't tell you why, except of course, neither of us is supposed to be here. 'It's reception,' I hiss, motioning for him to stop talking.

'Hello,' I go for calm and casual as I pick up the phone but really, I'm a bundle of nerves. Why are they ringing our room? Have we been discovered? On our walk upstairs, did someone notice us and inform the hotel staff that we are having an extra-marital affair? Would they even care?

I'm greeted by a pleasant, businesslike voice that says, 'Good afternoon, Mrs Brown. I'm sorry for disturbing you. This is the hotel manager speaking.'

'Yes?' I swallow nervously.

To protect me, Soon-to-be-divorced guy (AKA Tony, although I can't get accustomed to calling him that) had given the hotel staff a false name when we arrived and acted as though we were a married couple.

'A gentleman in reception is asking for you,' the manager informs me.

'A gentleman?' I repeat, my mouth hanging open.

Following my appalled gaze, Tony growls, 'Who?'

'Who is it?' I enquire dutifully, attempting to hide my alarm. They must be mistaken. No one knows I am here.

The manager pauses uneasily before continuing in a subtly quieter tone, 'He says he's your husband.'

CHAPTER 40: LUCY

Now

On the pretext of helping me with my shopping, Adie has accompanied me to the car park, but my cart only holds three bags of shopping and nothing heavy. Every time I see the back of someone's head that I think I might recognise or a car that looks familiar, I cringe, fearing it might be one of my friends. In addition to the fact that he calls me Sadie every five minutes, which would immediately give me away, I have no excuses prepared should I run into anyone I know. Beth would wet herself if she caught me using a false identity but would also congratulate me for being with a man other than my husband. She's always implying that Matt isn't good enough for me, and for once I think she's right. I hope this doesn't mean he's tried it on with her too. I mean, who hasn't my husband made a pass at?

'Don't you need to get back to your mum?' I suggest slyly, to prevent Adie from following me to my car.

'She'll be fine,' he huffs, whirling around to wave at Jonty who is pushing her trolley in another direction, towards Adie's top-of-the-range Volvo.

'Be with you in a minute, Mum,' he shouts. 'Now, where's your car? Oh, I see it over there.'

He points to my battered little car, which is so badly parked it takes up two whole parking bays, straddled as it is across the white lines.

'You mean you can hear it?' I wince as Casper spots us from the back seat and begins barking.

'You have a dog?' Adie exclaims excitedly.

'I wouldn't call him that exactly,' I giggle, embarrassed by the noise Casper is making. As we get closer to the car, he becomes even more excitable and starts howling and jumping up at the windows. Everyone turns to stare at us as though I were the worst dog parent in the world.

'He's lovely,' Adie enthuses, sounding sincere.

'Do you like dogs then?' I ask doubtfully because I recall reading in Rachel's diary that Adie wouldn't allow her to keep a dog because he had an allergy. Reading between the lines, I also got the impression that he was not a fan of pets in general.

'I love dogs,' he replies confidently, contradicting his former wife once again and leaving me with another mystery to solve.

He helps me pack the shopping bags in the boot, which feels like an incredibly intimate thing to do. When something spills onto the ground, we bump heads in our efforts to reach it first and when we see that it's a packet of sanitary towels, our eyes lock in embarrassed silence. My cheeks might be on fire but he's the first to look away, giving me an opportunity to discreetly slip the zero-leaks winged pads back amongst the shopping.

As I close the boot, he murmurs, 'So?'

'So?' Now that I can see the funny side, I find myself grinning.

There are moments, like now, when I want to forget about Rachel and who Adie really is and be Sadie for real. Because let's face it, her life is so much nicer than mine, which consists of a disgruntled, unfaithful husband, in-laws who hate me and a falling down house that is beyond our means.

He frowns and continues to hover awkwardly as I buckle Sophie into her car seat while fending off Casper's desperate attempts to escape from the back seat. 'I suppose I'd better let you get on,' he sighs regretfully.

'Yes,' I reply, hoping he can take a hint. 'But it was nice to see you again.' He follows me as I deliberately move around to the driver's door.

'Do you mean that?' he asks intently.

'Of course,' I stammer, unsure whether I do, but somehow knowing that my response should be a definite 'no'. Could I be succumbing to the charms of a murderer? Or is it just Sadie who has a crush on him?

Changing his tone, he states without any preamble at all, 'I'm taking the family to Burleigh House this afternoon for a picnic.'

I can't resist teasing him by asking, 'Is that with or without the nanny?'

'Without,' he chuckles and rolls his eyes. I must admit that I admire him for being able to find humour in the most trying of circumstances, it speaks volumes about his strength of character.

With a crinkly-eyed smile, he adds, 'And I'd love it if you joined us.'

'Oh, I couldn't possibly, I don't want to intrude on your family time.'

'Nonsense,' he tuts. 'You'd be a welcome addition. Bring your little boy too, he'll be company for Archie.'

I notice then, that although I haven't given him my answer yet, he has assumed that I am going to say yes. Does that smack of arrogance? I gaze at him for a moment, wondering what his intentions are towards me. Can a man like him — rich, handsome, successful and charming really be interested in someone like me? Romantically, I mean. Being common as muck, I'm more suited to being his cleaner than his girlfriend.

'If you're worried about being alone with a man you barely know, I can assure you that my mother will be there to chaperone,' he jokes.

But the joke backfires. Because now I'm asking myself does the thought of being alone with him scare me, as it ought to, or excite me?

Since Matt isn't expected back until tonight — and God help him when he walks through the door because I have so much to attack him with — I realise that Sophie and I could join Adie and his family on the picnic without being missed. That way, I would be able to see first-hand how he interacts with his mother and kids and learn from Jonty how she feels about Rachel's tragic accident. She might also be able to shed additional insight on the relationship between her son and daughter-in-law and the role the nanny played in all of that. Given my unwavering determination to uncover the truth, I would be a fool to pass up such an opportunity.

Fortunately, Jack has a friend's party to go to after school which eliminates one important issue; otherwise, he would expose me as the imposter I am, although I'll need to make sure I'm back in time to pick him up afterwards. As I attempt to convince myself that having a picnic with a male friend is completely harmless and that Matt or anybody else could not possibly object — just let them try — I decide what to do.

'In that case, we'd love to come,' I tell him, feeling myself blush again.

CHAPTER 41: RACHEL

Then

'You have to go, Tony,' I prompt, squeezing his hand, but he pushes me away and runs an impatient hand through his hair.

'I'm not abandoning you,' he says firmly.

My eyes are glistening with tears as I whimper, 'You have to.'

As I gaze at the dishevelled sheets on the bed with their incriminatory wet patch, I let out a small sob while stumbling on my words, 'If Adie comes up here and finds me, *us*, like this, there's no telling what he'll do.'

As I anticipated, that immediately awakens his masculine ego. 'And there's no telling what I'll do to *him*,' he growls, clenching his fists.

'How will getting into a fight with my husband help me or my children?' I ask irritably and with good cause.

His chin falls to his chest in defeat. 'If he so much as lays one finger on you . . .'

The fact that he has already given up proves to me that when men fail to rescue the women they love, it kills them, but it only makes us women stronger since they depend on us far more than we do them.

'We both know it will be much worse than that,' I answer truthfully, gazing at him for a moment. Instead of demanding, 'What are you going to do about it?' I hold back, knowing it won't help.

He collapses on the bed, groaning, 'God, Rachel. Do you want me to stay or go? Make up your mind, please.'

Leaning against him, I tilt my head to one side, and murmur in his ear, 'It means the world to me that you would stay and protect me, but I can't risk Adie finding out about us. That would give him even more ammunition to prove I'm an unfit mother so he can file for sole custody of my children.'

He studies me intently for a moment before haltingly suggesting, 'We could always run away together. Disappear.'

My face creases into a grateful grin as I see hope alight on his face. However, I have no choice but to crush it, like an insect in my hand, by shaking my head and insisting, 'Not without my children.' Then I frown and add in a venomous voice, 'Besides, Adie should be the one to disappear.'

'I'm beginning to think you're right about that,' he grimaces, pulling me in for a tight embrace. 'Letting you go to him kills me.'

'But that's what I must do if I'm to keep my children,' I explain, as I skilfully peel myself out of his grasp and slip on my jogging bottoms and T-shirt. He continues to gnaw away at his bottom lip as he watches me get dressed, and as I pull on my trainers, I risk one more look at him and see how his expression has transformed from one of defeat to one of resolve.

'I know it upsets you to see me distressed, like this,' I point out, with a smile meant just for him, 'But I must go down now before he comes up here. I'm sure the hotel manager won't tell him which room we're in, but knowing Adie, he'll find us somehow.'

Voice sharpened with anger, he explodes, 'I'll do it,' while jerking to his feet and gazing at me with emboldened eyes. He appears menacing, as though he were enveloped in a halo of red mist. I seem to have awakened the beast in him, like I do with Adie and all the other men I've ever met.

As my mind works faster, trying to decide what's going on in his head, I give him a shrewd look and pretend I don't know what he's talking about. Does he mean it though? I need to be certain that he is prepared to go through with it as much as I am. It's the only way I'll ever be free.

'Do what?' I probe innocently.

'Whatever it takes, for him to disappear,' he murmurs less confidently, coughing into his palm.

As I fake surprise, my eyebrows rocket up my forehead. Soon, I'm stammering through my tears, 'I knew you'd save me. I knew it from the moment I saw you.'

My body ripples with relief as I enter his waiting arms and allow myself to be held. We're both visibly shaking; him more so than me. But I remind myself cynically that it's not a competition. Tearing my gaze from his, I glare ferociously at the door and frantically cry, 'I must go,' urging him to, 'Slip out the back way when the coast is clear.' After that, I bolt from the room and as I stumble down the stairs two at a time, he calls out desperately, 'Text me as soon as you can, so I know you're okay.'

Okay? I doubt I will ever be okay again. It would be an understatement to say that I am terrified. As feared, Adie is waiting for me in reception. Fortunately, no one else is around. Apoplectic with rage, he hisses, 'Do you have any idea how worried we've been?' and wags a finger at me.

I reply savagely, 'By we, I assume you mean you and Fiona,' as I am suddenly just as angry as he is.

'You said you were going for a run, but you've been missing for hours. You want to think yourself lucky that I haven't called the police. Consider the impact that would have had on the children,' he warns.

My mind numb with disbelief, I screech, '*Missing?* How can a grown woman like me be considered missing?'

'You lied to our children's nanny about your whereabouts. As your husband, I have every right to be concerned.'

'Concerned husband!' I scoff mockingly, wanting to lash out at him. 'Why are you here really, Adie? And how did you know where to find me?'

'This is not the time for explanations,' he says condescendingly, with an arrogant lift of his head. Then, muttering under his breath, 'We must get you home first,' he takes a menacing stride in my direction.

'I beg to differ,' I retaliate, stepping back from him in horror. 'I am not going anywhere with you until I find out how you knew where I was.'

'Very well then, if you insist,' he scowls, casting a nervous glance around him as though afraid of being overheard. 'Since I was appointed as lasting power of attorney on your behalf, I have taken the precaution of installing a tracker on your car for your own personal safety and wellbeing.'

Jaw clenched in rage, I snap, 'Oh, of course, everything is for my benefit, isn't it? In other words, you've been spying on me. *How dare you.*'

In an unyielding voice, he continues, 'Rachel, unless you want me to call the doctor again and tell him you're having another of your breaks from reality, you are to come with me right now.'

'You wouldn't dare when we both know that's not true,' I whimper nervously, as I feel myself tremble all over.

He gives a devilish smirk. 'We both know I would.'

CHAPTER 42: LUCY

Now

As if my life weren't already full of unexpected twists, I find myself at Burleigh Park's Garden of Surprises, which offers sensory delights at every turn, such as sculptures, serene water features and a mirrored maze. It creates the ideal canvas for a summer picnic when combined with the undulating landscape, great lake, wildflowers, meandering pathways and old trees that roll down to the distant spires of Stamford. Whenever the kids and I come here for a picnic, we usually wind up in the deer park because admission is free, but Adie insisted on splashing out on a family ticket so we could access the private, walled gardens. I've never been inside before, and I'm in awe of the beauty of Capability Brown's lost gardens.

Adie also insisted on providing all the food and my mouth fell open when I saw the decadent wicker food hamper overflowing with champagne, artisan cheeses, a charcuterie, fresh fruit, chocolate truffles and gourmet sandwiches. Jonty carried the fringed rugs for us to sit on, and I just held Sophie's hand on the stroll here, feeling self-conscious in my long, flowy summer dress that I wore especially. After meeting my full-on, people-loving daughter, Adie's two kids, Beatrice and Archie, soon overcome their shyness and the three of them are now friends, despite the age difference.

As we walk side by side, searching for the ideal picnic location, Adie's arm accidentally brushes against mine and my skin reacts by tingling. To prevent him from seeing my red cheeks, I splutter, 'I knew you weren't an Aldi man. That feast looks like it comes from Fortnum and Mason.'

He laughs good-naturedly. 'You wouldn't be far out.'

'An egg sarnie and a packet of crisps would have done me, but I must admit my mouth is watering at the thought of all that delicious food.'

'A woman who appreciates good food is a woman after my heart,' he announces in a conspiratorial whisper.

As I stifle a giggle, Jonty playfully admonishes him, 'Behave yourself.' Then turning to me, she tuts in mock disapproval, 'My son is quite the lady's man where you're concerned. You'd better watch out, Sadie.'

Remembering what Rachel wrote in her diary about her husband's womanising makes my cheeks flush again. Even though Jonty is obviously joking, I take what she says as a warning to be on my guard against her son. As if he were somehow proud of himself, Adie's eyes lock with mine and his mouth curves into a triumphant grin. I turn away and observe casually, 'How about we sit down over there by the enchanted oak?'

'Great idea,' Adie says, and strides purposefully in the direction of the towering tree, leaving us to follow.

The next hour is spent picking at the delicious food, making small talk and creating wildflower necklaces for the children while taking in the expansive parkland views. I'm relieved that Adie thought to bring along some child-friendly snacks like cheese straws, cucumber sandwiches and sausage rolls, otherwise Sophie would have gone hungry. And when she's hungry, she's never at her best. As it is, she's having a wonderful time and is in her element being the centre of attention. Unlike me, because now that

I'm seated on the ground, with my ample white cleavage on show, I feel like a buxom wench who ought to be spouting cockney. I was aiming for *romantic lead in a period drama*, but I now regret my choice of dress.

When Sophie clambers to her feet, balancing her flower necklace on her golden curls like a princess's tiara, and starts to dance around, grinning and giggling, the other kids join in. Adie then springs energetically to his feet and engages them in a spirited game of tag. As I watch, I wish Jack was here because he would have loved to have been a part of this, but I don't give much thought to my husband. I feel like I fit in with Adie's family. The Dawson family, on the other hand, has never appreciated me.

Jonty looks at me shrewdly and announces, 'You're good for him.'

'In what way?' I ask, frowning.

'You're just what he needs after Rachel.'

In a faltering voice, I hear myself say, 'I hear you got on really well with your daughter-in-law,' before I realise it.

I get another sharp glance from her, but this time she scowls and demands, 'Who told you that?

'Nobody,' I stammer, surprised by her intensity, 'I just assumed . . .'

Before I can say anything more, Adie comes back to join us, and as he sits down beside me, I see them share a meaningful look. Then, before I know it, Jonty has gotten up and joined the kids, and I suspect this was contrived so that Adie and I could spend some time together alone.

'You look very pretty today if you don't mind me saying so,' he points out gallantly, breaking the silence between us.

'I don't mind at all,' I admit, blushing profusely. But then I go and ruin the compliment by declaring, 'But after all that food I feel incredibly fat.'

'You're not fat at all. Don't say that,' he protests angrily, then continues to flatter me, 'you have a very shapely and womanly figure.'

But didn't Rachel write in her journal that Fiona, the nanny, was exactly his type? Tall and slender, with long, dark hair. Nothing like me! I wish I knew who to believe. It's very frustrating not knowing who to trust.

'Would you have dinner with me one evening, so that I can cook for you again? You'd make a lonely widower incredibly happy if you said yes.'

'I can't believe you're playing the lonely widower card,' I exclaim incredulously, laughing aloud.

With a humorous shrug, he protests, 'Why not, if it works?'

'Who says it's working?' I chuckle, relishing his discomfort.

'Hmm,' he pulls a contemplative face before promising, 'I can assure you there is nothing improper about my suggestion.'

I'm not sure why, but when I hear this, I feel slightly disappointed. 'Can I think about it?' I wonder, no longer grinning or laughing, for I'm afraid there won't be any way back if I say yes to him. For the first time in my life, I don't know what I'm doing, and I confess that I enjoy this feeling. I'm in danger of committing myself to something beyond my control, and I'm not sure if I should be excited or scared. I feel like I've been a wife and mother for so long that I've forgotten what it means to be a woman.

'But what about Matt?' I think.

What about him? My inner voice argues churlishly, still angry with him.

'He's still your husband.'

Some husband! Inner voice wins.

I smile mischievously as I turn to face Adie and interrupt his reflective mood by stating, 'I've thought about it and the answer is yes.'

CHAPTER 43: RACHEL

Then

Under the watchful eye of the hotel manager, who came out of hiding to see us off, I had allowed Adie to march me out of the hotel and into the car park, his fingers pinching against the skin on my arm the entire time. Even though my head drooped onto my chest in shame, I wasn't yet defeated, and Adie, being Adie, knew this.

'We'll go back to the house in my car,' he'd ordered, bundling me into the front passenger seat, as if afraid I might do a runner.

'You haven't even asked me what I was doing at a hotel in the middle of the day?' I'd snapped as he climbed in next to me.

He'd given me a dark sideways glance and growled, 'I don't have to.'

Determined to provoke him, I'd pointed out in a scratchy voice, 'So you're not going to ask me who I was with?'

'We both know you were up there alone,' he'd said in a clipped tone, letting out a deep sigh and giving me a weary look.

'That's not true,' I'd stammered incredulously, 'I was with a man. We signed in together as Mr and Mrs Brown.'

'You signed in as yourself, Rachel, the hotel manager showed me the register,' he'd hissed, starting the car.

I protested angrily, 'You know that's not true. You're simply trying to make me think I'm crazy again when I'm not,' but this time he didn't respond, and we drove the rest of the way home in silence.

Once we were back at Rutland Terrace and he'd parked the car on the street, he took hold of my elbow and helped me into the entrance hall of number thirteen as if I were an old woman, calling out, 'Fiona, we're back.'

As I watch Fiona come in, she purses her lips in that prudish way of hers, and prattles, 'Rachel, I'm so glad to see you back safe and well.'

Hackles raised, I scowl, 'Why wouldn't I be? Where are the children?'

'They're in the kitchen having hot chocolate and cookies. I hope you don't mind, but I felt they deserved a treat after the day they've had.'

Her words stab at my heart because I ought to have been here to collect my children from school rather than letting her do it and giving her the opportunity to turn them against me.

'It won't hurt this once, but please ask my permission next time,' I reprimand curtly. As I stare at her, she boldly holds my gaze, and I am enraged by her audacity. Who does she think she is? I've also noticed that she has put on make-up and changed into a figure-hugging black dress since this morning. She is undoubtedly already tired of being forced to dress simply and look less attractive to those of the opposite sex.

'Would you please help my wife upstairs?' Adie speaks directly to Fiona, ignoring me. 'She's feeling very tired.'

'That won't be necessary,' I heatedly declare, adding, 'I'm not an invalid, Adie.'

As though she were doing me a favour, Fiona beams, 'It's no bother.' However, when she rushes forward to assist me, I brush her off none too gently and imply in an ominous warning tone, 'The day I can't walk upstairs by myself is the day you might as well take me out in a coffin.'

My remark momentarily stumps them, and I see the warning look they exchange, which isn't meant for me. Their cautious gaze then shifts as one, to linger on me, until eventually Fiona ventures:

'Of course,' she concedes docilely, reluctantly standing down, but I can tell she's still going to insist on accompanying me up those stairs, whether I like it or not. She would never consider refusing one of Adie's requests.

I rub my eyes sleepily, recognising that Adie is right and I *am* exhausted. I try to forget about this afternoon because I feel guilty whenever I think of not being there for my children when they arrived home from school. Perhaps Adie has a point, and I am an incompetent mother.

I'm about to trudge dejectedly upstairs when Fiona asks my husband, 'Did you tell her about the dinner?'

So, I'm *her* now, am I? I can't help but think as I tear my gaze away from her to stare at Adie, who to be fair, appears suitably wrong-footed. It seems to me that he is annoyed with Fiona for speaking out of turn.

'What dinner?' I ask, stunned.

Adie studies me intently, seemingly to establish my state of mind, before admitting sheepishly, 'Something came up while you were out, and I had to make a decision that affects you without consulting you.'

'Oh?' I observe dangerously quietly. *Now what?*

'Now that I've been promoted to director, the partners thought it would be a good idea for us to throw them a dinner. What with the recent move and everything,' he stammers, gesturing to me as if I were the 'everything' he is alluding to, 'I would have said no, but this is too important to decline.'

'What could be more important than my husband finding his wife in a hotel bedroom with a strange man in the middle of the afternoon?' I'll write in my journal later, but for now, I ask sharply, 'And when is this dinner?'

Before Adie can reply, Fiona interrupts, clapping her hands together in glee, as she often does when she's excited, 'It's on Saturday.' This gesture irritates me so much that I would like to hack off her hands with an axe.

With an indulgent grin at Fiona, Adie offers, 'Fiona has offered to help me host if you're not up to it.'

'I bet she has,' and 'Over my dead body,' is what I silently say to that. They clearly intend to pass Fiona off as the upcoming new woman in Adie's life in order to replace me. However, I sense some reluctance on his part, since his business sense will be telling him that, although Fiona will certainly dazzle them with her looks, she lacks the experience and sophistication to pull off such a significant event. But since they're no closer to getting their hands on my fortune, what do they hope to gain by parading her in front of the partners? That is the burning question.

I firmly tell him, 'No. I can manage.'

Behind me, I hear Fiona's sharp feline intake of breath as Adie nods his assent. She is obviously incensed that he did not push harder to place her in what she believes to be her rightful position alongside him as hostess. When I see her jaw is clenched in outrage, I know I'm right. But she's too smart to complain. Not one sarky word tumbles out of her glossy lips.

Mustering up the most patronising of smiles, I tell her, 'Don't worry, you can still help on the night. You'll make a fine waitress, I'm sure.'

CHAPTER 44: LUCY

Now

'Not this again,' Matt cries defensively, as he uncorks a bottle of red wine, but his eyes darting back and forth give him away because he realises I can see straight through his lies even though he continues to complain, 'Some welcome home this is, I must say. Most husbands wouldn't tolerate being attacked the minute they walk through the door.'

'*Most husbands* wouldn't have tried it on with their wife's employee of ten years,' I hiss, finishing the last of my second can of full-fat Coke, while he takes a huge, stress-relieving drink of his wine. I then head straight to the fridge and grab another can but as soon as I catch Matt giving me a sidelong look of guilt, I start to feel wretched. What became of us? He used to check out my curves. Nowadays he only looks at me to check that I've fallen for his lies, which I haven't. Not yet at any rate.

'She got the wrong end of the stick, that's all,' he mumbles vaguely, as though his explanation is adequate. It isn't. Not by a long shot.

'How so?' I demand, as I open my Coke and take a gulp, while stealthily shoving Rachel's diary out of sight under a stack of magazines on the table.

He sneers unpleasantly, 'You're always saying Kerry can't get a man and is it any wonder when she goes around looking like an old bag lady?'

I fold my arms tightly across my chest and sigh, 'I never said that.'

'As good as,' he insists, shrugging his shoulders and adding, 'so I made the mistake of trying to flatter her. God knows she needed it. I thought she'd be grateful for a compliment or two from someone like me.'

'Now you sound like your dad,' I point out sarcastically. But in the next minute my eyes well up with tears and I bite my lower lip as I ask, 'Should I also be grateful for *his* unwanted attention?'

He winces at that and as he shakes his head uncertainly and squeezes his eyes shut, he briefly reminds me of the young man I fell in love with.

'Mum said he never meant anything by it. And that you—'

'Don't tell me,' I scoff, pushing my face into his. 'I must also have got the wrong end of the stick.'

'No. But you might have overreacted. You've been under a lot of stress lately, Lucy,' he mumbles vaguely, averting his gaze from mine.

'And whose fault is that, Matt?' I yell hysterically, wanting to hurl my drink in his face. The bottle of wine too. Sod it, and Rachel's diary.

He hisses, 'Keep your voice down,' and runs his hands agitatedly over his face in frustration.

Holding my ground, I grind out through clenched teeth, 'Your lecherous old man put his hands on me in this very kitchen. And I want to know what you're going to do about it?'

He pulls out a chair and collapses on it, then buries his head in his hands, crying in anguish, 'Oh God, I don't know. I'm really struggling to believe my dad would do something like that.'

I take a huge risk by stating the obvious, 'The way I see it, Matt, you have two choices. Either you believe him or me.'

My words do the trick because his head jerks up and lines of pain appear on his forehead as he implores, 'I know you wouldn't lie to me, Lucy. In all the years I've known you, you never have. But can you swear on Jack's life that you couldn't have misinterpreted Dad's intentions?'

I notice that he omits to mention his daughter's name alongside his son's in that sentence, but I don't concern myself with that now, though I might ask him later if this was deliberate. He has to hear this, so I move in closer, to whisper, 'Not in a million years. And he also informed me that you were playing away from home.' I refrain from using the word 'again'.

'He said that?' Matt lets out an incredulous gasp.

I look away before I say something even more hurtful about his family. But when I hear his voice breaking as he groans tearfully, 'I'll go and have it out with them tomorrow,' I'm moved enough to put an arm around him, because as usual, I can't bear to see him in such pain. Before I know it, I'm pleading, 'And do you swear that you never intended anything with Kerry, that you were just trying to pay her a compliment?'

I melt when he looks at me with his son's innocent eyes, and as the layers of hurt, rage and betrayal peel away — much to my shame — it seems like I am not only a pushover but a disgrace to the female of the species. Unlike some of my friends, who identify as feminists, I've always been more of a Dolly Parton 'Stand by your man' type.

'Do you even need to ask?' he murmurs as he hugs me tightly.

'No,' I lie, reflecting on how depressing it is that husbands and wives are unable to be honest with one another, even in happy marriages.

I hesitate before asking, 'So, you do believe me then, about your dad?'

He nods, and sighs wearily, before mumbling into my breasts, 'I should have known better than to doubt you, Lucy, when you always tell the truth.'

He's wrong. The truth is I've lied to Matt more in the past few days than I have in my entire life. I'm not proud of it, but I've convinced myself that my suspicions about him cheating justify my dishonesty. But I also believe two wrongs don't equal one right, so when I saw in Rachel's diary earlier this evening that she had slept with shady Soon-to-be-divorced guy, I felt she had let herself down. Since I thought I knew her better than that jerk, I'm also sure she had been coerced into it. Otherwise, regardless of how many times her husband had cheated on her, she wouldn't have done it.

I realise now how hypocritical I was being considering I had already accepted Adie's offer to dine with him next Saturday. After all, a man doesn't invite a woman to dinner at his home unless he intends to make love to her. And when I said yes, I was aware of this. Rachel's lover might not have satisfied her, but I'm confident Adie would not have been such a disappointment to me, had I have allowed myself to be seduced by him. But after tonight, I've come to the realisation that there is no longer any chance of that happening and that I mustn't see Adie again. I owe it to Matt to give our marriage another shot now that I know he will defend me in front of my in-laws and that he didn't try it on with Kerry.

CHAPTER 45: RACHEL

Then

After midnight, I finally accept that Adie is not coming to bed — not my bed at any rate — and my body prickles with humiliation. Apart from a few creaks and groans that are normal for a property this age, the house is silent, but I can guess where my husband is — up one flight of stairs and down the landing, in Fiona's room. Everyone, even my children, appear to have fallen under that young harlot's spell. We'll see about that, as I get the impression Fiona isn't as patient as she likes to make out, so if I wait long enough, she's bound to make a mistake and show her true colours. The question is, how much time do I have left? A day? A week? A month?

To distract myself from the gruesome plans Adie and Fiona may have for my premature death, I have been working on a spectacular menu for Saturday night, which is bound to impress Adie's business associates. When it comes to Fiona stepping into my shoes, I'm determined to make it as challenging as possible for her. Earlier this evening I also spent time writing in my diary about what happened at the hotel and the events of the day. Tony (I preferred him when he was mysterious Soon-to-be-divorced guy) has been texting me constantly, declaring his undying love and saying how much he misses me, so it's clear he is still infatuated. Since he's the only one who believes in me and wants to help, I can't tell him that I no longer share his enthusiasm. The truth is I fear that what happened between us was a mistake, but I can't back out now. He's all I have.

When I realise how little I know him and that I have no idea what he does for a living, I'm prompted to text him to ask him. He responds right away: 'I work for the HSE as a Health and Safety Inspector.'

'That's nice,' I type, trying not to sound condescending but I think to myself that it sounds as dull as Adie's work in cyber security. I wouldn't say that aloud though because I wouldn't want to offend him. He obviously feels he has accomplished something significant, and who am I to deny him that? Not everyone can be a journalist who is passionate about uncovering the truth. Or the child of multimillionaire parents, destined from an early age to inherit a significant fortune.

He goes on to regale me with, 'I investigate all types of workplace accidents and determine who, if anyone, is at fault.'

I type mockingly, 'That could come in useful,' as I continue to brood over the fact that my husband and his mistress are plotting my murder. They might even be preparing to carry out the act tonight, while I'm asleep in my bed. By strangulation, knife, hammer or by lethal injection. Who can say? I wouldn't put anything past my evil husband. I shudder, knowing I have to change the way I think, or I'll wind up overanalysing everything and become what Adie terms 'emotionally unstable'.

My ears prick when I hear Adie and Fiona's laughter floating along the landing followed by the celebratory clinking of glasses as the last of yesterday's champagne is consumed. I imagine the sound of Fiona's hands clapping together in delight as she laughs at Adie's humourless jokes. He has never been good at comedy because he takes himself too seriously, as his mother will attest. I wish Jonty was here to comfort me. And I her, because after what happened to poor Sasha, she deserves a far better son than the murderous monster she gave birth to.

With trepidation, I text Tony again to make sure he hasn't had a case of cold feet or changed his mind since the last time I saw him. 'Have you decided what you're going to do about my situation?'

'I have indeed,' he declares, adding a victorious hand emoji.

'And?' I sigh with an unmistakable bone-crushing fatigue.

'I'm going to follow him.'

'Follow who? *Adie*?'

'You've got it in one,' he writes jubilantly. 'I'm going to put *my* investigative skills to use by tailing him. I've already installed a tracking device on his vehicle so there's no chance of him escaping me.'

'You've done what? Won't Adie find out? Is that even legal?'

'Less so than killing someone I think you'll find,' he reminds me, his words containing a tinge of rebuke.

'With a full-time job, how are you going to manage that?' I complain.

'As of right now, I'm on annual leave for two whole weeks. I've arranged it with my boss and everything.'

Even though I'm annoyed with him, I can't help but feel moved. 'You did that for me?'

'I told you I would help you, didn't I?' he boasts smugly, 'And now I can find out what Adie is up to 24/7.'

'But what do you hope to achieve by that?' I enquire, unconvinced.

'Evidence,' he states, attempting to convey to me the significance of this. 'The courts are more likely to accept your claim that he's an abuser who is using emotional control to defraud you of your money if we can prove that he's shagging the nanny while she's living under your roof or that he was somehow involved in the death of that other woman who was found in her apartment. He might even end up behind bars. If that happens, he'll wish I *had* killed him. We won't have to, though, this way.'

My lips part to speak but nothing comes out. It's not a bad idea, I'll give him that, and I'm surprised I didn't come up with it myself. I'm supposed to be the trailblazing journalist. But I'm not certain I want Adie to live. Not after all he's done. Alive, he'll be a constant danger to me and my children, won't he? And prison is too good for someone like him.

Giving in for now, I type, 'When are you going to start watching him?'

After a short delay, my phone displays a winking emoji and the words, 'I'm on it now.'

Irritably, I tap out, 'You can't be. Adie is at home.'

'He's not in your bed though, is he?'

'How do you know that?'

'Look outside the window.'

I take a deep breath to counteract the panic tearing at my insides, and then I jump out of bed and sprint over to the window. When I draw back the curtains and see that Tony is telling the truth, my pulse is loud and dangerously insistent in my ears. He's sitting in his car in the darkened street and is gazing up at my window. The white glow from the car's internal light projects a ghostly glow over one side of his face, making him a menacing figure. He raises a hand and waves when he sees me peering down on him. I recoil in horror at the sick, clownish grin on his face.

'Oh, my God,' the words tumble out of my mouth in a frantic rush.

His text message, 'Now I can watch you all the time as well, to make sure you're safe,' pings alarmingly on my phone. His words feel more like a threat than a promise, even if he wants them to sound comforting.

What have I done? It seems like I've made the situation worse. A few days ago, his passion for me may have thrilled and excited me, but now my misgivings about Tony are greater than they were before. When his next text message arrives, my anxiety is heightened.

'I've never felt this way about anyone before, and I don't plan on letting you go, unlike that waste of space, Adie. You're all mine now, Rachel.'

I smile weakly back at him through the window, pretending that everything is fine despite the cyclone in my chest, because it seems like I have two jailors now, each one as controlling as the other.

CHAPTER 46: LUCY

Now

As Matt takes a late shower, 'to refresh him after his flight,' he'd said, the sound of water thunders from the ensuite bathroom. My thoughts keep returning to Adie and Rachel while I lie in bed. I have yet to figure them out. I still haven't determined who the true villain is. One minute I'm certain Rachel is telling the truth, but whenever Adie demonstrates love for his children and mother, I tend to switch sides. Also, I think his grief over losing Rachel seems genuine. But what do I know?

Steam rises from Matt's shoulders as he returns to the bedroom, naked save for a small towel wrapped around his waist. The air is scented with Lynx body spray which makes me immediately suspicious because he doesn't typically wear it to bed. If he's after sex, I'm not sure how I feel about that. As my eyes search his face, I kill the mood by warning him, 'There's something else we need to talk about.'

'Oh?' he murmurs contritely, wanting to please me by showing an interest now that he isn't being accused of trying to get close to Kerry.

'It's about the house,' I say, my heart is pounding.

He turns to face me and flicks his damp hair away from his eyes before repeating, 'Oh?' in a high-pitched voice that doesn't sound like his. This is how I can tell he is already on his guard but is attempting to hide it.

Blood pulses in my ears as I tell him, 'I can't live here.'

I watch him visibly freeze. 'What? Why?'

I narrow my eyes at him as I ask, 'Be honest, Matt. Were you aware of what happened to Rachel?'

He screws up his face. 'Who is Rachel?'

I respond impatiently, 'The woman who used to live here,' assuming he must have heard that name before as part of the house-buying process.

When he shakes his head, indicating that he has no idea what I'm talking about, I go on, a little sarcastically, 'Didn't you know? Didn't the solicitor tell you?'

'Tell me what?' he scowls.

'She died here, in this house.'

'Shit!' he exclaims, clasping a hand over his mouth. Then, still reeling from this revelation, *and I know precisely how that feels*, he stumbles over to the bed and sinks onto it. 'How?'

'She was found at the bottom of the kitchen stairs.'

Matt's eyes are haunted as he mumbles, 'My God. How terrible. The poor woman.'

A wave of relief washes over me as I ask, 'I take it you didn't know then?'

'Of course not,' he protests fiercely, shaking his head as his clean, minty breath wafts over me. 'I would never have kept anything so significant from you. I can't believe you would think so low of me,' he complains, his face a picture of disappointment.

'I'm sorry, Matt, but I didn't know what to think,' I admit regretfully, unable to contain a tidal wave of tears as I snivel, 'It was such a shock. And although everyone claims her death was an accident, I'm not so sure.'

'Everyone?' he asks, pointedly raising an eyebrow.

That's when I realise how close I am to giving myself away. I can't tell Matt about Rachel's fears of being murdered without admitting how far I've gone with my interest in the Bellos, including meeting up with Adie.

'I read about it online after hearing about it from a gossipy neighbour,' I lie through my tears, careful to avoid his gaze, because it turns out I am still a terrible liar, even though I've had plenty of experience lately.

I'm surprised when Matt takes me into his arms and whispers into my hair, 'I'm sorry you had to find out like that. As you say, it must have been a huge shock. And of course, we'll sell the house if that's what you want.'

When I hear this, my face explodes into a gleeful smile and I blubber into his shoulder, 'Do you mean that?'

'You know I'd do anything for you, Lucy.'

'I would never have set foot in Rutland Terrace had I known that someone died here,' I garble, my throat thick with gratitude.

'I know you wouldn't,' he murmurs into my neck and puts a palm on one of my breasts, making it clear that he's got other things on his mind and doesn't want to talk about the house or the Bellos anymore. Although my husband is saying all the right things, and I have no reason to doubt him because he seems so sincere, I'm not done yet.

'So, you'll talk to the estate agent first thing in the morning?' I persist.

'Uh-huh,' he mumbles noncommittedly, preoccupied.

As his hands begin to explore the rest of my body, making my skin tingle, I realise I'm in danger of giving in to his advances before everything is resolved, so I poke him in the ribs and groan, 'I'm being serious.'

Taking the hint, he sighs and raises himself up on one elbow to look at me, 'It could take a while to sell because the property market is not as buoyant as it was when we bought the place. So, until we find a buyer, we'll have to continue to live here. Are you able to manage that?'

I nod grudgingly, to show I understand and am on board with that, but if I'm being completely honest, the mere prospect of spending even another night in this house makes me feel miserable. What other choice do we have, though? We can't afford to pay rent on another property, and it's not like we can stay with the in-laws. We'll just have to hope for a miraculously speedy sale. Miracles do happen, because for once Matt seems to understand how I feel and isn't putting obstacles in my way.

Because of this, I'm really aroused, but just as we're about to have sex, I hear my son sobbing and calling out for me.

Annoyed, Matt hisses, 'Leave him, he'll go back to sleep in a minute.'

I give him a dangerous look which can be translated to 'as if'. My kids, as I've said before, mean everything to me, and they come first, even if I'm gagging for sex as much as Matt is.

'You baby those kids too much,' Matt scolds, as I swing my legs out of bed.

'And you sound like your mother,' I retort over my shoulder as I yank the door open and hurry down the hallway to Jack's bedroom. There I'm faced with a child who is rumpled and exhausted, and who has adorable pillow creases on his face. My heart melts instantly. Compared to the love I have for my kids; sex can do one. But despite what Matt thinks, there has always been space in my heart for others, including him.

'Another nightmare?' I ask, making a pitying face.

Jack nods miserably. 'And I still don't feel very well.'

'You are a little warm,' I observe, moving to the bed to feel his forehead, adding guiltily, 'perhaps I should have kept you home from school today.'

'But then I couldn't have gone to Oscar's party,' he sulks.

'Quite,' I agree, grinning, because I now know why he pretended his cold had improved this morning and insisted on attending school. 'Wait here a minute while I go and get some tablets for you.'

As I rummage in the bathroom cabinet farther down the landing, searching for ibuprofen and only finding empty foil containers, I curse myself for spending the afternoon with Adie, contemplating sleeping with him, when my son was sick and trying to conceal it from me. I reflect on what kind of mother I am and resolve once again to do better. I'm ready to give a triumphant punch in the air when my hand settles on what feels like a full packet of tables based on its weight, but upon closer inspection, I see that it's not the harmless ibuprofen I was planning to give my son.

The prescription pill, Risperidone, is made out to a Mrs Rachel Bello and is classified as an antipsychotic drug on the label. The words 'All lies' and 'Not mine' have been disturbingly scrawled on the packaging.

CHAPTER 47: RACHEL

Then

Everyone is watching me. I feel like a prisoner. Even more so when Adie made the surprise announcement that he intended to accompany me on my morning run, something he has never done before. I sense the tension between us gathering, building towards breaking point. Although he insists on pretending that he didn't catch me cheating on him with another man in a hotel room, he must suspect me of something to want to monitor my movements so closely. Somewhere deep within me, a glimmer of rage ignites at the loss of my freedom. In my mind, I hear Adie's voice attempting to gaslight me into believing that my own family doctor had prescribed me those antipsychotic pills, even though I know this to be untrue. If only I could prove it, but now that Adie has been granted a lasting power of attorney on my behalf, he will be made aware if I attempt to access my medical records. I still don't understand how he was able to achieve this status without my knowledge, but I must assume it was done illegally, which would have cost him a small fortune.

Adie must have taken out a loan to pay for a solicitor who is willing to risk disbarment for engaging in illegal practices because he has no extra money due to all the gambling debt he has accrued.

Considering that a lasting power of attorney typically takes 8 to 10 weeks to complete in the UK and there is a four-week waiting period to allow for objections, which naturally did not occur, it is the only way I can think of that he could have completed it so swiftly. Adie will be counting on getting his hands on my inheritance so he can repay all his debtors. I don't know how long it will take him to realise the money is gone but I don't think it will be long.

A hand on my arm jolts me out of my thoughts and I realise Adie is talking to me. The pressure of his fingers wrapping tightly around my skin is biting. His voice, meant to be soothing, but sounding terrifying to me, echoes around the entrance hall as he chirps, 'Are we ready then?'

Fiona's jealous eyes linger on us as Adie and I leave the house together, like any other married couple, but she is preoccupied with one of the children vying for her attention, so she turns away impatiently.

The summer sky outside is reassuringly blue and as we jog towards Stamford Meadows, Adie keeps up with me with ease. Although he doesn't run frequently, he works out and is fit because he cares about his appearance. However, I'm still a faster runner than he is, and as my pace increases, he struggles to match it. Adie is fiercely competitive and detests being beaten at anything or by anyone, especially a woman, so he pushes himself harder than he should, causing him to break out in an unattractive sweat. We don't talk as we run, but occasionally I see him look at me out of the corner of his eye, as though he is itching to say something.

He finally stops to catch his breath, and I feel compelled to wait for him. That's when he remarks in a reflective tone, 'It feels like things have been a little difficult between us lately, don't you think?'

I nod without making eye contact because I don't want to give anything away in case he's trying to get me to say something I'll later regret.

'Hopefully, the new nanny is working out okay?'

'For me or for you?' I snap.

Faking confusion, he replies innocently, 'I meant for us. As a family.'

I laugh bitterly as I say, 'Oh yes, I couldn't be more delighted with her.'

His jaw twitches at that and whatever he was going to say next he doesn't. Instead, he ponders, 'Are you looking forward to the dinner party next Saturday? You don't think it will be too much for you, do you?'

'Do you?' I counter, giving him a spiky look.

'Of course not,' he lies. 'It can't fail to be a massive success with you in charge. And I can't wait to show you off to the partners.'

'I'm not a possession, Adie,' I reply churlishly.

'You're right. That was a stupid thing to say. I apologise.'

I gaze at him then, trying to figure him out because I can't recall the last time he apologised. Why is he suddenly being nice? Given that Tony isn't exactly melting into the background (Colombo, he is not), I begin to suspect Adie has already realised that he has a stalker. Perhaps he found the tracker on his car when he went out this morning. Let's face it, Tony couldn't be more visible if he tried, having jogged after us in his shiny shorts and hideous white socks. As for his car parked so obviously outside the house, practically outside our front windows — where Adie must have clocked it — I'm beginning to believe that Tony is a bumbling fool. But is he a dangerous one? I'm convinced Adie thinks I've hired a private investigator to dig up the dirt on him and that's why he is uneasy.

I believe I'm right when he suddenly comes out with, 'I was wondering if we should go away somewhere, just the two of us.'

'Really?' As my eyes widen in disbelief, his words function as a reminder that I must never underestimate how cunning my husband is.

'Now we have a full-time live-in nanny, there's no reason why we can't.'

'What for though?' I ask, coldly.

At the knockback, his smile slips lightly, but then he's beaming like the Adie I knew in the past. The one who could take a joke.

He bemoans in jest, 'Knock a man down, why don't you?' then more hesitantly he suggests, 'I was thinking of a romantic weekend in Paris, or wherever you might like. What do you think?'

What do I think? That I was spot-on when I predicted Adie was onto us and is fully aware that he is being followed. He is simply being nice to me now, in public, in front of Tony, to give him the impression that I have lied about him, or at the very least that I have exaggerated all his offences. Adie cannot know that this plan will never succeed, because even though it pains me to admit it, Tony is my lover and not a paid-for Private Eye.

'I want us to try, Rachel, so we can make our marriage work,' Adie is saying, and he sounds so sincere that I almost believe him. His acting skills have always been remarkable. But when he begs, 'Can't we put the past behind us for all our sakes?' he is clearly alluding to his affairs with other women, not forgetting his violent and abusive treatment of me.

From a short distance away, I hear a red-faced Tony coughing his guts up and I roll my eyes in annoyance since I realise he must have heard this too. Later, I expect him to have a hundred irritating questions for me.

'What will it take for us to get back on track?' Adie continues.

Without any hesitation on my part, I answer bluntly, 'The truth.'

'The truth about what?' he queries, bewildered.

I speak softly so that only he can hear me. 'Did you kill your first wife?'

CHAPTER 48: LUCY

Now

After Matt finally forgave me for not having sex with him so I could console our son instead we ended up having a surprisingly good weekend doing family stuff. On Saturday we went shopping at Morrisons (Matt thinks I'm crazy because I enjoy shopping for food, but what's not to love). Then, on Sunday, I prepared a homemade taco dinner from scratch, which the kids loved¬ while Matt worked on some DIY projects to get the house ready for resale. I wasn't present when he made the call to the estate agent, but he told me they would be coming out next week to revalue the house. Once the kids were in bed, Matt drank his red wine while I had my usual tipple of Coke. And yes, we did eventually make love. As always in our house, it felt rushed because of the kids. But at least we made the effort. As far as I know, he hasn't been to see his parents yet, but he swears he will do it as soon as he can, so I've promised myself not to keep nagging him about it. If he said he'll do it, then he will. That's good enough for me.

And now it's Monday morning again. The speed at which they roll around amazes me. Matt took the 6.05 a.m. train to Stevenage to attend a senior management meeting. Jack's cold is much better, so I dropped him off at school earlier and then I returned home to do the housework. There are four loads of washing to contend with, three beds to make, toilets to scrub, the dishwasher to empty and rogue socks and trainers to find.

But as I carry out these chores, constantly keeping a watchful eye on Sophie, who follows me about the house in her princess attire stuffing her mouth with cheesy Wotsits, something is niggling me. When I realise what it is, I sigh wearily and make myself stand up straight. My back hurts from bending over so long. I'm supposed to be at the shop today, but I don't think I can face seeing Kerry. What must that poor woman think of us? How am I meant to explain to her that Matt was only complimenting her to make her feel better about herself? Although I don't usually shy away from difficult conversations, this is one I do not want to have. Probably because I'm not sure who or what to believe anymore.

While I'm emptying the pockets of Matt's business suit — the one he took to Istanbul — in preparation for sending it to be dry cleaned, I find some receipts. Since Matt uses a company credit card and faces consequences for failing to keep paper receipts, I initially don't think much of it. But when I look closer, I see that he has used his own credit card this time, possibly by mistake. Given that both bank cards are black, this wouldn't be the first time he's done this, so he'll have to submit an expense form to claim the money back. But the bill for this fine-dining restaurant is for two people. Not one, as though Matt had eaten by himself, and not for four, the total number of JCB employees who travelled together on the trip. But two! I know this for certain because they'd ordered two of everything. Where were the rest of the group while he was dining out with one other individual at the romantic-sounding rooftop restaurant Beso? My next observation is that he spent a lot of money (money that we do not have) on champagne.

Is Matt cheating on me again? Was I right all along to doubt him? Does having it confirmed mean my day, my life and my world just got a hundred times worse? A vein throbs agonisingly on my forehead, and blood pulses in my ears. Thrum. Thrum. Thrum. Still clutching the receipts in my hand, I manage to stagger over to the bed and collapse onto it, sobbing. I go around in circles trying to work things out in my head, hoping there is a rational explanation for everything but I have a nagging sensation in the pit of my stomach that Matt wasn't telling the truth when he denied anything was going on with him and his new female coworker. He never tells the truth. Is he also lying when he says he loves me or that he would do anything for me? The problem with lies is that once you've become aware of one, everything else your loved one says is questionable.

The coworker's name was Katya. How could I forget the foreign-sounding name when she was giggling in the background while I was on the phone with my husband? Despair washes over me as I try to visualise what she looks like. Is she more attractive than I am? More amusing? But I refuse to go down that path again. So, I squash down those thoughts and concentrate on what needs to be done right now.

As I steel myself for what might lie ahead, envisioning life without Matt — and I must confess that my heart aches at the thought of him not coming home to his family every day — I let the crumpled, tear-stained receipts flutter to the floor. When I remember that he hasn't yet fulfilled his promise to see his parents either, he's lucky I don't take a sharp pair of scissors to his suit! Making a snap decision, I call out to Sophie, declaring, 'Enough with this housework. Let's go and see Kerry in the shop.'

I needed answers and I needed them now, so I have no memory of the drive into town. Only that Sophie was excited to see Kerry. Upon seeing the mascara smeared across my red, blotchy face when I burst into the shop, Kerry plucks Sophie out of my arms and tries to divert her attention away from my distress. I'm too numb to resist. The next thing I know, she's putting a cup of milky tea in my hand, 'For the shock.' Everything slows as I blurt out, 'Answer me one thing and I promise never to ask again. When Matt came over to do the accounts, did he put his hands on you?'

She slowly nods, while avoiding eye contact. I feel dread set in then and my breathing becomes difficult. As I watch Kerry's overgrown eyebrows dip sympathetically, I realise Matt wasn't wrong when he cruelly described her as a bag lady, but she is content with her life as a single woman living alone with her cats. Why not? Better to be known as a crazy cat lady than a cuckolded wife. I give her a nod in return and muster a weak smile, resolved to honour my word and refrain from asking her any more questions.

Meanwhile, the world continues to spin, so I shakily sit down. I was clutching at straws when I chose to believe what Matt told me. Even though none of this is my fault, my life is falling apart around me, and the shame of my husband's womanising clings to me like the smell of sex. As fresh tears prick at my eyes, I picture a naked Matt and his lover (whoever she may be) in a dingy hotel room with unwashed semen-stained bedsheets.

If that cheating scumbag of a husband was here right now, I'd kill him.

CHAPTER 49: RACHEL

Then

Over the weekend, our relationship deteriorated even more since Adie, of course, denied everything. He was furious that I had the audacity to bring up the subject of his first wife, Caitlin, as I had been forbidden from discussing her since the day we were married. However, Caitlin was my friend — or rather a close colleague. We clicked right away when she started working in the sales team at the broadsheet newspaper where I was employed. She had a head full of gorgeous red Irish curls and was adorably self-conscious about the cute gap in her upper middle teeth. After just three years of marriage, she died after jumping off Stamford bridge, a known suicide spot. I wonder if Adie plans to pass my death off in a similar way.

Because of what happened to Sasha — I can't get the death of that poor girl out of my thoughts — I know my husband is capable of murder, so I now have my doubts about what happened to Caitlin. It's odd to think that I never would have met Adie if she hadn't died, as we met at her funeral. Even though he was overcome with grief at the time, he was so charming that I soon fell under his spell. Adie has repeatedly tried to convince me that Caitlin was suffering from severe depression and deliberately took her own life but I am certain she would not have done such a thing. She had too much to live for, and life adored her. Even if he did not! The comparison between her situation and mine is terrifyingly similar.

I'm relieved that it's finally Monday because Adie left for London this morning; after curtly informing me that he wouldn't be returning for a few days, leaving Fiona and I alone in the house. I can't help wondering if she knows about Caitlin's existence. Most of our acquaintances are under the impression that I am Adie's first wife and it's unlikely he would have revealed too much, even to her. He has too much to hide.

Still, it wouldn't hurt to find out how much she knows. So, at the very next opportunity I get, I decide to test her. This comes about when I ask her to help me make the canapés for the dinner party ahead of Saturday night. The oriental prawn and squid fishcakes, steak and béarnaise profiteroles, pea and mint fritters, mac 'n' cheese and sticky pork belly bites can be all prepared in advance and frozen. Everything else, including my showstopper DIY marshmallow bar, will be made closer to the event.

As I sink my fingers into the gooey fish mixture and roll it into a ball, I mumble vaguely, 'Does the name Caitlin mean anything to you?'

'Should it?' Fiona shrugs, and I assume from her response that Adie hasn't told her about his previous marriage.

'Only if you know it,' I reply disingenuously, grabbing her attention.

'Who is she?' she asks, sneaking a sly glance at me.

Just as I'm about to reply, there's a loud knock on the door of the boot room. We can hear a male voice impatiently yelling, 'Is anybody there?' even from down here in the kitchen.

'Whoever can that be?' I groan in irritation as I head to the sink to wash my hands.

'I'll go if you like,' Fiona offers, seeing the state of my hands.

'Would you?' I smile appreciatively, even though being nice to her is the last thing I want to do.

After barely a minute, she returns, her face displaying concern. 'It's that man,' she hisses.

'What man?'

'The weird one who's been hanging around the house,' she informs me, shuddering. 'He gives me the creeps.'

I take a deep breath and bite my lip because I already know the identity of the creep she is referring to. Tony. Or as I've decided to call him, White Socks, as it suits him better. It's either that or bumbling fool.

'You're not going to answer the door to him?' Fiona exclaims, raising her eyebrows in horror as I wipe my hands on a tea towel.

As I walk out of the room, I mutter, 'I'm sure he's perfectly harmless,' although I'm seriously beginning to doubt that. He's been texting and calling me nonstop since he heard Adie declare that he wanted our marriage to succeed. To avoid raising Fiona's suspicions, I've had to turn my phone to silent. I don't want her to think there's another man on the scene as she will automatically assume I've left the door open for her and Adie.

Tony is slouching listlessly on my doorstep as I open the door. It's clear that he is feeling insecure about us and wants to express it. Despite my attempts to reassure him that my marriage to Adie is basically over, he couldn't look more wretched if he tried. Honestly though, once you become aware that your husband is plotting your murder, there is no turning back.

'What are you doing here?' I hiss in a voice laced with venom.

'I miss you. I wanted to see you,' he laments pitifully.

With my eyes darting up and down the street, I warn, 'You can't be here. What if Adie came back?'

'Who gives a damn?' he shrugs melancholically, adding in a bitter tone, 'you're going to go back to him anyway.'

'Is that what this is about?' I'm annoyed but not surprised.

I detest men who try to guilt their partners into doing what they want or who play the victim. It's simply another form of manipulation. As a result, I start to feel sorry for his soon-to-be ex-wife. It's not surprising that she found somebody else. Right there on the spot, I decide that once this, whatever *this* is, is over, he will have to go. Of course, I'll always be grateful to him for trying to help me, but I don't feel enough for him. He used to be someone I found attractive and enjoyable to be with, but now I think he's a joke. That I ever found him desirable or funny is unbelievable. That was my sex hormones talking because I had been ovulating when I met him. My increased sexual appetite aways lets me know when I am.

Then, realising that he has become a liability and won't be as easy to dispose of as I first thought, I attack him by saying, 'You're jealous, so you thought you'd ruin all our plans and go back on your word,' because my almost-knight in shining armour has somehow turned into my tormentor.

CHAPTER 50: LUCY

Now

I drive to the Caterpillar building in Peterborough all the while fighting back tears. Once there, I park recklessly and walk unsteadily towards the main entrance doors, still in disbelief over Matt's betrayal. When Kerry realised that I was intent on visiting Matt's former workplace and couldn't be persuaded otherwise, she wisely kept Sophie with her at the shop. Since Matt prefers to keep work and family life separate, or at least that's what he told me, and I foolishly believed him, I've never gone to any of his places of employment before. He was always reluctant to let me meet his coworkers for the same reason. But all that's about to change now that I'm on a mission to gather facts! I'm determined to find out who the female coworker he had the affair with is and whether he's still seeing her. Did he take her to Istanbul with him? Or is it Katya he's sleeping with?

The building is intimidatingly large and made of hostile grey concrete. As I walk through the glass reception doors, I brace myself to be questioned by the stylish receptionist who sits at a desk and taps at a keyboard with gleaming red nails. According to her name badge, she's called Natalie. She glances up and smiles when she sees my shadow hanging over her, but I notice it doesn't reach her eyes. *She looks like a Natalie*, I can't help thinking, taking in her blonde ballerina bun, slim figure and midnight-blue eyes.

'Yes?' she enquires, cheek twitching with irritation at being disturbed.

I swallow what feels like a giant pebble as I spell out, 'My name is Lucy Dawson, and my husband Matt used to work here until two years ago.'

She gives the smallest of nods. 'How can I help you?'

I explain earnestly, 'Matt has a special fortieth birthday coming up, and since he's still so fond of his former coworkers here — he talks about them all the time — I was wondering if I could speak to them so I can invite them to his surprise party.' I laugh nervously as I add this.

My laughter dies when I realise my hurriedly prepared explanation isn't working. The blank expression on her face tells me she doesn't believe me.

'What are the names of the people he used to work with?'

'That's the problem,' I murmur conspiratorially, 'I don't know.'

'But you mentioned that he was always talking about them,' she continues, looking around nervously, as if for back up.

She's got me there. Thinking quickly, I bluster, 'He had nicknames for them, so I never got to know their real names.'

'That wasn't very politically correct of him, and it isn't the behaviour we expect of our colleagues here,' she points out primly, her lips pursed.

I look away before I utter something that might get me thrown out. 'I quite agree,' I mumble, swallowing my pride to placate her. Then I stammer, 'Did you happen to know Matt?' ruining everything.

She looks alarmed, as though I had just accused her of having an affair with my husband. *Did she?* Everyone is a suspect until I know differently.

'I've only been here three months.'

To my surprise, she picks up her phone and murmurs noncommittedly, 'I'll talk to the office manager. She might know. She's been here for years.'

'Oh, I'm so grateful. That's very kind of you,' I gush.

She gives me another dubious look and then adds curtly, 'Please wait over there,' pointing to a yellow modular sofa as if she can't wait to get rid of the distraught, red-eyed human being in front of her.

While I wait, a fresh ripple of sadness washes over me, as I think of what Matt has reduced me to, lying to strangers who are just doing their job and are trying to make a living, the same as everyone else.

'So, you're Matt's wife,' a voice booms. 'It's a pleasure to meet you.'

I wipe away a stray tear as I stand up to shake the heavily ringed hand that is being held out to me.

'Are you okay?' The woman asks in concern, studying my face.

'Don't mind me. It's nothing really,' I apologise, feeling stupid. I change the subject and exclaim, 'So you know my husband?' in a cheerful tone.

'I do,' she confirms with a wide grin, sitting down beside me and urging me to follow suit. She has a friendly and inviting manner that puts me at ease. 'We worked together for over a year. How is he doing at his new job?'

I reply, 'Really well, thank you,' but as he never confides in me, I'm not sure if this is true or not.

'And he's coming up to forty I understand?'

'Yes,' I answer guiltily since I can't admit that Matt still has five years to go before he reaches that milestone, or she'll know I was lying before.

She observes bluntly, 'He looks so much younger.' Then, with a start, she says, 'I apologise for not introducing myself. I am the office manager and my name is Julie.'

'How long have you worked here?' I begin.

'For ever,' she grimaces with a filthy laugh, drawing attention from everyone in the building. I've never heard someone laugh so loudly.

Although she is extremely nice, I have a suspicion that this is not the woman Matt was seeing when he worked here. While not unattractive, she is more sergeant major material than lover and must be in her fifties.

'You can put me down as coming to the party. I'd love to see Matt again.'

I pounce on her words, 'And who else was he close to, do you think, that I ought to invite?'

'Let me see,' she mumbles thoughtfully, stroking her chin. 'Brian in accounts and Toby in supply chain would be a good call. They were as thick as thieves. Other than that, I can't think of anyone else.'

As innocently as possible, I press for more, 'He mentioned that he was close to someone else. A female colleague.'

'No,' she declares with confidence, her eyes wide with disbelief. 'As far as I know, Matt wasn't friends with any of the women here, so you must have got the wrong end of the stick about that.'

I narrow my eyes, thinking this doesn't sound right at all. 'Oh, I understood they travelled together sometimes,' I persist slyly.

'Really?' she exclaims, stunned. 'That definitely did not happen,' she emphasises with a firm, no-nonsense shake of her head.

As Julie and I conclude our chat, I'm filled with a crushing sense of disappointment that Matt has told me yet more lies. I'm so affected by this that I struggle to maintain my composure as I politely make my excuses and leave. As I exit blindly through the doors, shame and humiliation follow me, and tears well up in my eyes once more. Since Julie has proven to me that Matt did not have an affair with a female coworker, I ought to be relieved. But that doesn't mean it didn't happen with somebody else. Just not here, as he claimed. Someone in Julie's position would have been the first to hear about an office affair as it would have caused quite a stir, and everyone would have been gossiping about it. Out of the two of them, I believe her over Matt. The only thing I know for certain is that Matt had the affair, but it wasn't with a coworker like he said. So, who was the mystery woman? Why did he lie about her identity? He must have regretted not telling the truth when I insisted he leave his job.

Feeling totally justified in what I am about to do, I take my phone out of my bag and dial an unsaved number that I've committed to memory. My next move is not an act of revenge, but something I feel I am owed. After the hellish day I've had, it's easy to convince myself that I deserve it.

'What time do you want me Saturday night?' I ask Adie.

CHAPTER 51: RACHEL

Then

I glance out of the window and notice the Russian woman from number nine — I believe her name is Alina — dodging Tony on the street and casting a suspicious glance over her shoulder at him. He's still out there. However, he doesn't pay the slightest bit of attention to my attractive neighbour, who I assume most men's eyes would want to follow. His gaze is fixed on the house. And me, as I glare back at him through the windows of the library. The last text message I received from him was in response to mine demanding to know why he was loitering outside the house rather than finding out what Adie was up to in London.

'There's no point in following him there, where I'd easily lose him,' he'd grumbled, before saying, 'I'd rather be here with you. Why won't you let me see you? Don't you love me anymore?' Given that I've never once used the word 'love' to him I angrily declined to respond. Not only is he deluded, but he is most likely a psychopath. I guess that's the danger of making friends with strangers on trains. Whatever was I thinking?

There is movement behind me as Fiona enters the room. 'Is he still out there?' she hisses, her voice bordering on hysterical.

I nod without turning around, hoping she'll retire to her bedroom now that the children are in bed, and she is no longer needed. *She never was.*

'Who is he? What's he doing? What does he want?' she demands tetchily as she comes to stand beside me so she can see for herself. Although it's getting dark, he's still clearly visible and hasn't moved in over an hour.

'That's a lot of questions, which I do not have the answers to,' I rebuff her coldly, assuming that she'll be reporting all of this to Adie on his return, if not sooner. I imagine they talk constantly on the phone as lovers do. I myself haven't heard from him all day. Nor do I expect to as he was furious with me the last time I saw him. As for Fiona, if she discovers that I am lying and that I really do know Tony, she's smart enough to work out the rest on her own. The town will be abuzz with rumours of our affair then. Adie will no longer be able to pretend at ignorance then.

'Should I ring Adie and tell him to come home?' she frets, gnawing at the skin around her fingernails.

'That's not your place to do so. You forget yourself.' I almost spit out the words as I turn to glower at her.

'I'm sorry,' she murmurs, face flushed with shame. 'It's just that he's freaking me out by being out there. Are you sure you don't recognise him?'

'He isn't breaking any laws, so I don't see what we can do. And I've told you before, I haven't a clue who he is,' I continue, raising my voice.

'Well, he seems to know you.'

Jaw clenched, I tell her in a clipped voice, 'That will be all, thank you, Fiona. I expect you'd like some time to yourself now you're off duty.'

Her face gets even redder when she realises she's being dismissed. For a second or two, she looks as if she's going to put up a fight, but then she droops her head and shuffles out the door without saying another word.

It's not just her I'm angry at. Tony is the one I'm furious with. I could murder him for making my situation worse. Not better, as he'd promised to do. To let him know how I'm feeling, I pull the curtains shut fiercely, preventing him from seeing into my life. I wish I could get rid of him as easily. I'm just as mad at myself. Not only for succumbing to flattery and allowing myself to be seduced into having unsatisfying sex with a man I've quickly grown to detest, but also for not taking the proper precautions.

When I think of all the times Adie has told people 'My wife is feeling unwell' the joke is on me, because it's turned out to be true. I have been feeling unwell recently. A missed period — albeit just two days late — as well as nausea, frequent urination, exhaustion and tender breasts are all early indicators of pregnancy. So, despite having taken a pregnancy test this afternoon and it turning out to be negative, I'm certain that I *am* pregnant, as a home test wouldn't necessarily show up a positive result until ten days after conception. The fact that I am expecting a child is not something I will be disclosing to anybody else. Least of all the father.

When I think that we only had unprotected sex once, a headache begins to threaten my temples, because how unlucky can one person be, but then I remember that I was ovulating at the time. I might not have given in to Tony's advances so readily without that added complication. This is when conception is most likely to happen, according to the research I did, making sure to delete my search history afterwards, in case Adie has gained access to my passwords and is spying on me. Again, I wish I had been aware of this little-known fact earlier. Because of all the other medication I've been prescribed — illegally, I might add, and against my will — the contraceptive pill is no longer effective. So, I have to presume the baby is Tony's since I can't recall the last time Adie and I made love. Besides, I always insist that he wears a condom.

I'm not heartless, which is why I don't want to think about how I will live with this decision in the future, but I've already made up my mind that I'm not keeping the baby, which I tell myself is roughly the size of a poppy seed and cannot feel physical pain. Anyway, how could I bring an innocent child into our dark world of secrets and lies? It wouldn't be fair to it.

Even if Adie could be persuaded into believing the child was his, which I seriously doubt, he'd use it against me, to gain complete control of me and my money. He would ruin my life and the life of the child without giving it a second thought while persuading everyone else that he was the perfect husband and father. Even knowing the baby wasn't his, he'd never let me keep it if we got divorced. He would do this just to spite me. And what of Tony? If he learned that I was expecting his child he would be bound to claim paternity and insist on a DNA test to prove it.

My palms start to sweat as I decide to visit the pharmacy first thing tomorrow to request a prescription for the morning-after pill. The emergency contraception apparently works for up to five days following sex, so the timeline still works. Failing that, I'll arrange for a private, early termination. It will be my secret. Nobody else has to know.

CHAPTER 52: LUCY

Now

As I close the front door behind me, I wave to Alina who is going into her house with her two boys. She gives a shy smile and lifts a hand in acknowledgement. I don't smile back because I'm going to have dinner with, and probably sleep with, a man who isn't my husband, leaving my babies at home with their lying, cheating father. I refuse to feel guilty though. After everything Matt has done to me, I deserve a night of fun. Matt is my first and only lover. I thought he'd be my last. I can't tell you how much that grieves me in one sense. It has also been much harder than I thought to keep quiet about his unfaithful behaviour over the last few days. Trust me, there have been times when I've wanted to ram every piece of kitchenware I own into him.

There's a very good reason why I haven't confronted Matt yet about the receipts in his pocket, what he did to Kerry and all the other lies he's told, and that's because I want to experience this all-consuming rage and sense of moral injustice for just one more night, long enough to be with Adie. I want to enjoy my time with him without any of the guilt I would otherwise feel. That might not make sense to a lot of people, but it does to me.

I'm walking because Matt thinks I'm going on a boozy night out on the town with the girls, but as soon as I turn the corner, I phone a cab to come get me and take me to First Drift. Matt would normally have complained about having to babysit his own kids for the night but given all the lies he's told me recently, he dared not object, even after I told him I was meeting up with Beth, who he can't stand. He's right about one thing though, I do plan on having a drink or two tonight, if only to boost my confidence.

I don't take offence when I see the driver eyeing me in his rear-view mirror, I'm flattered instead. I've lost a load of weight recently and when I looked in the mirror earlier tonight, I thought I looked okay, maybe even more than okay. Like my old self in fact. I'm wearing the same floaty dress that I wore to the Burleigh House picnic because Adie said it looked good on me. Strangely enough, I'm no longer concerned about exposing too much cleavage. *Bring it on*, I say.

I ask the driver to stop and let me out at the top of the lane so I can walk the rest of the way. I'm not sure why, but I don't want him to know my precise destination. I'm beginning to see how much deceit is involved when starting an affair. You need to stay on your toes if you don't want to be found out. Regardless of what happens between me and Adie, I don't intend to make a habit of committing adultery, unlike Matt. I couldn't live with myself.

When a bright red MINI Clubman passes me at speed, churning up dust and debris and taking over the entire road, I dive out of the way to avoid being hit. I realise it's Fiona when I catch a glimpse of the driver. Did she try and run me over on purpose? She seemed in a right strop based on what I saw of her. Clearly, she had just left Adie's place. But that can't be right, can it? On the phone, Adie had told me that she'd left, finally. 'Good riddance,' he'd cheered, having returned home to discover her stuff gone, her house keys on the table and a curt note with her forwarding address. Feeling shaken from the encounter with the former nanny, I decide to bring this up with Adie later. But I won't let it spoil our evening.

When he answers the door, a dazzling smile bursts across his handsome face. 'Come in,' he exclaims, 'it's great to see you,' and leans in to kiss me on the cheek. For a moment or two, our first kiss feels awkward, but then I relax and follow him through the house into the kitchen, taking in the gleaming surroundings like I did when I first came here.

'The kids are in bed,' he tells me, uncorking what looks like an expensive bottle of white wine. 'Are you joining me?' he asks, gesturing to the bottle.

I chuckle and sit down at the kitchen island, saying, 'Too right I am.' I then observe with an eager smile, 'Something smells delicious.'

'We're having roasted figs with blue cheese and serrano ham followed by pan-fried sea trout with asparagus and hassle back potatoes,' he boasts, then enquires, 'I hope you're okay with that.'

I nod, and mumble, 'Perfect,' even though it sounds a bit fancy for my liking, but I obviously don't say so. I've never had figs before, and I'm worried I might not like them.

'You do like figs, don't you?' he asks, sensing that something is amiss.

'I love them,' I lie. *Again.* 'By the way,' I begin, as he pours a small amount of wine into my glass and waits for me to taste it. He only fills it to the top when I nod in approval, 'I saw Fiona on the way here, coming out of your road. She didn't look very happy, and I swear she would have run me over if I hadn't jumped out of the way.'

'Fiona?' he frowns and stops whatever he is doing. 'You must be mistaken.'

'No, I don't think so. I'm certain it was her. I assumed she'd been to see you.'

He gives a headshake. 'No. I haven't seen her since she left.'

'Perhaps she's stalking you and did a drive-by,' I suggest, figuring that since it wouldn't surprise me, it shouldn't surprise him either.

'You could be right,' he grimaces, and then he changes the subject by putting his phone on the table in front of me and asking, 'would you mind picking out some background music for us on Spotify? The login is 1844.'

As I select Billie Eilish, thinking he won't like Taylor Swift or Rhianna, since Matt doesn't, I can't help but compare Adie's openness with Matt's secrecy. Matt would never allow me access to his phone, which he keeps locked and never lets out of his sight.

'Good choice. I love this one,' Adie raves as 'What Was I Made For?' starts to play through the built-in speakers throughout the house.

As he runs a hand through his hair, it's then I notice it.

'You've taken your wedding ring off,' I gasp.

'I thought it was about time,' he sighs and stares at his finger as though he can still feel the weight of the gold band that used to hang on it. In a caramel-smooth tone, he murmurs, 'How about you, Sadie?'

Is it my imagination, or does he sound suspicious when he says my name, as though he's figured out my identity and is about to expose me. But if that were the case, I wouldn't be here right now, having dinner with him. Surely, he'd refuse to have anything more to do with me after discovering that I'd lied to him. Not just him, but also his mother and kids.

Assuming I'm wrong, I obediently remove my ring under his watchful gaze. I feel such a fraud, and so very disloyal as my mind shifts to the husband waiting for me at home. I still love Matt. I shouldn't be here. *He doesn't love you though*, good old inner voice reminds me. *If he did, he wouldn't hurt you the way he does.* But as Adie's gorgeous brown eyes hungrily travel down my body, I feel as if I am also on the menu tonight. The truth is I want nothing more than to be consumed by him.

I'm about to propose that we skip dinner and go upstairs — we can always eat later — when he scares me by announcing in a deadly serious voice, 'I think one of us has a confession to make.'

CHAPTER 53: RACHEL

Then

'I think I'm going to be sick.' I yank my eyes away from our startled dinner guests, who are seated at the dining table gawping at me, to fiercely glare at Adie who is once again uttering those now-familiar words, 'Apologies, but my wife is feeling unwell,' as he helps me to my feet. Until a few moments ago, I believed that everything was going smoothly. The menu was a huge hit, and I was praised for how well everything had been cooked, especially the pan-fried sea trout with hassle back potatoes. More than a dozen bottles of wine, hand-selected by Adie to complement the dishes, have been demolished so far. I was mildly surprised to see him cut back on his alcohol consumption tonight, likely because he doesn't want to risk anything going wrong. I obviously haven't touched a drop, but even if I had, that wouldn't explain why I suddenly feel nauseous.

With a trembling hand, I tuck my hair behind my ear and give our guests a feeble smile while I try to form a coherent sentence. But I stall when I notice Adie biting his lip and displaying uncertainty. This makes me question whether he has drugged me again in the hope that I will make an exhibition of myself and prove that I'm as unstable as he makes me out to be. Would he really jeopardise his own dinner party though? It's difficult to believe he'd want to be embarrassed in front of these powerful executives.

'Please excuse me for a moment,' I finally manage to say, but even to my ears, my voice sounds shaky and unlike my own. I trail off when I see Adie hold up a hand, seemingly warning me not to say anything else.

I'm on the verge of tears, so I let Adie lead me out of the room. He keeps one bone-hard hand on my bare back the whole time. In a calculated attempt to outshine Fiona, who had been instructed to dress in a black skirt and white blouse to mimic standard wait-ress attire, I wore my long, slinky, barely-there black number. I also informed Adie's business associates, who I was disappointed to find were all white men in their fifties, 'Fiona is an employee, not a guest so she will not be eating with us.' I realise this was cruel of me, but the injured look she sent me was worth it. In retaliation, she wore the shortest skirt she could find and is braless beneath her silky top. I couldn't help noticing that the men were entranced by her and their eyes were on stalks as they followed her jiggling breasts around the room.

As soon as we're out of the room, I bolt towards the down-stairs cloakroom, slamming the door behind me to keep Adie out. There, I throw up what little dinner party food I had eaten. I feel better instantly.

Adie taps impatiently at the door. 'Are you okay, Rachel? Do you want me to come in?'

'No,' I bark as I splash my face with water and pinch my cheeks to restore some of their colour. 'I'm fine now. I'll be out in a minute.'

I hear him sighing from the other side of the door, so after flushing the toilet, I open it to find him standing there. He looks me over, trying to figure out if I'm telling the truth. When he squints his eyes at me and insists, 'You can't be better that quickly. You ought to go to bed and rest,' I'm enraged.

'And ruin a perfectly good dinner party? I don't think so,' I reply scathingly, arching both eyebrows.

'You don't think it could be food poisoning, do you?' he asks, looking worried.

When I realise that our guests, not me, are the ones he's worried about, I try to reassure him by stating confidently, 'Definitely not.'

He observes, unconvinced, 'Well, something obviously made you sick.'

'Whatever it was, I'm better now and I'm ready to go back in and join the others,' I stubbornly insist, not wishing to discuss it anymore.

I walk past him then with my back straight, and when I notice Fiona hovering close by, with her unsightly loose breasts, I realise that she must have followed us out of the room and is now eavesdropping on our conversation. 'This is my house. That is my husband, and those children upstairs are also mine,' I'm tempted to scream at her. Instead, I punish her by telling her, 'You'll be pleased to hear you won't need to wait at the table anymore.' I expect her to be relieved because I am aware that she feels this duty is beneath her. And there's real venom in my voice as I add, 'But if you could start clearing up the kitchen that would be a big help,' demonstrating that I'm not done with her yet.

I return to the dining room and as everyone glances up inquisitively, I pull a playful face and purr seductively, 'I'm so sorry, gentleman. I do hope you'll forgive me for abandoning you.'

One of the more attentive males asks, 'Are you quite well now, Rachel?'

As a good hostess should, I nod and grin flirtatiously, before asking, 'Anyone for more wine?' A cheer goes up from the table, and I laugh along. It's this pleasant scene that greets Adie when he comes back into the room, looking less worried, and dare I say it, a little impressed. The look I give him is meant to convey: 'See, I told you I had everything under control.'

By the time I'm finished with him, he'll regret trying to replace me with a cheap tramp like Fiona, who we both know is inferior in every way to me. Now that she's out of the picture and everyone's attention is on me again, with Adie appearing to approve for once, what could possibly go wrong?

When I hear the loud hammering at the front door, I realise I spoke too soon. As I recognise the voice yelling out my name, 'Rachel, I know you're home, so answer the door,' I'm immediately filled with a sense of dread.

Across the table, Adie glowers at me with such accusing eyes that my heart nearly stops. Menace oozes from his every pore, making me flinch.

'What the devil?' he growls, as he slams down his glass and scrambles to his feet, toppling his chair in the process. Our guests, meanwhile, stare at us incredulously. They are aware that something is going on, but unlike my husband and I, they are clueless about what it is. Or what it means.

Even though my mind is numb with disbelief, I get up too and claw at Adie's arm, pleading, 'Wait. I'll go,' but he shrugs me off violently. So, I'm forced to chase after him in the hope of getting to Tony before he does.

CHAPTER 54: LUCY

Now

As I tuck into my second serving of figs with blue cheese — which are, incidentally, quite delicious — I can't express how relieved I am to learn that my secret remains safe as Adie is the one with the confession to make. While he was baring his soul and confiding that he'd deliberately concealed stuff from me, I felt horrible, as I'm the big fat liar with something to hide. If I were a decent person, which I obviously am not, I would leave now and never see him again, because he deserves better. I'm temporarily forgetting I have a lot of doubts about Adie. Because according to Rachel's diary, he's an abuser, a philanderer and quite possibly even a murderer. If that doesn't put me off the man, then nothing will.

When he admitted Rachel was not his first wife and that he'd been married before, saying she passed away in similar tragic circumstances to Rachel, I was initially appalled. But when he explained that she had died by misadventure after falling from a bridge onto the A1, I heaved an enormous sigh of relief. At least no one was blaming the poor man for her death. I wonder why Rachel didn't mention a first wife in her diary.

'How come you never mentioned Caitlin before?' I stammer, still in shock. Losing one wife is a tragedy, but losing two — well, some might argue that's just too coincidental.

He surprises me by agreeing, 'Most people would be suspicious, and wisely so, of a husband who lost two wives to tragic circumstances.'

To lift the mood, I reveal mischievously, 'I'm not most people.'

His eyes sparkle as he reaches for my hand, 'I'm glad to hear it.' My skin tingles when he strokes the inside of my palm with his fingertips. Feeling like I'm on fire, I push my plate away, which is out of character for me, and instead of feeling hungry, my stomach flutters with butterflies.

'Have you ever had an affair?' I ask out of the blue.

After rolling his eyes at this unexpected question and shrugging contemplatively, he answers honestly, 'I've thought about it,' which I think is brave of him, although Rachel claimed he was a persistent womaniser, just like Matt and most of the men I know, including my father-in-law. My eyes guiltily hit the floor, as I assume that Adie is lying.

My face must be a picture of disappointment as I run a tongue nervously around my lips before asking bluntly, 'Why didn't you?' And then I search his face for the truth, hoping Rachel was mistaken about him.

When he scowls and declares crossly, 'Call me old fashioned, but I believe in marriage vows,' I think I have my answer. His eyes flicker with something like fear, as he adds carefully, 'How about you? Have you ever cheated?' as if it matters to him.

'Chance would be a fine thing,' I splutter, almost spilling wine down my dress.

This causes him to smile. 'I don't believe you.'

Smirking to myself, I ask, 'Am I that obvious?'

There's a pause as he swallows down the rest of his food before replying with a playful grin, 'You're not the type.'

I snort, 'Who says?' and cast him a sidelong glance while pretending to be insulted.

The two of us silently lock eyes. I don't move from my seat. Not one inch. It feels as if my muscles will never unclench again.

My throat is thick with desire as I mutter, 'How can you tell? Is it because I'm not wild or exciting enough?'

He's staring at me intensely, as though I've suddenly become a burden. When he next speaks, he is more distant than he was a moment ago.

Since my arrival, the mood between the two of us has been like the build-up of pressure before a thunderstorm, but something has just destroyed it. I wonder what triggered this. Is the ghost of Rachel seated between us as we eat together? Is she going to remain there for ever?

Realising that although it's been two years since her death, it's probably still too soon for Adie to contemplate starting over with another woman, I prompt him gently, 'Is something wrong?'

He closes his eyes tightly, as if unwilling to recall a memory, so I give him another gentle nudge, 'Adie?'

He responds by gulping loudly, his Adam's apple jerking up and down, before giving an exasperated half smile. I get the impression he's trying to spare my feelings as he jests, 'What could possibly be wrong? I'm having dinner with a beautiful woman and drinking fine wine.'

Now that he's back in the room, so to speak, my mind focuses on just one thing. *He thinks I'm beautiful.* Ignoring the faint puckering of his forehead, I suggest helpfully, 'Shall we have our main course now?' thinking it might be better if we stopped discussing affairs since it's obviously a painful experience for both of us. Me because of Matt. And him, well, because, despite his denials to the contrary, he obviously cheated on Rachel and is now full of remorse, which is something, I guess. After all, everyone deserves a second chance. *Matt is already on his third*, I think wryly.

I start when Adie abruptly stands up, his cheeks blown out as though he were preparing to take on the world. When he reaches out for my hand this time, he softly draws me into his embrace. And then, as 'Every Breath You Take' by The Police plays on the sound system, we slow dance. His wine-infused breath feels unbelievably warm on my neck as he whispers, 'Beautiful, Sadie . . . didn't you know? The main course is you.'

I'm on the verge of giggling out loud when he comes out with this because it sounds like something a serial killer might say before cannibalising one of their victims. I tend to laugh inappropriately when I'm nervous, but I'm not convinced this *is* what I am feeling.

Could it be the danger of being with Adie that I find exciting? Is that what makes him so addictive, I wonder, and why I can't get enough. Does it reveal a dark side of me that I never knew existed?

CHAPTER 55: RACHEL

Then

As I squeeze past an enthralled Fiona who is standing in the centre of the entrance hall, mouth agape, I have a hunch that she is enjoying the spectacle that is unfolding in front of us. However, I pay no attention to her because rumblings of panic are rolling around in my stomach as I listen to Adie's and Tony's muffled voices coming from the half-open front door.

Adie snarls, 'You're the private investigator who's been following me.'

I shudder in revulsion as I hear Tony snort in his awful, whiny voice, 'I'm no investigator, pal.'

They are facing each other when I swing the door fully open. Tony is dwarfed by Adie, whose face is tight and unreadable. I sense he is about to pounce on Tony, who, on the other hand, looks like he is about to have a heart attack. He is bright red in the face and is breathing heavily.

'I'm not your *pal*,' Adie sneers, pushing his face into Tony's. 'And it wouldn't be the first time she's hired a PA to check up on me,' he adds with an accusing glance in my direction.

'That isn't true,' I get in quickly, feeling gaslit once again.

But nobody is listening. Instead, Adie turns to confront Tony, demanding, 'Now, what do you want with my wife at this time of night?'

Around me, I hear sharp intakes of breath as Tony spills the beans by boasting, 'We're together. Her and me. We're having an affair.'

When he gestures possessively at me, I resist the temptation to lash out at him with my fingernails and rip his face to pieces. The bloody fool.

Tony juts out his chin and violently cracks his knuckles as he yells, 'And I've had enough of you messing her around.' He jabs a finger at Adie, insisting, 'She's coming with me now.'

'Don't be ridiculous,' I hiss, incensed. 'I'm not going anywhere with you.'

'Quite right,' Adie mumbles, fixing his dark gaze on me. In a dangerously quiet voice, he then warns, 'Although if what he is saying is true, Rachel, and I'm beginning to believe it is, then you *will* be leaving.'

A desperate, gnawing fear takes hold as I realise Adie is serious. Feeling like indignation is my only option, I scoff, 'Surely, you don't believe him. This man is deluded and unwell. He's been stalking me for days.'

Before Tony can protest, I slam the door shut in his astonished face without making eye contact. I immediately turn to face Adie, tears pooling in my eyes as I try to reason with him, 'Whatever you think is going on, you're wrong. You're insane if you think I'd do something like that.'

I can tell he doesn't believe me because he knows that I will say and do anything to keep my children. This is why he throws back his head and laughs nastily, stating, 'That's ironic coming from you.'

'What's that supposed to mean?' I complain sulkily, folding my arms.

He lets out a deep sigh. 'It means that I'm tired of your lies and having to play along with them just to keep this family together. I even had to turn a blind eye to your infidelity when I caught you red-handed at the hotel.'

'You're a fine one to talk when you're shagging the nanny right under my nose.' As I get into my stride, I wag an irate finger at him. 'Don't pretend you're not. I've known about it for ages. I hear what the two of you get up to at night when you think I'm asleep.'

His brow creases with incredulity as he barks, 'That's absurd. You should talk to your therapist again as you clearly need help.'

'That's another lie,' I burst out triumphantly, 'because since when did I have a therapist?'

As he reaches his breaking point, he snaps, 'Since for ever.'

I ignore his remark and gesture to Fiona, who is shaking her head and giving me a disdainful look. 'And she isn't the first. There have been many others, haven't there, Adie? Including poor Sasha, whom you had silenced because she was blackmailing you.'

Even as our dinner guests shuffle into the room, eyes down, dragging their feet and appearing mortified, I continue my venomous attack, 'And I am fully aware of all your gambling debts too.'

When Adie hears this, his face is a picture. However, I don't get to enjoy this win because the business associate who is in charge, interrupts me abruptly, by saying in a disappointed tone, 'We're leaving, Adie. We'll expect to see you on Monday morning. You can explain everything then.'

'This is all a misunderstanding,' Adie explains somewhat pathetically, looking like a diminished man as he anxiously wrings his hands. 'My wife frequently loses touch with reality due to a mental health condition.'

Bristling, I lean in, to hiss, 'Ha. More lies.' Spittle flies from my mouth as I shriek at Adie's work colleagues, 'You should stay and find out what your favourite employee is really like.' Then with a spiteful dig at Adie, I snort, 'I bet your big bosses would be surprised to learn that we're talking about tens of thousands of pounds of debt. But you were hoping to use my money to pay it all back, weren't you? After you had killed me, that is.'

This sends shockwaves through the room and everyone turns to stare at each other, eyes wide in disbelief. The incriminating words had fallen out of my mouth before I could stop them and I instantly regret them, but I feel compelled to make things worse by laughing uncontrollably as I go on to splutter, 'But the joke is on you because the money has all gone.'

A few of our guests give Adie pitying looks. One shakes his head in embarrassment. Someone else makes a disapproving grimace. But they all turn to leave together at the same time and shuffle quietly out of the door. Even though they've shown some sympathy for Adie's situation, I get the feeling that he won't have a job when Monday morning comes around. Unlike Tony, Adie is not an idiot. He will also be thinking along those lines.

The ensuing silence is disturbed by Adie asking in a surprisingly composed voice, 'What did you do with the money, Rachel?'

'I gave it away so you couldn't get your lying, cheating hands on it. What will you do about your gambling debts now?'

As though he can't believe it, Adie puts his head in his hands and cries brokenly, 'You've ruined us. And you did it just to spite me.'

CHAPTER 56: LUCY

Now

I feel alive when I smell freshly cut grass, hear bees buzzing and feel the summer sun warming my face. While I hang the washing on the line to dry — kid's socks, towels, bedsheets and a faded bra of mine — I sing along loudly to Queen's 'Don't Stop Me Now', because what Freddy wrote is accurate . . . *I'm having such a good time*. Last night Adie didn't tell me I was 'fine as I am', as Matt does. He said I was beautiful, lovely, gorgeous and perfect. These are words I never imagined I would hear. And he made me feel all of those things. Sex with him was amazing. I was blown away by it. I had no idea passion and intimacy like that existed. Now that I understand how a man and a woman should make love, I squirm in embarrassment that I've tolerated Matt's selfish efforts for so long. I might have lied to my husband, broken my marriage vows and slept with a known womaniser and suspected killer, but for now at least, I'm okay with that. And, hey-ho, housework is suddenly much more enjoyable.

When I go back inside the house, I'm greeted by silence and feel a sharp stab of isolation. I love my family and dislike it when they are not here. I don't need time away from my kids like some mothers do. My life revolves around Jack and Sophie.

But because I arrived home late last night — I sneaked in at around 2 a.m. hoping to find Matt asleep — he offered to take them to the park this morning. This was unusually considerate of him as he typically works on DIY projects around the house on Sundays, but he is making an effort for once and is trying to make amends.

I can't avoid speaking to him for ever about the failure of our marriage and the need for us to part ways. On that I am determined, but I can't pretend it doesn't break me. I only hope we can find a way of co-parenting together and remaining friends. Thanks to Adie, I now have the self-confidence to start over, with someone else, if I want to, whereas Matt always made me feel like a burden. I got the impression he felt he was too good for me and could do better. His parents supported this view.

The tears come as I cradle a coffee in the kitchen. A quick cry will set me right, as always. Along with a chocolate biscuit. Soon, I'm grinning again, because, after last night, how could I not? I wish I could tell Beth all about my newfound sexuality — I'm sure we'd have a giggle over every minute detail, and she'd be thrilled that I'd met someone else. But I can't. If she knew who Adie really was, she'd think I was crazy. And perhaps I am. 'Crazy in Love' as Beyonce would say. And there I go again . . .

I twist in my seat impatiently to check the time. It's still only 11 a.m. and I suspect Matt and the kids will be another half hour. I worry about Sophie. I wish they were back already. I want to hug Sophie's small body and kiss Jack's freckled forehead till he squirms to escape.

Feeling bored, even though I have a hundred and one household chores to do, I cautiously make my way up the dimly lit concrete steps — I can never do this without thinking of Rachel — and then up the stairs to our bedroom, where I've been hiding her diary in my underwear drawer. I know Matt would never stoop so low to look through what he calls my 'period knickers', because I happen to prefer a full brief to a thong. My friends are the same. We women would choose big-girl pants any day of the week.

I lie on the bed and flick through the pages of the diary — which still smell of Rachel's perfume — just in case I missed something before. Rachel never once mentioned Caitlin, Adie's first wife, which I find strange, considering she wrote about everything else. *But hold on — what's this?* Out of the middle of the diary, a slip of folded paper I had not previously noticed falls out and lands in my lap.

I open it with shaking fingers and instantly recognise Rachel's familiar handwriting. Because it is dated 7 July, the day she died, it truly feels like a message from the dead.

Adie has taken my children and left, claiming he was going to spend the night at his mother's. When I heard this I laughed out loud, because even his own mother can't stand him and will likely throw him out once she finds out what he has done. She's bound to be on my side and will tell him that the children should be with their mother. I suspected him of taking Fiona with him to Jonty's, but he denied this, saying she was going home to her parents because she couldn't stay at the house after what happened at the dinner party. What a night that ended up being, thanks to that idiot, Tony. I loathe that man and can't wait to be free of him. He may have had his uses, but he's too much of a liability to have around. To top it off, I'm still pregnant. I couldn't go through with taking the morning-after pill in the end. Nobody knows I am with child and that's how things must remain, at least for the time being, while I consider my options.

As I realise that Rachel was pregnant when she died, I gasp in horror and clasp a hand to my mouth. This means that two lives were lost rather than one. One of them an innocent. Too many questions crowd my mind at once and it feels as if all the air is being forced out of my lungs. Once again, I don't know what to think. Whose child was it? Rachel's husband's or her lover's? Was Adie aware of her pregnancy? Would the baby have been loved if it had been born? Although Rachel did not go ahead with her decision to terminate the pregnancy, she did consider it, and this saddens me, given that I am desperate for another child.

But wait a minute, according to Rachel, Adie left and took the kids with him, so he couldn't have been present on the night she died, absolving him of any blame. Unless he sneaked back later and succeeded in getting his mother to unwittingly provide him with an alibi. He has consistently maintained that he loved Rachel and was devastated by her passing, yet he coldly abandoned her and deprived her of her own children, which was unforgivably cruel. As for that creep Tony, or Soon-to-be-divorced guy, as Rachel sometimes called him, I'd like to give him a piece of my mind. Where was he when Rachel needed him the most? Why wasn't he consoling her in Adie's absence? Knowing she possibly spent her last hours on this earth alone is unbearable to me.

I'm still reeling from this revelation when I hear Matt's car pull up outside and doors slam as the kids noisily spill out onto the pavement. I stand up and make my way to the window, where I see Matt pacing up and down, eyes darting everywhere, as he hugs his phone to his ear. He is acting secretive and there is something fishy about the way he keeps checking out the downstairs windows as if on the lookout for me. What is he up to now? More importantly, what woman is he speaking to this time?

CHAPTER 57: RACHEL

Then

I'm left standing where Adie left me when I watched him load the children into the car before driving away. He returned only to retrieve a hurriedly packed holdall. I presumed he had already driven Fiona home because for once she was nowhere to be seen. In my family's absence, I keep replaying last night's scene in my confused mind, but I am still struggling to accept the reality of what happened and my self-destructive role in it.

Holding onto Adie's arm, I'd begged in disbelief, 'Please don't go.'

I wasn't concerned about Adie leaving — just the children — since my one and only desire had been to rid myself of my husband one way or another. Losing custody of my kids had always been my worst fear, and now it had come true thanks to Tony, the man who was meant to save me.

'I mean it, Rachel. We're leaving,' Adie had snapped coldly, forcibly shaking me off. 'I should have done it years ago.'

'But you can't take my children,' I had gasped in disbelief as tears pricked at the corners of my eyes.

'How long are we going to pretend that Beatrice and Archie are yours?' he'd barked and my whole world collapsed at that point.

'What?' I'd stammered, narrowing my eyes suspiciously.

He'd softened his voice to mumble, 'The children are mine and Caitlin's, remember? We've talked about this.'

'You're lying,' I'd screamed, and raised my hand to strike him, but he'd caught it in his and dropped it as though he could not stand to touch me.

'No, I'm not,' he'd insisted, shaking his head. 'After you lost your job at the paper because of your delusional behaviour, I thought having a baby of your own might help you, but you wouldn't even consider it.'

A baby of my own? I remembered thinking, 'Should I tell him?' but in the next breath I was glad I didn't when he'd sneered, 'I'm so glad I never got you pregnant because you'd be a nightmare as a mother.'

I had bitten back a reply because my temper was fraying once more.

'You don't even like the children,' he'd sighed wearily after pausing to examine me closely. 'And I can assure you the feeling is mutual.'

I'd scratchily pointed out, 'That's not true,' and placed both hands behind my back to stop myself from lashing out at him again.

His voice had dripped with disappointment when he told me, 'That's because you don't what *is* true and what *isn't*,' adding in a firm voice, 'But I have to go. I can't do this anymore. The affection I once felt for you has been destroyed by your illness and has emotionally exhausted us all.'

I exploded then, 'You're only saying that because all of the money has gone and I'm no longer of any value to you.'

He started at my feral tone and snorted angrily, 'Unbelievable,' before storming towards the front door, muttering one last insult over his shoulder, 'you're a fantasist, Rachel. I've said it before and I'll say it again, you need help.' This time I did not try to stop him.

That was more than twenty hours ago and since then, no one has thought to check up on me. Not Adie. Not the children. Not even Jonty, who I thought was on my side, because she was meant to be my friend. Or did I make that up too? Was Adie right to call me a fantasist? Or was this simply another tactic to convince me that I am losing my mind? Maybe the children are mine, after all. I love Beatrice and Archie, so he's wrong about that. If I didn't, I would hardly leave them my fortune.

Still wearing my slinky black dress, I wandered the house all night long, seeing shadows everywhere. I pictured the children still here, sound asleep in their beds, having read them a bedtime story and put them to bed myself. Since they loved me the most, they insisted on me doing it rather than their father. The world Adie had described was nothing like the one in my imagination, which is a much gentler, kinder, routine-filled place where I'm not plagued by ghosts and unpleasant memories.

I guess some of what Adie said is true. I didn't slam out of poor Sasha's flat that day as I had told myself I had. Born into a life of privilege and entitlement, where I was used to getting my way, Rachel Beiersdorf was not going to allow someone like Sasha Walker to blackmail her or her husband. Who did the common tart think she was? Nor was I going to part with any of my money either. So, in a jealous rage — Sasha had slept with my husband and attempted to extort me out of my fortune — I strangled her with a piece of her own clothing.

If my memory serves me right, it was a cheap off-white T-shirt, two sizes too small for her. Sasha did not want to die that day, or any other I imagine. She fought valiantly until the very end, like a warrior, when her eyes nearly exploded out of her head and she slumped lifelessly to one side, her blonde head lolling against me, until I shoved it away in disgust.

Tony was quick to comment on my scratches and bruises, presuming my husband had physically assaulted me, which ironically served my purpose. Adie, though, was too preoccupied with the false accusations of sexual harassment he'd been accused of to notice these defence wounds.

There's something about a house at night, especially an old one like this with its atmospheric setting, which has always fascinated me. Generations of people have lived and died here and taken their secrets with them, as I shall one day. Can you be too secretive? Too distant. Too cold? Much like 13 Rutland Terrace is. Despite my resistance to the move, I now recognise that the house's dark and secretive personality compliments my own.

Although I continued to listen to the unique sounds the house made for some time. A creak here. A sigh there. A dripping tap elsewhere. I eventually grew tired and returned to where it all began — the grand entrance hall with its high ceilings and shuttered windows, which block out the moonlight at night and the ferocity of the sunlight during the day.

When I see the front door being quietly pushed open, I am reminded with a heavy heart that I forgot to lock it the night before. It's nearly midnight, a time when thieves take their chances. My instinct is not to run, but to fight back, to the death if necessary, because I'm sick of being made to feel like a trespasser in my own home. For a moment, however, I picture Adie returning with Beatrice and Archie, and I wait for them to rush into my arms, exclaiming, 'We've missed you, Mummy.'

I convince myself that it *is* Adie when I see the menacing silhouette of a man step inside, his shoes making a faint shushing sound on the expensive geometric tiles. I pinch myself hard to make sure my eyes aren't deceiving me, but it's only when he hesitantly asks, 'Is that you, Rachel?' that I realise my mistake. I was right the first time, it isn't Adie, but a thief. The one who stole my life from me tonight.

Poised for action, I flip a switch and the room is suddenly flooded with bright light from the glass chandeliers, temporarily blinding us both.

'Come in, Tony,' I offer with an inviting smile meant only for him, 'I've been expecting you.'

CHAPTER 58: LUCY

Now

'Have you seen the magnet that was on the fridge?' I ask Matt again, this time in an exasperated tone since he clearly didn't hear me the first time. He continues to look blankly at me as if it might be a trick question, before gulping and saying in a small voice, 'What magnet?'

'The one of Rachel and her family, Dumbo. You know, the couple who lived here before us?' I refrain from adding 'Don't tell me you've already forgotten about the poor woman who died in our kitchen?'

I sigh, dragging a hand through my hair as I niggle, 'Well, have you seen it or not? It was here a minute ago.'

When he suggests in a bored tone, 'Perhaps the kids took it,' he doesn't look at me.

'Not helpful. Have you seen what the time is? They've been in bed ages,' I tut dismissively.

'Has it fallen off?'

I shake my head and grumble, 'I've already looked,' wondering why I'm so bothered. But it's the only picture I have of Adie. Having decided to come clean and be honest with him about who I am and what my intentions were from the beginning (i.e.

to learn the truth about Rachel), I'm aware that he probably won't want to see me again, and I wouldn't blame him, so this memento will serve as a reminder of the time I spent with him.

When all I get from Matt is radio silence I turn to look at him properly for the first time this evening. His eyes are tired and bloodshot from drinking all day. He can't seem to keep his hands still and his shoulders are slumped over the table. When I catch a glimpse of what he is concealing in his clenched palm, a warning scream echoes through my mind. As I struggle to hold back all the dark thoughts that are now racing through my mind, he gives me a strange faraway look, as if he were someplace else.

'What have you got there?' I demand, hating how scared I sound.

Matt gnaws his lip and his eyes are haunted as he replies, 'Nothing,' but I know I don't imagine it when I see his hand tighten possessively around the magnet. Although he acts indifferent, I can detect fear in his eyes.

'Why are you hiding Rachel's picture magnet in your hand?'

I watch him stare down at his hand, which seems to have opened on its own accord because he appears astonished to see it there. He looks like my husband. He smells like my husband. But he doesn't sound like my husband when he groans, 'I thought I threw it away.'

'Yes, well, I retrieved it from the bin,' I reply defensively, sensing something is going on that I don't understand. At least not yet.

He looks up at me with the saddest of eyes and asks accusingly, 'Do you have any idea what day it is today?'

Not liking the direction this conversation seems to be taking, my voice rises in panic and my shoulders go up a notch as I answer, 'Sunday.'

'7 July to be precise,' he murmurs, continuing to gaze at the picture in his palm. I inhale sharply when I see him gently caress

Rachel's face with his forefinger, and I stutter, 'What's going on, Matt?'

'Today marks two years since her death.'

'How do you know that?' I scowl, wishing now that I had never heard of Rachel Bello.

'Because I was here, Lucy,' he exhales dramatically and squeezes his eyes shut before sobbing, 'I was here the night Rachel died.'

'You couldn't have been. You're not making any sense,' I garble, panicked. Because it *is* beginning to make sense, slowly but surely.

'I remember now,' I exclaim, my eyes wide with shock, 'that night two years ago when I discovered you crying your eyes out in the kitchen and you confessed to having an affair. You claimed it was over because you wanted to save your marriage. She took it hard, you said.'

'I lied,' he snivels pathetically, his face collapsing. 'When I realised she was using me, I was the one who took it hard.'

'Are you saying that you were having an affair with Rachel?' I'm incredulous. Matt is Tony (AKA Soon-to-be-divorced guy who, according to Rachel's diary, had never been in love with his wife and thought of her as his sister). How could I have not known this? Why didn't I guess? 'That's why you were so desperate to buy this house . . .'

He wipes his tears on the back of his sleeve and admits, 'I wanted to be close to her and it was all I had left of her.'

'Oh, my God,' I splutter as I make my way to the table, knowing that I must sit down before I fall down. 'You were in love with her. Weren't you?'

Through his tears, he nods and continues as though my feelings were insignificant, 'I would've done anything for Rachel.'

'So, you lied about everything,' I hiss, pulling a repulsed face.

His voice is hardly audible, as though he is afraid of saying the words out loud, 'I didn't mean to hurt her.'

'What did you do, Matt?' I scream in fear, my mouth hanging open.

Ignoring my question, he curls his lip and snarls, 'I was ready to leave you, my family, everything for her. And I told her so. But that wasn't good enough for Rachel. Nothing was.'

'It was you,' I gasp, clasping a hand over my mouth. 'You killed Rachel.'

He whispers conspiratorially, 'It was an accident,' and then shushes me brutally as if afraid someone might overhear but we are here alone. Or are we? Is Rachel with us even now. When it dawns on me that she was trying to destroy me the entire time I was trying to save her, something inside me dies. It's true what they say . . . there is always one more twist to any horror story, the one the reader doesn't guess. And Rachel's diary was no different. Because of her, my husband has just told me something no wife should have to hear, but he doesn't seem to want to accept responsibility for his actions, which leads me to suspect that Rachel's death was no accident. He wouldn't have been able to tolerate her rejecting him. I blame his mother once again, for allowing her golden boy to believe he is infallible. But this time I won't let him get away with it.

'You were right about Rachel,' I taunt him spitefully, wanting to hurt him as much as he has hurt me, while knowing that is impossible. 'She didn't love you and was using you. She said so in her diary.'

'What diary?' he asks, blinking in bewilderment.

'It doesn't matter,' I snarl. 'What matters is that you were willing to abandon your family for a woman who couldn't care less about you.'

'Don't say that!' he barks, but as he scrambles to his feet, the photo magnet of Rachel and her family flies off the table and hits the ground.

As if it were Rachel herself that I was attacking, I stomp on it viciously until it shatters into pieces, and I bawl, 'Why not? It's true. She would have told you about the baby if she truly cared for you.'

Silence. Not a word from Matt. Just the ticking sound of a clock. The humming of the freezer. A creaking from upstairs as the foundations of the house sleepily expand and contract. And then . . . Matt grabs my arm and demands menacingly, 'What baby?'

He only has slits for eyes and is more frightening than I've ever seen him. But that doesn't stop me from revealing harshly, 'Rachel was pregnant with your child when she died, which means you killed them both.'

'That's not possible,' he growls from behind me, but I'm already halfway up the stairs. I can't breathe down there in the kitchen. I need fresh air.

I feel his hands on me before I reach the top, dragging me back down. As we struggle silently on the stairs, I manage to free one arm, and then with a tremendous effort I shove him hard, screaming, 'Get off me, Matt.'

In slow motion, as though I were dreaming, I see him tumble backwards down the stone steps. When bone hits concrete, a loud cracking sound echoes around the room. Matt's body, twisted at an unnatural angle, face thankfully turned away so I can't see it, twitches for a few seconds before becoming motionless. At first, I believe it to be a simple fall, nothing major, like the one I had the day we moved into Rutland Terrace. I expect him to get up any minute, rubbing his head and complaining that I pushed him on purpose. *Did I . . . ?* But when I see the red halo of blood pooling around his head I realise that I have killed Matt, my first love and the father of my children, and he is now with Rachel again, the woman he worshipped yet murdered in cold blood.

CHAPTER 59: RACHEL

Then

'Tony, why have you come back here? What is it you want exactly?' I enquire politely, as though we were strangers meeting for the first time on a train, as indeed we once were. I would give anything to go back in time so I could catch a different train that day. After robbing me of my children, he is deserving of nothing but my contempt.

'I want *you*, Rachel,' he whimpers, putting my teeth on edge.

'You hardly know me,' I sigh, thinking that although this is true he is still the father of my unborn child. He will never learn this from me though.

'I fucked up, didn't I?' he grovels, tugging at the thick, sandy hair that he is so vain about, and sounding more like a boy than a man, a boy accustomed to being pampered and mothered.

'You did, indeed,' I agree, chuckling sourly, despite the fact that none of this is funny at all.

'I don't know what I was thinking when I interrupted your dinner party,' he mumbles apologetically, as if it were a minor transgression, and showing no remorse for what he did. Men who play the victim are something I despise. I want to tell him that if he tried being a woman, even for one day, he would understand what it's like to live with misogyny.

I say sharply, 'I am genuinely interested in why you did that when you must have known it would not end well. For me, that is.'

'But, don't you see, now that Adie's gone, we can be together. That's what you want, isn't it? I mean, that's what you said.'

'I said a lot of things,' I point out scratchily, 'but you're forgetting that he also took my children and getting them back is all that matters to me now.' As I say this, I am overcome with memories that, according to Adie, are not my own — such as when the babies were born and placed in my arms, feeding them their bottles of milk, and hearing them say 'Mama' for the first time — but I refuse to accept his version of events. How could my precious Beatrice and dear sweet Archie not be mine?

'We'll get them back together,' Tony promises, swaggering towards me with an absurd amount of misplaced confidence.

If he thinks that I'm about to fall for his nonsense a second time, he's seriously mistaken. He reminds me of a pushy salesman, now that I think about it. How come I didn't see that right away? Is it because I was in a dark and vulnerable place, having met him on the day I went to see Sasha.

I keep him at arm's length by slowly backing out of the entrance hall until he's compelled to follow me. My body ripples with anger as I hold out a forceful palm to stop him from advancing any further and haughtily demand, 'And how do you propose on doing that?'

He clears his throat and mutters awkwardly, 'I thought I'd move in here with you, so we can be together.'

'What would that solve, you silly man, other than providing Adie with additional evidence that I'm having an affair?' I snap nastily.

As I watch Tony's eyes narrow and his chin protrude defensively, I discover that he is more complex than I had originally believed. He takes himself very seriously in addition to being a conceited and self-absorbed individual. Experience has taught me that men with the greatest egos are also the most dangerous because they can't stand to be made fun of and will always seek revenge. Deciding that this might work to my advantage, as I intend to be free of him permanently, I consider changing tactic.

He becomes even more whiny as he argues, 'Just because you've been seeing someone else doesn't mean you can't still see your kids or get custody of them. No court would refuse you access.'

Unless Adie can prove they aren't mine. Because I have no rights whatsoever if I am not Beatrice and Archie's biological mother.

'I wish things were that simple,' I snip, pulling a cynical face.

'They could be,' he insists stubbornly, 'if you'd let me look after you.'

'Look after me!' I hiss. 'What a joke that is when the one job you had was to kill my husband, so I could be free, and you couldn't even do that.' I give a mocking shrug and add, 'I mean, how difficult can it be?'

'I'm no killer, Rachel. I told you once before that we could get custody of the kids without having to do that,' he warns, biting down on his cheek.

'Oh, really?' I arch a sardonic brow. 'And do you see my children anywhere right now, Mr Know-it-all? Ha. No. I didn't think so.'

'There's no need for—' he stammers as if having trouble speaking.

Smugly, I interrupt him, 'There's every need. Because the truth is there was never going to be any you and me, Tony, or whatever your real name is since I don't believe you are who you claim to be.'

I pause to let this sink in, and when his face turns an ugly shade of red, I know I am right. He is no match for me, verbally or otherwise, and so I gloat, 'Not that it matters to me, because had you done as I asked and got rid of my husband for me, I was going to dump you anyway.'

'Rachel, you don't mean that. I know you don't,' he begs, advancing decisively in my direction. 'I love you, and you love me. I could tell you were the one for me the instant I laid eyes on you.'

'And I could tell what a weak and pathetic man *you* were,' I reply cruelly, stepping back from him as though he were the devil. 'I don't want to be with you. I never did. Don't you get it? I was using you, that's all. You can't even make love properly. It was the worst sex I ever had. You must be insane if you think I could ever be interested in someone like you.'

I may have gone too far with the manic laughter but it seems to have done the trick as his expression has darkened and his eyes are now filled with a deep and abiding hatred. I begin to believe that I was right before, and he *is* insane. Most of us are, you know. My instinct now is to flee, but he startles me by snaking out a hand and wrapping it around my throat. The force of his anger is impressive, as is the pressure on my throat, and I realise once again that I have underestimated him. I hear the wobble in my voice as I attempt to cry out for help and I despise myself for it because I'm sick of men controlling me and pushing me around.

If I want to live, I have to keep quiet so as not to aggravate him further . . . but do I? Isn't it all too hard?

In my ear, he growls, 'Bitch,' while brutally shoving me backwards until I run out of wall and I'm standing above the kitchen stairs. Sensing what he is about to do, my eyes lock with his one last time. Mine are meant to be begging for my life, but instead, I glare at him, before managing to gasp defiantly, 'I dare you to do it, or are you too much of a coward?'

Then, with an evil grin, he lets go of me, and as I fall, hearing my bones break as they strike the concrete steps, my mind drifts to my friend Caitlin, who died in a similar manner. I shudder at the memory of her shocked and terrified expression as I pushed her off the bridge that day, just because I could and because she had what I wanted — Adie and the children.

CHAPTER 60: LUCY

Six months later

Adie took a while to forgive me for all the lies I told him. He eventually came around once he found out about the baby. There's no way of knowing who the father is, but Adie insists that he doesn't want a DNA test when the baby is born because he wants to raise it as his own regardless of paternity. For this, everyone admires him. Every single one of my pals adores him, even Beth, who I suspect has a secret crush on him because she keeps telling everyone what a catch he is. I do not disagree as I couldn't ask for a more perfect partner and he's already a fantastic father, so I know our unborn child will be in excellent hands if anything should happen to me.

I'm expecting another boy, but I haven't told anyone this yet, not even Adie, because I'm still unsure if I want it to be Matt's or Adie's son. Speaking of babies, I haven't mentioned Rachel's pregnancy to Adie. What good would it do when it wasn't his? To everyone else, the baby never existed because she wasn't far gone enough for it to show up on the postmortem results. Although I owe Rachel nothing after she succeeded in destroying my family, I do believe that women should take care of one another in a world that is essentially dominated by men.

After a long day on my feet, Adie and Jonty have ordered me to come upstairs and lie down on the bed, if not for my sake, then the baby's. I had forgotten what it was like to be six months pregnant. I have to keep an eye on my weight because I'm on the large size already. It can be annoying at times when Adie monitors my diet as though he were a professional nutritionist. The days of being allowed to drink full-fat Coke are long gone. Jonty looked in on me a while ago, bringing me some herbal tea and a potassium-rich banana for my swollen feet and ankles. According to the midwife, I may need to be placed on bed rest if I'm not careful since I run the risk of developing preeclampsia.

When I first met Jonty, I sensed that I could be a daughter to her and her a mother to me as I imagined that was the kind of relationship she had with Rachel, but I was later proven wrong, as this was all in Rachel's head. Jonty couldn't stand her. And now she grows increasingly distant with me. Whenever I ask her what is wrong, she acts all aloof and avoids the subject.

I sit up in bed, which seems much harder than it should, to take a sip of my now-cool tea. As I try to get comfortable, I can't help but notice my unkempt reflection in the spotless mirrored wall that runs the length of the room. Adie's bedroom — I don't think of it as ours — because it isn't to my taste with its severe black minimalistic style and industrial grey colour scheme. I can't get used to being a brunette either, although Adie claims to love it and says it suits me. When I had to stop bleaching my hair due to the pregnancy, I agreed to take it a few shades darker than my natural dark blonde in order to please him. But I must admit I like the longer length.

The sky outside my window is darkening with heavy clouds, and I imagine how cold the January air would be against my skin if I were permitted to go outdoors. I wouldn't dare challenge the popular belief that Adie has the greatest of intentions, but he does have a tendency to suffocate me. Since I moved in with him three months ago, I feel like a prisoner, with both Adie and Jonty supervising my every move. Rutland Terrace is now sold and Adie deserves all the credit for handling everything, because, following Matt's death, I was in no fit state to do anything, much less deal with estate agents. While Sophie has barely noticed Matt's absence, Jack has mourned his loss the most and hasn't been himself since.

When I hear my son shouting for me from his bedroom along the landing, I mutter aloud, 'Oh, not again, the poor love,' because Jack's nightmares have, understandably, gotten worse rather than better since his father passed away. Before I can get out of bed and hurry to comfort him, the door swings open.

With a practised smile, Adie offers, 'It's okay, I'll go.'

Though I'm not entirely sure where Adie sprung from, I suspect him of hovering outside my door. I'm not sure if I should insist on going myself, so I hesitate. Ultimately, because it's easier, I give in, 'Are you sure?'

'Of course,' he nods as if it is no problem at all and quickly exits.

'It's okay, Jack,' Adie murmurs reassuringly from across the landing. 'It was just a bad dream, but you're okay now.'

On hearing this, I slump back against my pillows, but a minute later I'm sitting upright again when I hear Jack exclaim tearfully, 'Where's Mum?' only for Adie to respond, 'Your mum's not feeling very well, Jack.'

Even though I want to be with my son, I stay where I am because I know Adie won't like it if I interfere. Still, I puff out my cheeks in annoyance because since when was pregnancy classified as an illness?

Adie returns to the room a few minutes later. I smile warmly at him because it is expected of me and enquire, 'Is everything okay?'

He nods, crisply and decisively, but his eyes flicker with uncertainty. I lift my eyebrows to ask, 'Is anything wrong?'

'No,' he sighs as he takes a seat beside me on the bed. 'I just didn't want to have to bother you with anything, that's all.'

'Oh?' is all I can say to that, as I feel like he's going to bother me anyway. There's something about his expression that is concerning me for some reason. I can't really explain it, but it makes me think of the moment he eventually told me the truth about Rachel. I still recall being shocked by how vindictive he sounded when he remarked, 'She was a manipulative lying bitch, a fantasist who became obsessed with her fortune thinking everyone, including, me was out to get it.' When I naively observed, 'That doesn't sound like Rachel,' he flew into a rage and kicked out at something on the floor. I became scared at that point and have since learned to keep my opinions to myself when it comes to his deceased wife.

Without looking at me, he mumbles, 'If you feel up to it, I need you to sign some documents.' I'm intrigued enough to ask, 'What kind of documents?' as he takes a brown envelope from his trouser pocket.

'Nothing for you to worry about, darling,' he promises and leans in to give me a kiss on the cheek. He smells of a perfume that I do not recognise.

Once he's out of the room, I mutter to myself, 'I'll be the judge of that,' as I slide the legal-looking document out of its envelope and onto the bed. He has taken out a one-million-pound life insurance policy in my name. Though saddened — alarmed, even — I'm not shocked.

Bile rises in my throat as I push the paperwork aside to retrieve Rachel's green journal from under my pillow. I've taken to writing down my thoughts in it, continuing where she left off.

Adie was right when he called Rachel a manipulative liar and a fantasist but she didn't lie about everything. Much of what she wrote in her diary was true. Her affair with my husband for one thing. It's Adie I have been wrong about all this time, having chosen to overlook every clue that Rachel left me. But yesterday, when I overheard him talking on the phone to someone I can only assume was Fiona, the truth hit me with a horrible clarity because he was telling her how much he missed her.

Rachel was also right when she claimed her husband and nanny were plotting her murder to inherit her wealth, except Matt got there before them, so they were spared the trouble. And then I showed up, determined to find out what really happened to Rachel, to become a thorn in their sides. After learning that Fiona was back on the scene, I searched through Adie's phone (he must have forgotten he had previously given me his login details) and discovered a screenshot of my LinkedIn profile taken on the day I first showed up at his house. Being a cyber security expert, he must have run facial recognition software on his CCTV footage to establish my real identity. So, they knew who I was from the very beginning, and I have to assume they were all in on the deception. Adie, Fiona and even Jonty.

Once I showed up, like the proverbial bad penny, Adie couldn't openly be with Fiona, not without raising my suspicions. He had to silence me if he wanted to hold onto Rachel's fortune, and if he couldn't . . .

I now fear my life is in danger, as Rachel's was. If anything should happen to me and this house is sold, I hope the future owner discovers my diary and realises that the couple who lived here before them were not who they seemed. Adie, my partner, wants me gone so he can be with his new woman (the one he thinks I don't know about) and become a million pounds richer.

THE END

ACKNOWLEDGEMENTS

The dedication at the front of this novel refers to my older brother John who continues to bravely battle a cancer for which there is no cure. Growing up in a houseful of six siblings (of which I was the youngest), he was my confidante and best friend, and to this day I can still tell him anything. When I was going through a painful divorce some years ago, he went out of his way to check in with me every day to see how I was coping, even though he was struggling with ill health at the time. Love you, big bro.

The concept for *Before Us* came about because of my interest in old historic houses, their atmospheric setting and the generations of people who live and die in them, taking their secrets with them. One of the things I frequently do in my novels is to make a house one of the main characters. It might be of interest to you to know that 13 Rutland Terrace in Stamford has featured in one of my books before. It appeared in *The Godmother*. The Georgian terrace in question is an iconic landmark in my hometown. All descriptions of number thirteen are my own (I have never been inside it), and as far as I know, nobody has been murdered there. I mention this to avoid upsetting the current owner(s).

For those of you who are local to the area, you will likely recognise popular landmarks throughout this book. If you've never been, I recommend a visit. It's a lovely market town, known for its olde-worldly bookshops, stately homes, afternoon tea, quaint coffee shops and cobbled passageways. *The Sunday Times* once voted it 'Britain's top place to live'.

When readers ask, 'What is the favourite book that you have written?' I invariably answer, 'The last one,' since that is typically true for many authors. But I must say that *Before Us* truly captured my imagination in a way that has solidified it as a firm favourite. I like to write about unreliable narrators, and Rachel's dark and secretive personality presented some challenges. She proved a tricky one to get my head around. Lucy, on the other hand, was considerably easier because she was a relatively open book. I hope that, for once, I was successful in making her a mostly likeable character that readers can root for.

I would like to say a massive thank you to everyone at Joffe Books for all their hard work in getting this story ready for publication. They have been an absolute pleasure to work with. Go Team Joffe. As always, special thanks go to Kate Lyall Grant, Joffe's publishing director. If you are not from the UK, please excuse the English spellings. Oopsie-daisy, it's just the way we do things across the pond. Apologies also for any swearing but this is down to the characters and has nothing to do with me. Lol. The same goes for any blaspheming.

Now for the best bit where I get to thank my lovely readers for all their support, especially all the bloggers and reviewers. You know who you are! Your loyalty and friendship mean everything. As do your reviews. ☺

THE JOFFE BOOKS STORY

We began in 2014 when Jasper agreed to publish his mum's much-rejected romance novel and it became a bestseller.

Since then we've grown into the largest independent publisher in the UK. We're extremely proud to publish some of the very best writers in the world, including Joy Ellis, Faith Martin, Caro Ramsay, Helen Forrester, Simon Brett and Robert Goddard. Everyone at Joffe Books loves reading and we never forget that it all begins with the magic of an author telling a story.

We are proud to publish talented first-time authors, as well as established writers whose books we love introducing to a new generation of readers.

We won Trade Publisher of the Year at the Independent Publishing Awards in 2023 and Best Publisher Award in 2024 at the People's Book Prize. We have been shortlisted for Independent Publisher of the Year at the British Book Awards for the last five years, and were shortlisted for the Diversity and Inclusivity Award at the 2022 Independent Publishing Awards. In 2023 we were shortlisted for Publisher of the Year at the RNA Industry Awards, and in 2024 we were shortlisted at the CWA Daggers for the Best Crime and Mystery Publisher.

We built this company with your help, and we love to hear from you, so please email us about absolutely anything bookish at feedback@joffebooks.com.

If you want to receive free books every Friday and hear about all our new releases, join our mailing list here: www.joffebooks.com/freebooks.

And when you tell your friends about us, just remember: it's pronounced Joffe as in coffee or toffee!